Special Excerpt

Thunder rumbled softly to the west, but the air was dry for the moment. A cool night wind had dried the thick, scummy water on my skin, leaving a filmy, greasy residue behind. The truck jerked violently to the left, plowing through a deep puddle, and I rolled with it, bracing my foot against the wet, matted hair of the carcass for support. The steer lay stiffly on its side, legs jutting straight out, and rocked slightly with the motion of the truck. Then we were over the top of the foothill and shuddering down the other side into the deep hollow where the Sawyer brothers lived. I pulled my eyes away from my bloody hand and twisted around so I could see through the two-inch gap in the wooden slats.

The weak headlights splashed over a tangle of old fig trees that had never been pruned. A quagmire of rotten figs blanketed the ground beneath the trees. As we got closer, I heard a low buzzing fade in and out. It took me a moment, but when a wasp landed on the steer and crawled around, I realized what was causing the buzzing. I had never heard or seen wasps out at night before, and it made my skin crawl.

wormfood

jeff jacobson

MEDALLION
P R E S S

Medallion Press, Inc.
Printed in USA

Accolades for Jeff Jacobson's *Wormfood*

"Poignant and thoughtful yet violent and gritty, *Wormfood* is a triumph of a first novel. Think Joe R Lansdale meets Harper Lee in a roadside diner that serves human flesh. Part coming-of-age story, part cautionary tale, part redneck thriller, *Wormfood* is much more than a horror novel but just as disturbing. Jeff Jacobson is a writer to watch out for and I'm looking forward to reading his work for years to come.

"*Wormfood* is not just a great horror novel, but a great novel, period. Exciting, fast-paced, entertaining, and with that extra touch of heart that lifts it from the realm of pulp into high art . . ."

—Trent Haaga, screenwriter of *Deadgirl*

"Jacobson's evocative prose goes down like Southern Comfort in *Wormfood*, a terrifying mixture of *The Petrified Forest* and the very best nature-runs-amok drive-in flicks. A first-rate horror thriller with memorable characters and an action-packed climax that will leave you dreading rainstorms forever."

—Gregory Lamberson, author of *Personal Demons* and *Johnny Gruesome*

"This is a claustrophobic encounter of the weird kind . . ."

—Mort Castle, editor of *On Writing Horror*

wormfood

jeff jacobson

DEDICATION

For Deb

Published 2010 by Medallion Press, Inc.

The MEDALLION PRESS LOGO
is a registered trademark of Medallion Press, Inc.

Slightly different versions of Chapters 14 and 15 originally appeared in *F Magazine #5*, and earlier drafts of Chapters 20 and 21 originally appeared in *Hair Trigger #24*.

Typeset in Adobe Garamond Pro
Printed in the United States of America

ISBN: 978-160542101-8

10 9 8 7 6 5 4 3 2 1
First Edition

ACKNOWLEDGMENTS

A lot of fine folks helped out and showed me such unbelievable kindness that a mere thanks doesn't seem to be enough. But this is the least I can do. Your willingness to go above and beyond the call of duty for this goofy writer is appreciated more than you will ever know. So many, many thanks to:

My family—Saw and Mad, Mom and Dad and Clay.

The wonderful writers and teachers and mentors and students and friends in the Columbia College Chicago Fiction Department— including my teachers Don De Grazia, Anne Hemenway, Gary Johnson, Eric May, Devon Polderman, and especially John Schultz, who gave invaluable advice and encouragement.

The fantastic team at Medallion Press, especially Adam Mock, Paul Ohlson, Lorie Popp, Helen Rosburg, Emily Steele, and Jim Tampa.

Some of the people I'm honored to call my friends—Gus and Jen Alagna, Christian Behr, Jay Bonansinga, Mort Castle, David Chirchirillo, Craig Christie, Jen and House Domonkos, Tom Egizio— Webmaster extraordinaire, Mark Ferguson of Hard Boiled Records, Trent Haaga, Heather Jack, Dave Janczak, Brian Kustek, Gregory Lamberson, Jack Mazzenga, and Lou and Sandy Phillips, and so many others.

The musicians who helped fuel the writing of this novel—AC/DC, Johnny Cash, The Cramps, Deadbolt, Motorhead, Murder by Death, The Ramones, the Reverend Horton Heat, Southern Culture on the Skids, and The Ventures.

And finally, my wife, Deb, who gave me unwavering support and patience. I love you, little one.

CHAPTER 1

Grandma woke me up with her .10 gauge, shooting at the ground squirrels again. I think that was the morning it all started, when the worms got loose and the Sawyer brothers stole the dead steer and Fat Ernst had us break into Earl's coffin and I tasted Misty Johnson's sweat and that witch crawled out of the darkness under her lawn mower and a whole hell of a lot of blood got spilled.

Yeah. It started with Grandma and her Browning.

Those squirrels pissed her off like you wouldn't believe, burrowing into the rich black soil and eating her vegetables. She grew nearly everything we ate in her garden out there behind the trailer, from tomatoes that swelled up like water balloons about to burst to red onions the size of softballs to ears of corn so sweet they tasted like they were half sugar cane.

So when the squirrels snuck in and tried to eat the results of her hard work, Grandma went to war. And she didn't take prisoners.

The shotgun blast faded into the soft whispering of rain striking the roof. I rolled over in bed and checked the alarm clock. It was dead, dark, and silent on the floor next to my narrow mattress. At first I thought one of the storms had knocked out the power again, then realized that Grandma had unplugged the clock. I guessed our talk last night about me working for Fat Ernst hadn't gone over as well as I had hoped.

My watch read 7:32.

The Sawyer brothers would be showing up any minute now.

Grandma hated them even worse than the ground squirrels.

The shotgun ripped another hole in the morning air. Grandma didn't believe in traps or poisons; they took all the satisfaction, all the *fun* out of the job. Instead, she loaded her own shells, using number 9 steel shot, so we didn't have to worry about lead poisoning. She didn't even have to get rid of the little corpses. The Browning .10 gauge blasted them into instant fertilizer.

I stumbled into the bathroom, pulling on a pair of shorts and a T-shirt as I went. No time for a shower. I stuck my toothbrush in my mouth, took a deep breath and flexed my chest and both arms in a classic bodybuilder pose. In the mirror, nothing much happened. A scrawny sixteen-year-old with a bad haircut grimaced back at me. It looked like I'd been in an accident and couldn't move very well.

My name is Arch Stanton. Me and Grandma lived in a single-width trailer dumped at the end of a long dirt driveway out in the hills. Grandpa died nearly five years ago, heart attack. Mom and Dad had been dead for over twelve years. They were coming back from a week-end in Reno when Dad apparently took one of the mountain turns a little wide and hit a minivan filled with a family of six. Head-on collision; killed everybody but the family's youngest child. When they performed the autopsy, they found that Dad's blood had an alcohol level of .09 percent. Just enough to be legally drunk in California. All of the insurance money, everything, went to the child who survived.

Me and Grandma needed money. We needed money bad. I had tried to tell her the night before, over dinner, tried to tell her that something had to be done. "I know you don't want me working for . . .

him, but jeez, Grandma, we're two months behind with our rent. You can't just ignore that," I had said slowly, quietly. Fat Ernst owned the trailer and the land, and the only reason he hadn't kicked us out yet was because I worked like a dog in his restaurant.

Grandma just looked at me, her crinkled face curiously flat.

I looked at my plate. "I know you don't like it. I don't like it. But we don't have a choice." I sighed, figuring it wouldn't be a good idea to mention that, along with my regular job at the restaurant, Fat Ernst had me helping the Sawyer brothers tear down an old barn. They needed me for my weight, a whopping one hundred and seven pounds, perfect for climbing up into the rotting rafters and knocking sheets of corrugated metal off the roof.

Grandma crunched her lettuce. "We get along just fine."

"No, we don't. We—" I broke off and flung my arm at our reflection in the sliding glass doors, gesturing at the dark, invisible field beyond. "We don't own anything."

"We'll manage."

I attacked my chicken breast, sawing it into ragged chunks. "How? How? Where are we gonna go? You refuse to go on welfare, so—"

"Nobody, nowhere, is ever gonna have to give us money or food. You should know that, Arch. We raised you to be strong. I'll never, ever accept charity from anybody."

"Grandma, this welfare, it isn't charity. We pay taxes, so we deserve it."

Grandma gripped her fork tight. "Deservin' it's got nothing to do with it. I never accepted no charity, and I'm sure as hell not about to start now. Me and your grandfather survived the Great Depression just fine. You and me'll survive this just fine."

I shook my head. I had already tried explaining that the world was a different place now than in the 1930s, but Grandma told me I'd understand when I got older. Well, I understood just fine.

That's why, after our talk, I had crept through her dark garden, plucking a few tomatoes, a couple onions, and some ears of corn I didn't

3

think she'd notice. Fat Ernst gave me five bucks for every bag of produce from Grandma's garden. Believe me, I wasn't proud. I hid the bag of vegetables in the closet by the front door, nestled between Grandpa's Springfield 30.06 and his stack of Encyclopedia Britannicas—the only thing Grandpa ever read besides Louis L'Amour novels. I figured that was a safe place since Grandma didn't like to see Grandpa's stuff. Hurt too much, I guess.

It was 7:40. Now I was officially late. I retrieved the bag from the closet and carefully placed it in the bottom of my backpack. I grabbed an apple out of the fruit bowl, something that Grandma kept full no matter how little money lay in the dark blue jar on top of the fridge. The apple was getting a little brown, but I wasn't going to complain. I bit a healthy chunk out of it and glanced out the window over the sink.

The trailer faced north, providing a wide, unobstructed view of a large, flat field that lay between two low foothills. A twisted, very dead oak tree waited patiently to collapse out in the middle of the field, surrounded by petrified cow patties and thick weeds. Beyond the foothills, the desolate, high country wildness rose into a low sky full of dark clouds.

Ten yards from the northwest corner of the trailer, Grandma stood at the edge of her garden, as still and patient as Death himself. She wore Grandpa's old rubber boots and his faded overalls. A gigantic straw hat covered her head and the shotgun rested easily across the handles of her mud-spattered walker.

I swallowed another piece of the apple and was about to take another bite and find my shoes, but then I froze. The sweet taste of the apple soured as I realized I was looking at a small black hole, set about a quarter inch from the brown skin. A nice, neat wormhole.

Then I heard the low rumbling of the Sawyers' truck.

The truck, a pitch-black 1960 one-ton Dodge, riding awkwardly on four giant tires, lurched impatiently up the long muddy driveway like a hungry beetle. It rumbled up to the trailer, followed by rolling clouds of blue exhaust. A grinning bull skull, its splintered white horns curling out to a wingspan of over four feet, proudly rode above the curving, decidedly aggressively aerodynamic lines of the truck at the front of the hood. A heavy steel bumper protected the grille. Yellow and orange flames flickered over the front tires. The words "SAWYER FAMILY HIDE AND TALLOW SERVICE" had been spray-painted on the doors in jagged, dripping letters.

The truck stopped ten feet from the back steps but the engine continued to idle. Clouds of blue smoke drifted slowly over the garden, enveloping Grandma. She leaned on her walker, keeping the shotgun close, and glared at the truck through her ornate cat's-eye glasses. Her voice sounded as if each word were elegantly sheeted in ice as it rose above the rumbling engine. "What do you want?"

The driver's door popped open and Junior stepped out onto the running board. Junior was built like a furry fire hydrant. His hair flared up in a stiff pompadour, like Elvis on steroids. Giving Grandma an easy grin over the wide hood, he said, "Howdy."

"Howdy," Bert echoed and waved from the passenger window. He was long and lanky and looked like a bone-thin greyhound with some sort of skin disease. He smiled at Grandma, shifted a giant wad of chewing tobacco from one side of his mouth to the other, and spit a ball of nearly black phlegm into the weeds at the edge of the garden.

Grandma wasn't impressed. "When you no accounts came roaring on in here, you must've missed the sign that stated clear as daylight that we shoot trespassers around here. I'll ask one more time and that's it. What do you want?"

"We're pickin' up Arch," Junior said. His grin was gone. "We got a job to finish."

"Is that right," Grandma said. It wasn't a question.

"Yeah, that's fuckin' right," Junior shot back. "Holy fucking Jesus," he said pretty much to himself. "You want me to draw you a picture? Where is he?"

I moved over to the sliding glass door but couldn't bring myself to open it.

Grandma was silent for a moment. "You boys could stand to learn a little about respect."

Junior laughed and I winced. He shouted, "All I know is Fat Ernst is paying us five bucks to collect Archie's skinny ass. He didn't say nothin' about respect, so go fuck yourself, you old goat."

Grandma fired sideways with deadly ease, shotgun braced against right hip, riding the kick with her walker. The blast obliterated a squirrel that had been furtively darting through the tomatoes. She broke open the side-by-side and neatly caught the empty shells as they popped out. Without taking her eyes off Junior, Grandma slid two fresh shells into the shotgun and snapped the barrels into place. The gun blast echoed away and died in the foothills.

I knew it wouldn't take much for Grandma to start shooting at the Sawyer brothers, so I gritted my teeth and slid the glass door open with an escalating *whish*. It sounded like a sudden catch of frightened breath.

My tennis shoes lay on the wooden stairs like two animals that had died in the night. The Sawyer truck waited off to my right. Junior said, "Mornin'. 'Bout fucking time."

"Mornin', sunshine," Bert said.

"Mornin'," I said, jamming my bare feet into the filthy tennis shoes. They felt cold and slimy against my skin.

Grandma didn't say anything for a long time. Finally, fixing those cat's-eye glasses on me, she said, "Where you headed?"

"Grandma, I'm just gonna go to work. Earn some money," I said quietly, moving down the steps.

"Thought we talked about this last night," Grandma said.

Junior shook his head. "No hurry here. Take your time. Shit." He banged his hand flat against the cab's roof. "Let's go! We got work to do."

Grandma casually brought her shotgun around until the barrels were aimed at the truck. I knew she was just looking for an excuse, itching to send nearly four hundred tiny balls of steel shot through Junior's head at over thirteen hundred feet per second, cracking open his skull like a walnut under a hammer, squirting blood, bones, and brains out into the damp air, drenching the weeds beyond the driveway with the remains of his head.

And I knew Grandma well enough to know that she might not need an excuse.

So I did the unthinkable. I stepped in front of Grandma's shotgun, moving sideways toward the truck. Something sour and foul sagged and cracked inside of me. It felt like I had just broken something sacred. "It's gonna be okay, Grandma. Really. I'm just gonna go make some money. I'll see you tonight, okay?"

Grandma didn't answer. At least she kept moving the shotgun so that the barrels were never aimed directly at me. Her expression didn't change. I was sure I could see the pain of betrayal behind her glasses. I wanted to say something that would make everything better, anything to repair the crumbling canyon between us.

But nothing came out of my mouth. As Bert opened the passenger door, I finally turned away and stepped onto the running board. Grandma's voice stopped me. "You be careful out there."

I nodded back at her and climbed into the truck. Bert twisted sideways and pulled me inside. The cab smelled like an unholy, fermenting mixture of cheap whiskey, cow shit, and blood. I landed in the middle of the wide bench seat. Bert slammed the door.

Junior nodded at Grandma over the hood and said, "By the way, Ma said to say hello. Said she hasn't forgotten, understand? Said to tell you she's keeping them forty-four teeth safe and sound."

Grandma didn't say anything. She didn't move. Nothing.

Junior dropped behind the wheel and jerked the long gearshift into reverse. I didn't know what the hell he was talking about. As we rolled backward out of the yard, I watched Grandma through the bug-spattered windshield, a stout figure silhouetted against the faded white trailer, standing perfectly still next to her garden. I raised my hand and waved once.

Grandma didn't wave back.

CHAPTER 2

The truck hit the narrow blacktop strip of Road E backward hard enough that my head cracked into the compound bow hanging in the back of the cab. Junior wrenched the huge steering wheel around, stomped on the brakes, and shifted savagely into first gear, slamming the gearshift into my thigh.

I readjusted my backpack on my lap and tried to slide over a little on the tattered seat, but not too much. I didn't want to get any closer to Bert; I was afraid of catching fleas, or maybe even something worse. I just tried to hold my breath and focus on the dancing hula girl stuck to the dashboard. Actually, the figure wasn't dancing so much as shaking spastically in the vibrating, shivering truck.

We headed west, passing waist-high cornfields and grazing land so green it looked nearly black under the dark, oppressive sky. The town of Whitewood lay to the south at the mouth of a little sliver of a nearly forgotten valley, shaped like a crooked finger that curved up into the high mountain desolation in the northeastern corner of California's vast Sacramento Valley. The town existed in a gray zone, in the hazy border between the long, agriculturally rich Sacramento Valley and the unforgiving volcanic mountains. Mount Shasta loomed over the town to the northwest, and Mount Lassen waited quietly behind the hills to the southeast.

The business district ran for about three blocks, lined with empty, boarded-up buildings, ending in the town's only stoplight. It hung suspended from a cable stretched across the street, and high winds killed the light every few weeks. A couple of gas stations, a hardware store, and a poorly stocked grocery store were scattered along the eastern edge of town as if pulled like magnets to the rush of the freeway. The largest structure in town would probably be the high school football bleachers.

Junior casually scratched his balls with his left hand and yawned. He always wore jeans that were two sizes too small. I guess he figured he was showing off his package, but every once in a while he'd drop down on a barstool at Fat Ernst's and I'd hear that quick rip, like a gasp of relief from the jeans. Split jeans never slowed Junior down much; he always kept an extra pair in the truck.

His finger stabbed at the filthy windshield, pointing at the road ahead. "You see what I see?" he asked in a happy, lilting voice.

A jackrabbit hopped tentatively out of the weeds under a barbed wire fence and out onto the asphalt about thirty yards up the road, near the intersection where Road E crossed over Highway 200. The rabbit's ears twitched once; then it froze.

"Go get it," Bert said in a rush, under his breath. Like cats stalking a bug, neither brother moved a muscle for several seconds. Junior flicked the headlights. Once. Twice. He eased off the gas and we coasted quietly for a moment. He cautiously shifted down, still coasting. Junior flicked the headlights one more time, then popped the clutch and the truck shot forward as if stung by a wasp. The rabbit never moved.

A quiet thump.

The brakes squealed and I damn near lost a few teeth kissing the hula girl.

"Goddamn!" Junior shouted. "You see that? Goddamn!" The

truck slid to a stop at the edge of Highway 200 in a cloud of exhaust and melted rubber.

Junior pulled a clipboard wrapped in a plastic grocery bag from under the seat. He made a neat little check mark on the paper. Blurry snake tattoos slithered up his arms. The clipboard was carefully placed back into the bag and returned to its spot under the seat. "And there's our fucking quota for the week."

One of the Sawyer brothers' jobs was driving around, picking up roadkill for the county. They'd collect anything dead off the highways. Rabbits, possums, skunks, squirrels, raccoons, cats, dogs; anything, as long as it was dead or dying, always trying to reach the quota early in the week, in order to take advantage of more free time. That way, they could work for Fat Ernst earning money for odd jobs here and there, like tearing down the barn, unclogging sump pumps, or digging out septic tanks.

In addition, Junior and Bert ran the only hide and tallow business in Whitewood. They'd haul dead livestock back to their place, way back up Road E, past Grandma's trailer, past where the pavement ended up in the hills. Usually they would collect dead cattle, but sometimes sheep and hogs as well, boiling the carcasses down into glue or dog food. The Sawyer family used to own a legitimate slaughterhouse and sold meat all over the place, but it didn't surprise anybody when they got shut down one day by the health inspector.

Later, the health inspector disappeared.

Stories and rumors and hushed whispers floated through the bars and grocery store about it. Most of these stories were about Pearl Sawyer, Bert and Junior's mother. She'd been around for as long as anyone could remember, living in that same house. I had never seen her. Supposedly, she never left the house anymore. Not since her own accident with the lawnmower.

Junior kicked his door open and jumped to the pavement. Bert did the same. I climbed out too, if for nothing else than to get some fresh air. Thunder crackled far off to the west, far enough that I thought it might be a while before the full force of the storm reached us, but the clouds above were slipping across the sky and tumbling over each other at a frightening speed. The air smelled brilliantly clean, almost sweet.

Junior grabbed a snow shovel from the back of the truck, sauntered over and yelled, "Thank you!" down at the dead rabbit.

Faded stickers were plastered along the truck's rear bumper. "Gun Control Is Hitting What You Aim At," and "I Love Animals—THEY'RE DELICIOUS." Rickety slats of wood enclosed the truck bed and a large steel beam jutted out from the back of the truck. Several black plastic garbage bags lay clustered around the base of the beam near the cab. They looked plump. Full.

I got closer and saw that the rabbit was just a bloody patch of light brown fur. Long ears lay flat against the wet pavement. One vacant eye stared up into space, unmindful of the falling rain. Bert grabbed an empty garbage bag from the back and whipped it open.

I thought I heard a low, mechanical hum, but the rain smothered the sound before I could tell what it was.

Junior slid the shovel under the dead rabbit with a thick, grating sound, and Bert held the bag open as his brother tilted the snow shovel sideways and dropped the lump of fur inside. The rabbit hit the bottom of the black plastic like a sock full of sand. The low sound came again, and this time it got louder.

We all turned and stared in silence as a very long, very gray hearse rolled slowly past the front of the truck, heading south, down the highway toward town. A long line of cars, mostly Cadillacs with a few late-model pickups mixed in, wound slowly out of the hills, solemnly following the hearse. Little orange flags, hanging wet and limp in the rain, adorned the hood of each vehicle.

It was Earl Johnson's funeral procession.

Earl Johnson was, well, *had been* the richest rancher around White-wood. He owned nearly three thousand acres in the northeastern end of the valley, stretching up into the foothills around the reservoir.

The cars continued to stream slowly past us; California's elite ranchers were in town to pay their respects. I guessed it didn't matter if anybody had actually liked the man. He had had plenty of money and power, and his funeral was the social event of the year.

I was kind of ashamed, but part of me was glad he was dead. Last year, I'd applied for a job at his ranch. Well, it was more of a contract position. I'd heard that Earl was looking for somebody to kill coyotes. So I walked out to his house with Grandpa's 30.06 and found Earl out near the dog pens.

I explained that I'd had considerable experience with the rifle and I'd be more than happy to kill some coyotes. If he wanted, I was prepared for a demonstration and had already picked out my target, a knothole in a stump, maybe an inch in diameter, just over two hundred yards out in the field, with the creek bank as a backdrop for safety. I pointed it out, pulled the rifle up, and fired, all in less than three seconds, blowing the knothole out the back of the stump. But that son of a bitch had just laughed in my face, told me to get the hell off his property and to come back when I'd grown a pair. Turned out he held a grudge against my grandfather and wasn't about to hire me anyways.

I wasn't the only one who wouldn't miss him.

"Fucking cheap bastard," Junior snapped.

Bert hawked up a large ball of phlegm and spit nearly fifteen feet at the funeral procession.

Junior viciously flung the snow shovel into the back of the truck and stalked toward the highway. "Who the fuck do these people think they are?" he yelled at the passing cars.

"Bunch of rich motherfuckers, that's what I say." Bert spit again.

Junior turned to me and Bert. He was trying not to grin, but it looked like he had just farted in church and was secretly proud of himself. "We oughta pay our respects. It's the right thing to do."

"Yeah, goddamn, it's only right," Bert said with a serious tone and tossed the rabbit bag into the back. I glanced around at the empty fields and the dark sky. I didn't want to get left out here, nearly two miles away from Fat Ernst's restaurant, so I held my breath and climbed back up into the truck.

CHAPTER 3

Junior jammed his cowboy boot down on the gas and the truck shot out onto Highway 200, gigantic tires singing on the slick asphalt. Within seconds, we had pulled up behind the last car in the procession like a shuddering black caboose finally catching up to the end of a creeping train for the dead.

We followed along for a while, but it didn't take long for Junior to get sick of the slow pace. He kept fidgeting, squirming around and slapping at the steering wheel. "Hey," he said finally. "I wonder if Misty's somewhere up there."

"Holy shit, you're right," Bert said in a rush.

Misty Johnson. Earl's only child. I'd heard that she was failing her senior year; she'd been working too hard at partying and not enough at school. I was seriously thinking of failing a class just so I could maybe see her at summer school.

"I mean, it's her goddamn dad's funeral. She oughta be up there, right?"

Bert nodded so enthusiastically I thought his head might fall off.

"Gonna get me some of that sweetness, oh, you best fucking believe it all right." Junior slapped the steering wheel again. "I'd make her gag, you goddamn got that right. Just too damn big for her purty little mouth, yessir." Junior grabbed at his crotch so violently it looked like he had hurt himself. "Uhhh! Uhhh! Uhhh! That sweet blond hair in my left hand, beer in the other—oh yeah! Yeah!"

"Do it!" Bert shouted.

"I'll fuck her tonsils out!" Junior yelled at the funeral procession, thrusting his hips against the bottom of the steering wheel. My chest got all hot and tight and I started grinding my teeth together. That son of a bitch. He made me sick, talking about Misty Johnson like that. I wanted to grab the back of Junior's head and slam his face into the windshield, mash that grin into a thousand pieces.

"Then I'd pull out and come right in her eye, just like that!" Junior howled, using both hands as a visual aid.

"You'd be coming in 3-D." Bert snorted and collapsed against the door in a fit of herky-jerky giggles.

"Fuck this shit," Junior said suddenly. "Let's go say howdy." He wrenched the wheel to the left and the truck leapt into the oncoming lane. Luckily, there wasn't any traffic for as far as I could see.

Bert waved to the people in the funeral procession as we gathered speed and passed car after car. I leaned forward slightly and glanced out the window. Most of the drivers, almost always thick ranchers sporting even thicker mustaches and cowboy hats so wide the brims resembled goose wings, glanced over at the truck, then ripped their gazes away to stare fixedly at the cars in front of them.

This pissed the Sawyers off even more. I figured they wanted some kind of reaction: fear, anger, annoyance, anything but the inescapable certainty that they were being ignored. Personally, I was glad people were ignoring the truck. I sure as hell didn't want anyone knowing that I was with Junior and Bert.

"These stuck-up assholes; what's that word? Arrogant. That's it. These fuckers are just goddamn arr-o-gant," Junior yelled. "Hey, Bert. Climb in back, give these rich fucks a taste of the working man's life."

A wide smile split Bert's gray, peeling face. He popped the passenger door open, swung out, and clambered up the slats of wood. I ducked down a little, slid over, and pulled the door shut. Junior leaned across me and shouted out the open window, "You fuckers think your shit don't smell?" He shoved his arm past my face, thrusting his fist at the window and extending his middle finger. "Fuck all you cunt lickers!"

We had passed about a dozen or so cars by now; the hearse was maybe thirty or forty cars ahead. I glanced out the back window.

Bert grabbed the plastic bag that contained the rabbit and held it up triumphantly, then plucked a huge knife out of his cowboy boot. It looked like something Rambo would carry. The goddamn blade must have been a foot and a half long. Grinning at me, he jabbed the knife repeatedly into the soft parts of the bag. After carefully wiping the blade clean on his jeans, he slid the knife back into his boot and gave the bag a little shake. It leaked.

Junior hit the horn hard with his fist and "La Cucaracha" suddenly blared out at the world from under the hood. I tried to sink even lower in the seat, holding my right hand up near my face. Junior kept screaming "Cocksuckers!" at the passenger window.

Bert leaned against the wooden slats and began to swing the bag around his head like a lasso, whooping and hollering, "Yeeeemother-fucking*haaaaaaaaaaaaaaa*!" Dark spatters of blood suddenly appeared on car roofs, windshields, hoods. Bert kept swinging the bag, sending fresh drops of blood out into the air in long, streaming arcs.

People in the funeral procession suddenly started to pay attention to the Sawyer brothers.

Junior, who was getting tired of leaning across me to tell folks exactly what he thought of them, their cars, their children, their animals, and their bank accounts, finally just said, "Here. You drive."

I shook my head. "I don't know how to drive. Sorry."

"What are you, fucking retarded? It's easy. Here." Junior grabbed the back of my neck and yanked me across his lap while sliding under me at the same time. The truck lurched and stuttered. I heard Bert fall against the cab.

In the passenger mirror, I saw the black plastic bag hit a Cadillac's hood and slide up the windshield, leaving a wide, clotted smear of blood in its wake. The bag bounced off the roof of the Cadillac and sailed into the air, finally splashing into the irrigation ditch that ran parallel to the highway. The ditch carried water from the reservoir down into the valley. At the moment, it was overflowing with muddy water.

Junior said, "It's easy. Just steer us in a straight line and keep the speed up. That's the gas pedal." He pointed at one of the three pedals on the floor. "There's the brake in the middle and the clutch on the left. If you gotta shift, just push in the clutch. Easy."

"But—," I started to say.

"Just drive, you fucking idiot," Junior hollered, then twisted his upper torso out the passenger window and laughed like a fucking lunatic at the procession, flinging broken shards of glee that danced out into the rain. "Fuck you . . . fuck you . . . and you, too, motherfucker!"

I clutched the steering wheel so tightly it hurt. My right foot found the pedal on the far right, just dumb luck that it happened to be the gas pedal. I kept my left foot hovering in midair above the other two pedals, just in case. I was acutely aware of every little shudder and shake of the truck, every dip and crack in the asphalt, every sway and every bounce. I knew how to drive in theory, having spent most of a semester in a drivers ed class. But the reality of sitting behind the wheel of a one-ton truck, a goddamn stick shift no less, was an altogether different experience.

I flinched as the roof groaned and buckled. Bert was climbing up onto the top of the cab, dragging another bleeding bag behind him. I kept driving, keeping the needle frozen between twenty and twenty-five miles an hour. Actually, this driving thing wasn't so hard. I eased the steering wheel over to the left and the truck drifted over like a dumb, obedient dog. I casually slid the truck back over to the right. This wasn't rocket science, I decided. I gently pressed down on the gas pedal and, sure enough, the needle slowly climbed up to thirty miles an hour. We were over halfway down the procession by now.

Fresh drops of blood hit the windshield and mingled with the raindrops as Bert swung the new bag around in wide loops. I found the windshield wipers and cleaned off the glass. Much better. *This isn't so bad*, I thought. In fact, it was kind of fun. I pressed harder on the gas. Thirty-five miles an hour.

Junior, protruding halfway out the passenger window and grandly flipping off the funeral procession with both hands, kept yelling, "Suck my fat fucking cock, you fat fucking cunt lickers!"

I kept my eyes on the highway and hit the gas harder. The faster I got away from the funeral procession, the better. The needle, slower now, tenaciously crept toward the very tall, very thin number forty-five. An escalating whine grew from the front of the truck. I found the clutch, and with a little grinding that made my teeth ache, I managed to shift into fourth gear.

Another black plastic bag landed in the back of a brand-new Ford and burst open like a rotten tomato. Bert seemed to be enjoying his new game. Through the rearview mirror, I watched as he enthusiastically jabbed at another bag. Junior chuckled at his brother. "There goes the quota for the week."

Up ahead, I could see the junction of Highway 200 and Road DD rapidly approaching. Highway 200 dead-ended in a simple barbed wire fence, closing off the solid bank of the freeway, some three hundred yards beyond the junction. Fat Ernst's Bar and Grill waited just past Road DD, on the east side of the highway, and I decided I'd head for the parking lot to get past the funeral procession as fast as possible. All I had to do was get to the junction first. I figured the hearse would turn right and head west, going up into the foothills to Earl's house.

Junior flopped back inside, breathing heavily. "These goddamn rich assholes. Think they know everything. Fuckers." He started to unbuckle his pants.

I tried again. "I don't know how to drive. Or stop."

Junior glanced through the windshield, said, "Looks like you're doin' a helluva job to me," kneeled on the seat, facing me, and jerked his pants down. He stuck his ass out the passenger window and screamed in ecstasy, "Lick my ass! Lick it! Lick it!"

I kept increasing the pressure on the gas, and before long the needle hovered around fifty miles an hour. I had this driving thing down cold. Just fifty yards to go.

It never occurred to me that that the hearse might be turning left, heading to the cemetery, down Road DD to the east.

Now, looking back, I can see everything in slow motion: Junior swinging his ass back and forth out the window; Bert launching bag after bag from the back of the truck; and the goddamn hearse turning left, right in front of me. I stomped down on one of the pedals, hoping it was the brake, and jerked the steering wheel to the left.

But it was too late.

I got a brief flash of the back end of the hearse disappearing under the hood, as if the bull skull were attacking the long gray car, trying to eat the smaller vehicle, simply trying to swallow it whole as groaning, gnashing shrieks of metal filled the air. A shadow flashed across the windshield as Bert belly flopped onto the hood, sliding into the skull. I suddenly felt curiously weightless, until the steering wheel reached out and punched me in the chest.

And then everything got dark, numb, and quiet.

CHAPTER 4

Later, Heck told me what had happened. He'd seen the whole thing from the restaurant; he'd been nursing one of his morning Bloody Marys while Fat Ernst sulked behind the bar. Fat Ernst hadn't been invited to the funeral and was taking the snub personally.

Heck told me, "That Sawyer truck hit the hearse like it was pissed off. The hearse, man, it didn't have a chance. Went spinning across the highway and *pow*! It hit the bridge hard, man. Craziest thing I ever saw. "Damn hearse flying, then"—he punched his palm—"right into that bridge. Crunched that back end like steppin' on a bag of chips. You could just imagine what happened to the coffin inside, man."

At the time, all I knew was that something was stabbing into my ribs, and for a moment there in the darkness, I got scared that I was wrapped up in black plastic and Bert was jabbing at me with his knife. Then I realized that I was on the floor, wedged against the pedals. Gray light filtered into the cab through the cracked, filthy windshield. I tried to blink the black spots out of my eyes.

The world under Junior's seat—the clipboard wrapped in plastic, several wrinkled *Hustler* magazines, Junior's extra pair of jeans, empty beer bottles, fast food wrappers, a dog leash, and a gigantic Maglite—slowly swam into focus. I heard, "You stupid fucking idiot," and glanced up in time to see Junior's fist swinging down at me. His knuckles smashed into my forehead, slamming my head into the steering column, and great pinwheeling fireworks exploded behind my ears.

"You owe me, cocksucker. You owe me big-time." Junior's pompadour spilled forward and hung in his face. Greasy hair stuck to his tongue as he snarled, "My truck better . . . Holy fucking Christ." Junior glared through the windshield. "Where's the fucking skull?"

He quickly zipped up his jeans and wrenched his buckle tight. "If it's broke you're dead." He thrust his cowboy boot against my chest and shoved me against the pedals. "I'm getting real goddamn irritated here." He punched the passenger door open and jumped out, "Bert! Where the fuck are you?"

I grabbed the driver's door handle. The door sprang open and I slid out to the asphalt. I righted myself on my knees and gingerly felt around. No broken bones, just a lot of future bruises. I touched a raw spot above my eye and my finger came away covered in blood. Still, I could move without too much pain.

I grabbed my backpack and limped around the front of the truck. It didn't seem too badly damaged, thanks to the steel bumper. The bull skull was gone, though. The truck faced roughly west, sitting sideways in the middle of Highway 200, maybe twenty yards south of Road DD. I heard Junior shout, "Goddamnit, Bert! The skull's broke!"

I cautiously stuck my head around the right headlight and stared back up the highway. The hearse lay sideways, half submerged in the surging water, crumpled against the bridge. A cloud of steam or smoke enveloped most of the accident. I could see enough to notice that the back door hung limply on its hinges. The coffin was gone.

Straight up the highway was Junior. He swayed unsteadily up the yellow line, carrying the bull skull in his left hand. One of the horns was gone, broken off. Smoke rolled across the highway behind him.

For a moment, nothing moved but the smoke. Then all hell broke loose.

I heard car doors opening, slamming shut. Shocked, angry voices. Men with permanently sunburned faces in dark, Western-cut suits boiled out of their cars and pickups, stomping toward the intersection. Stocky women in dark blue and green dresses that hugged their ample hips and hung to midcalf followed their husbands out of the cars, some wearing the soggy remains of their potluck contributions.

The first Cadillac in the funeral procession, the one that had been following the hearse, sat quietly in the middle of the intersection. Finally, the driver's door swung open and Slim Johnson, Earl's younger brother, jumped out. A thin trickle of blood ran from his thinning hair down his white forehead, across the hat line, and continued down his red face. He looked naked without his John Deere hat.

"Sonofabitch!" he screamed, literally shaking with rage. His scarred, leathery hands clenched and unclenched into bony fists. It looked like Slim's wife and the rest of Earl's family were in the car. They didn't seem to be in much of a hurry to climb out. I wondered if Misty was in there. Many of the men from the funeral procession had reached the second car in line, but hung back, waiting to follow Slim's lead.

It didn't take long. Slim stalked forward, down the center of the highway, shaking a finger at Junior. "Sonofabitch!" he screamed again, apparently the only word he was capable of choking out. A vein throbbed alarmingly in his temple. He stomped down the highway in his ostrich skin boots, his finger vibrating spastically like a dousing rod that had just found the ocean. "Sonofabitch! You hear me, you little sonofabitch?"

Junior ignored Slim and tucked the bull skull under one arm. "Bert! Let's go!"

In the weeds next to the hearse, Bert called out weakly, "Junior?"

Off to my right, across the muddy lake that Fat Ernst liked to call a parking lot, the screen door slammed shut. Fat Ernst and Heck worked their way down the steps and started across the acre of mud. At first glance, Fat Ernst looked like somebody had haphazardly shaved one of those bears that were trained to ride a unicycle around a circus ring. When he got closer, you could see this guy was maybe a little uglier than a shaved bear. He had named his restaurant to try and convince people that this big, waddling German had a sense of humor. But all it did was give everybody permission to call him "fat" to his face.

The smaller man was Heck. He sported a potbelly so perfectly defined it looked like he was trying to hide a bowling ball under his shirt as he hopped through the mud with his ambling gate. Heck, short for Hector, ran a bait shop up near the Split Rock reservoir. He never had a whole lot of business since not many people bothered fishing up there; carp were about the only fish that could live in the brackish water.

Bert called, "Hey, Junior? Junior?"

Meanwhile, Slim had caught up with Junior in the middle of the highway. "You listen to me when I'm talking to you, you little—" Slim started to yank Junior around, but Junior twisted out of the rancher's grasp and shoved the bull skull into Slim's chest.

"Fuck off!" Junior shouted up into Slim's face. "Look what you fucking did to my truck!" Dark spittle flew out of Junior's mouth and landed on Slim's cheek. Slim did an admirable job of ignoring it, even as it slid down his cheek and collected at the corner of his lips.

Slim's voice dropped dangerously low. "Now, now you listen to me—"

Junior jerked the skull up in a quick, savage motion, cracking the heavy bone into Slim's chin. Slim's head popped back as if he'd suddenly found something amazing in the clouds above him; then he took two stuttering steps sideways.

He turned, and I thought he was going to say something to the group of ranchers behind him, but he toppled face-first onto the hood of his Cadillac instead. He slid down and his chin bounced off the front bumper, snapping his teeth shut with a solid crack that made me wince. It knocked him straight out; his eyes rolled back and he dropped to the asphalt, landing on one knee and his left ear.

None of the men from the procession moved. Somebody brave shouted, "Hey, that ain't right," but that was all.

The passenger door of Slim's Cadillac opened and the one and only Misty Johnson stepped out. Everything stopped for a second. Even the rain. She slammed the door and said, "Junior, didn't your mother ever teach you any manners, you goddamn dumb redneck prick?"

CHAPTER 5

Misty had hair the color of blond sin, curling slightly around her bare shoulders. A black dress clung to a body with curves like those on old cars from the late forties, early fifties: curves that hinted, suggested, promised the exquisite soft heat underneath. Man, oh man, those curves. There was something about the precise mathematical nature of those smooth angles that triggered something in my brain like goddamn voodoo; overloaded, overheated the circuits, sent the synapses barking at each other in different languages, fogged up the connections in a monsoon of lust. Maybe it was wrong to feel that way about somebody who had just lost her father, and at the man's funeral no less, but I didn't care.

Junior pointed the bull skull at her. "You better watch your mouth, talking about Ma." He turned back and ambled down the highway toward his truck, still looking for the broken horn. "Bert! Let's go. Get the lead out!" Then he saw me and stopped. His heavy-lidded stare froze my blood.

"I . . . I told you I didn't know how to drive," I stammered.

Junior just shook his head ever so slowly. He never took his eyes off of me. "See this?" He shook the skull at me. "You're gonna pay for this."

"Hey, Junior? Junior?" Bert crawled out of the weeds next to the hearse. Although his right arm hung at his side at an unnatural angle, I could see that the broken horn was clutched in his fist. He lurched toward the truck, holding his right wrist close to his waist, and met Junior at the double yellow lines in the center of the road.

Junior looked Bert up and down for a minute. They exchanged a few quiet words.

Misty leaned forward, crossing her arms and resting them on the top of the door frame. She watched silently, her perfect chest framed in the car's window frame, and looked at me.

Junior helped Bert toward the truck.

I blinked and watched as a couple of the men skittishly came forward and helped Slim to his feet. Fresh blood oozed from Slim's mouth. He jerked his arms free, glaring at the world, and shook one callused finger at Junior and Bert. "You . . . you little sonofabitch."

His fragile composure was beginning to crack again. I couldn't wait for it to shatter; then he'd go after Junior like some wild dog. Hell, this was something I'd pay to see. Slim swallowed and his top lip kept twitching as if he'd had a stroke. "I'm talking to you, boy, so you'd best—"

Junior turned back to the procession one more time, speaking slowly and loudly so everyone could hear him clearly. "Why don't you take that bony little dick of yours, stick it right up your tight ass, and start farting, motherfucker." He shoved Bert into the passenger seat. Bert's right arm hit the dashboard and he screamed. I tried not to grin.

Fat Ernst and Heck finally reached the back of the truck. My boss was wheezing terribly, something exercise always did to him. Even though his lungs were shot, having to haul all that bulk around meant he still had muscles like boulders, buried underneath deceptive layers of fat. Once, when a trucker was mouthing off, I saw Fat Ernst casually reach over the bar and pop the guy in the jaw. It wasn't a big, swinging roundhouse punch, either. No, it was just a little jab, but I heard the trucker ended up enjoying his meals through a straw for the better part of a year.

Slim ignored Fat Ernst and Heck and kicked the truck's back tire with one of his ostrich skin boots. I don't think it hurt the tire much.

"Howdy, Slim," Fat Ernst breathed.

Slim kicked the back bumper.

Junior tossed the bull skull and the horn on the floor of the cab next to Bert's boots and turned to Slim, smoothing out his pompadour with both hands. "Do it again. C'mon. Do it again! I got witnesses. When I drag your ass to court, I'm gonna tell everybody how you assaulted our truck."

"You little . . . little . . . sonofabitch," Slim said in one long, hissed exhale. I don't think anything scared Slim more than lawyers. He yelled, "Where is that useless goddamn deputy?" and looked down the highway, as if the police car might just happen to be driving along. He whirled and pointed at Fat Ernst. "Call Ray! Get him out here right now!"

Fat Ernst finally caught his breath enough to string more than three words together. "Well now, Slim, I don't know exactly what happened here, but—"

"Get on the goddamn phone! I want Ray out here now! Right now!" Slim started to say something else, but Junior jumped into the truck and started it with a roar, drowning out the rest of Slim's words.

I stepped smartly out of the way as the hide and tallow truck backed away from the smoking hearse. It swung around in reverse toward the restaurant. The gears ground together like a mouthful of steel shavings as Junior forced the gearshift into first. He beeped the horn twice and waved, then flew back down the highway the way we had come, passing the funeral procession once again.

"Sonofabitch!" Slim screamed.

"Now, just take it easy, calm down and . . ."

But Slim wasn't listening. He stormed back to his Cadillac, ripped open the driver's door, and got in. The back doors popped open and family members hastily crawled out as Slim gunned the engine.

Misty stepped away and shut her door. Slim's and Earl's wives, I didn't know which was which, clung together, watching Slim with wide, horrified eyes. Even Fat Ernst managed to get out of the way.

Slim stomped on the gas but nothing happened. The Cadillac didn't move. The back bumper was caught underneath the bumper of the burnt-orange Cadillac behind it.

Slim tried again, and the front tires started spinning on the wet asphalt. The bumpers gave a protesting, grinding sound, but held. The front of Slim's car drifted back and forth across the intersection. He screamed something and punched at the steering wheel. Then he jerked the short gearshift into reverse and stood on the gas again. The Cadillac rocked backward, and both bumpers curled down to the asphalt. Then it was back into drive and the car surged forward, lifting the bumpers up once again.

The metal held for a brief moment, long enough to get the front tires spinning and the car floating back and forth across the road. Then the bumper of the burnt-orange Cadillac gave way with a high, twanging sound and a couple of sparks.

Slim's Cadillac shot forward as if fired from a slow-burning cannon. I could see Slim wrench the wheel to the left, saw the front tires turn as well, but they couldn't find purchase on the rain-slick asphalt at that speed and the Cadillac shot through the muddy parking lot and plunged into the cornfield, where the engine promptly died.

Nobody said anything for a minute.

Then, from the cornfield, I heard a faint "Sonofabitch!"

And just when Fat Ernst opened his mouth, one of the wives started to scream. But she wasn't looking across the highway at the cornfield. She was staring down into the ditch. Several of the men and their wives rushed forward to see what was wrong. I walked across the bridge and stood a ways behind Fat Ernst.

Right on the other side of the intersection, by the short bridge where Road DD crossed over the irrigation ditch, the ditch split in

wormfood

two. One branch, the main one, kept going straight, due south toward the freeway. The other branch forked off to the left, following the road to Slim's and Earl's ranches in the northeastern end of the valley. A large wooden gate used to regulate the flow of water was sunk into the concrete where the two ditches met. Normally, the gate would have been down, cutting off water to the smaller ditch, but today it was open, and the dark water rolled and boiled at the junction where the smashed hearse lay.

It looked like parts of Earl were swirling around in the water.

Somebody led the wives away from the edge of the bridge as more parts of Earl's corpse slowly emerged. I caught sight of the toe of a black cowboy boot, an empty arm of a blue suit with a clenched, swollen fist sticking out of one end, and some just plain unidentifiable meat. "Jesus Christ," I whispered and swallowed. Stray strands of white hair floated up, and I quickly looked away before the rest of the head followed.

"Damn. That ain't gonna be easy, finding all of him to put back in a box," I heard Fat Ernst murmur to Heck. Fat Ernst froze suddenly, eyes wide. "Jesus, you don't think . . . They weren't gonna bury him with his belt buckle, were they?"

I'd heard about Earl's belt buckle a few times in the bar. I guess he'd won CAA Cowboy of the Year a few years ago, and as a prize they'd given him a giant silver and gold belt buckle. The gold had been sculpted into a relief showing a cowboy and his horse crossing a mountain meadow at night. Dozens of small diamonds had been set into the silver sky, representing stars. Way I heard it, the buckle wasn't cheap, not by a long shot.

Heck nodded. "That's what they said, man."

"Jesus," Fat Ernst repeated. Both men touched their own large belt buckles, but I didn't know if it was just to reassure themselves that their own buckles were still there, or if it was out of sympathy, like Catholics making the sign of the cross. Fat Ernst grunted. "I'll bet Slim ain't too happy about not getting his hands on that buckle."

"What the hell is that?" Heck asked.

I saw something roll over in the water. It looked kind of long,

29

cylindrical, and gray, like a small hose or something. But the water kept surging around, and it was gone before I got a good look at it.

"I reckon part of the lower intestine," Fat Ernst said knowingly. "I heard he'd been down on the bottom for something like two weeks. So Hutson couldn't embalm Earl. Read that they can't do it to bodies that have been in salt water too long."

Pieces of the corpse were starting to float down the smaller ditch, toward the foothills. "Guess he wants to go home," Fat Ernst said hoarsely, trying not to laugh. Heck snorted, covering his mouth.

"Did you see what happened?" Misty asked me.

I was suddenly painfully aware of the blood on my forehead, collecting and clotting into a stiff scab in my eyebrow. "I, uh, no . . . not really."

Fat Ernst didn't know what to say either. "Ah . . . we . . . uh, were real sorry to hear about the loss of your father."

Misty gave a quick nod, keeping her eyes on the ditch.

One of the farmers came over, took a look and screwed up his face like he'd just bitten into a rotten lemon. "Dear Lord . . . You think we should try and maybe . . . I don't know, maybe try and *collect* him? For later, I mean . . . to be buried?"

"Shit, I dunno," Fat Ernst said. "I'd say just wait. You can get all the parts later on, downstream, if need be." The man nodded, looking relieved. Suddenly, Fat Ernst noticed me. "What the hell are you doing?"

I looked at my shoes. "Uhh . . . nothing."

"Exactly. Get into gear and get to work. You ain't getting paid to stand around and gawk."

I nodded and stepped away from the edge of the ditch. It was time to get to work. As I walked across the highway through the gentle rain toward the spinning neon sign, I glanced back and saw Misty watching me. I turned around and kept moving. I heard Fat Ernst tell Heck, "Just can't get decent help these days." Then, quieter. "Swear to God, that boy is dumber than a box of dirt."

CHAPTER 6

Fat Ernst had big plans for his restaurant. He had it built next to where he knew they were putting in the freeway. Actually, he bought up a lot of land where he thought they might build the freeway, just in case. That's how he owned the land where Grandma and I lived. Paid off one of the county commissioners to make sure they put an off-ramp next to the restaurant, so folks going down the freeway could pull off nice and easy, spend some money, have some food. But before they could get around to planning the on- and off-ramps, the commissioner had a heart attack. The next guy who got put in charge just happened to be part owner in a gas station farther south down the freeway, on Highway 14. So the off-ramp never got put in next to the restaurant. They didn't even bother to build an overpass, just killed Highway 200 right there.

Well, that pissed Fat Ernst off so much he showed up at the next city council meeting, ranting and shouting about how the council was nothing but a bunch of commie motherfuckers.

The next day, a county health inspector showed up at the restaurant. Closed Fat Ernst down. Fifty-three counts of health violations. Fat Ernst didn't have much of a choice; he had to comply. Spent even more money, got the restaurant fixed up enough to where he could reopen.

Then somebody else came out a week later, cited him because he didn't have any designated handicapped parking. And this was back in the days when nobody gave a shit about wheelchair access. They must have really searched the books to find that law. Fat Ernst had to put up a handicapped parking sign, right next to the front stairs. All that did was to make him mad enough that he parked his bone white Cadillac there every day in a sort of protest.

The restaurant was built in the midst of cornfields, on about an acre of land mostly covered in cheap gravel. Fat Ernst wanted plenty of parking space, in anticipation of all the customers he figured would be eating there, but it only made the place seem even more isolated and empty. He never bothered to resurface the lot, and so after a few years passed it looked like some sort of bombed-out no-man's-land, with giant craters all over the place. When the rains came, the lot was one giant lake of mud.

I trudged across this lake and didn't even bother to try and keep my feet dry. Mud seeped into my tennis shoes and I could feel the silt and grit working its way between my toes. I glanced back over my shoulder at the intersection.

Everyone was still gathered around the ditch, but nobody seemed to be doing anything except talking and pointing at the water once in a while. I couldn't see Slim, but he'd gotten the engine of his Cadillac started; it rose higher and higher every few seconds before dropping back into idle.

I shook my head and walked up the five warped wooden steps to the restaurant. The building sat about two feet above the ground, resting on six-by-six wooden stilts that were sunk into concrete blocks. Two large windows flanked the front door. Beneath the left window there was a sign Fat Ernst had hung and never bothered to take down. After about five years, the thing had gotten so tattered and frayed you could hardly read it. It read something like *"Whitewood's Biggest*

wormfood

Party—Every Saturday Night!" But nobody ever really showed up.

Above the front door was another sign. This one had the words carved into a large, flat chunk of wood. It read "NO WEAPONS ALLOWED" in old-fashioned block letters, as if the place were some sort of saloon in the old West. I kicked open the front door and slammed it behind me.

The restaurant didn't look much better on the inside. Six tables, covered in peeling Formica, were evenly spaced out in the front half of the building. Dead pheasants and ducks had been awkwardly mounted on the walls between the occasional neon beer sign around the dining room. The dusty eyes of three ragged, moth-eaten buck heads followed me as I wound my way through the tables.

The restrooms were off to my right, on the south side of the building, just past the jukebox. An unbalanced pool table sat near the jukebox, with wood wedges jammed under the legs. Directly in front of me was the bar. It ran nearly the entire length of the building, stretching from the door to the restrooms all the way to the kitchen doors on my left.

I banged through these swinging doors, unzipping my backpack. The kitchen was crammed into a narrow sliver of a room directly behind the bar. Everything was set up in one long row: first the stove, then the silver counter, adjacent to the sink, and finally the wheezing refrigerator.

The kitchen didn't have any windows. Smudged yellow light came from two bare bulbs that hung from the cobwebbed rafters. I twisted the hot water handle and let the water warm up a little before cupping my hands and splashing it on my face. Soap would have been even better, but there wasn't any. Finally, I just stuck my head under the faucet and let the warm water run across my forehead for a while.

After wiping myself down and getting most of the blood off with an old dishrag, I pulled the soggy bag out of my backpack and winced at the sight of the crushed vegetables. It looked like someone had taken a short-handled sledgehammer to the tomatoes.

Since the coffee was already sluggishly gurgling to itself, it was time to light the stove. Fat Ernst thought it was a waste of gas to leave the pilot light on all night and would always blow it out. Then he'd reach behind the stove and crank the gnarled handle closed, turning the gas off.

Every morning I worried that maybe he'd forgotten to shut off the gas after blowing out the pilot light, so I'd lean over the stove and sniff cautiously. I never did smell anything; but just to be on the safe side, I'd step back and flick a lit match at the stove. This morning the match landed in the middle of the white film of grease that covered the long black griddle, and the match sizzled quietly a moment before dying.

It didn't explode, so I squeezed my shoulder between the back of the stove and the grease-spattered wall and twisted the handle back around. Deep inside the stove, I could hear the gas start to hiss. Now it was time to move fast.

I yanked open the oven door with my left hand and at the same time popped a match with the thumb on my right hand. I'd had lots of practice. I reached into the oven with my right hand and pushed the burning match up into the back corner and with a slight *whoosh*, the pilot light burst into life.

I scraped some of the grease off the cast iron griddle and heard the front door squeak open. Fat Ernst's voice came barreling through the swinging doors and bounced off the walls in the cramped space.

"I don't know what kinda hog pen you waded through before tracking all this shit across my floor, but I suggest you clean it up right quick. This floor ain't gonna mop itself."

I sighed, stretched. It was going to be a long day.

After filling up the bucket in the sink, I grabbed the mop leaning in the corner and went out front. Fat Ernst had left his own muddy tracks right into the bathroom. Another part of the morning ritual. I'm not sure what the hell kind of coffee Fat Ernst drank, but I'd learned to hold my bladder until the afternoon. Nobody used the restroom after Fat Ernst.

wormfood

Starting in the usual corner, between the jukebox and the front window, I sloshed a little water on the floor, then leaned against the wall, watching the intersection through the window. A few people had managed to get the driver's door of the hearse open and helped Mr. Hutson climb out. They eased him back to the bank and sat down with him, holding handkerchiefs to his bleeding head.

Most of the cars had left, but now there were a few guys in waders walking around carrying fishnets. They had a large ice chest set near the bank. One of the men, wearing camouflage waders that came up to his chest, wrapped a red bandana around the lower half of his face, so he looked like a bank robber. He carefully clambered down into the ditch, using the mangled back door of the hearse as a support. Somebody handed him a fishnet with a long telescoping handle and a two-foot ring. I guess they were pretty serious about collecting up the rest of Earl.

Heck watched the activity at the ditch bank for a while, then shook his head and walked back to the restaurant. At the top of the steps, he tried to stomp some of the mud off his boots. He didn't get much off, but I appreciated the effort.

"Mornin'." He shut the door and joined me at the window, leaning on the tables as he shuffled forward. "Goddamn shame," he said with a grin, showing perfect white teeth that seemed a little too big for his mouth. "Couldn't happen to a nicer guy, man."

As we watched a tow truck pulled up, surveyed the scene, then backed up to the hearse. One of the men suddenly detached from the group and rushed over. It was Slim. He waved his hands around wildly for a moment, then pointed toward the cornfield. I guess he wanted his Cadillac pulled out of the cornfield first.

"What an asshole," Heck muttered. "Both them brothers were cold-hearted sonsabitches, man. Can't say I'm sorry one's gone." He turned and tottered over to the jukebox. "I'd say this calls for a celebration." He leaned over it, whistling a tune I couldn't quite place. "Let's see here . . ."

I watched the tow truck pull away from the hearse and drive across the highway to the cornfield. Then I jammed the mop back into my bucket and splashed some more water on the floor.

I don't know why Fat Ernst was so hell-bent on keeping the floor clean. He didn't give a damn about the sanitary condition of the kitchen, but he sure wanted a clean floor out front. It wasn't even in good shape; the varnish had worn off in a vague trail from the front door to the bar and the wood was starting to crack in other places.

"Who the hell are these people?" Heck snarled at the jukebox. His finger slid slowly down the glass, marking each record. "No Johnny Cash. No Flat and Scruggs. No Bill Monroe or Grandpa Jones. Not even any goddamn Hank Williams."

I just kept mopping, concentrating on all the mud near the door. Heck would spend a few minutes grumbling about the piss-poor selection on the jukebox every morning. He kept hounding Fat Ernst to change the records, but my boss refused to take out anything. He figured he knew what his customers wanted, and that was mostly Southern-fried classic rock. If I had to listen to "Sweet Home Alabama" one more time, just one more time, I was gonna shove my mop through that goddamn jukebox.

Heck kept ranting. "Oh, sure, there's that no-talent sonofabitch Hank Williams Jr. on here, still living off his daddy's name, but I'd rather listen to my wife's cats fucking." He shook his head in disgust.

I knew Heck well enough to know that when his wife got mentioned, it was time for a drink. "Piss on it," he said with an air of finality, and pushed away from the jukebox. He swung those bow legs over one of the bar stools and sank onto it like a plant wilting in fast motion in some grade school science film.

He swiveled around, watching me as I sloshed the mop at the mud near the front door, and said, "Why don't you slow down there for a minute and have mercy on an old man. Get me something to drink. Something. Anything. No, no, wait." He rubbed a hand over his wrinkled scalp. "That won't work. Wife hasn't been cooking much

36

lately. Been feeding me too damn much cat food these days, and if I have a beer it's gonna raise holy hell with my insides." Heck nodded, handing down one of the great truths of the universe. "And I don't have to tell you that I don't need to spend all day in the crapper. Hell, no."

I heard the toilet flush. Once. Twice. I splashed water across the floor in a frenzy of black bubbles, backing closer and closer to the kitchen doors. Fat Ernst filled the doorway, hitching up his jeans and clasping a silver belt buckle the size of a baby's head. He shot me a quick, sharp look. "Hey, boy. You get that griddle warmed up. Fry Heck an egg and a couple of those sausages."

"Over easy," Heck said.

"Then you get your ass in the shitter and clean it up. It ain't pretty."

I nodded quickly, gritting my teeth. Only ten more hours. Then the day was done. Only ten more hours.

CHAPTER 7

That night, the rain finally slowed to a foggy drizzle as the dim sun slowly sank behind the mountains to the west. A faint light still reflected off the low clouds, but in time that too was gone, leaving the valley shrouded in misty darkness. Happy hour at Fat Ernst's came and went with no one except Heck around to enjoy it.

Despite the lack of customers, Fat Ernst kept me plenty busy around the restaurant, scrubbing the toilets, taking out the garbage, and taking stock of the inventory. Mostly that meant recounting the bottles behind the bar, but this time I had to check on the food in the refrigerator as well.

Fat Ernst was getting low on just about everything, especially meat.

Around eight, I was mopping the goddamn floor yet again when I saw an Ash Spring Sheriff's Department squad car splash through the muddy expanse of the parking lot. Deputy Ray himself climbed out, making sure his felt cowboy hat was in place, cocked at just the right angle. He squinted at himself in the side mirror, carefully positioning the toothpick in the corner of his thin mouth.

Shaped like a tall, crooked fence post with a fresh pumpkin impaled at the top, his Adam's apple jutted out several alarming inches from his thin, twisted neck. He licked his fingers, smoothed out his scraggly eyebrows, patted down his long sideburns, and tucked his hair back behind his ears. Ray was always hoping he might meet a woman who simply loved a man in a uniform.

I turned away from the window and was listlessly sliding the mop around under the pool table when he swaggered in, grinning like a dog that had just discovered he could lick his own balls and couldn't wait to tell folks about it. Heck was still perched on his bar stool, but just barely. He stared dully at the shot glass in front of him. Ray ignored me and nodded to Fat Ernst, who was watching bowling on the little black-and-white TV behind the bar.

"Howdy, Ernst. How's business?"

"Fabulous," Fat Ernst replied in a dead tone. He never took his eyes off the television. "What'll you have?"

"Better just make it a shot and a beer. Gotta go check out the dam later on. Sheriff's worried the reservoir might be rising."

"It ain't gonna flood."

"Rain sure as hell came down in buckets today, though. Boy, oh, boy. Like a cow pissing on a flat rock." Ray approached the bar and hollered at Heck. "Hey, Heck! How you doing?" He slapped Heck on the back in a friendly manner.

Heck's head slumped forward from the blow and his chin bounced off the bar. His dentures popped out and skittered across the bar like a frightened frog.

"Whoa—hey, there." Ray's toothpick danced under his thin mustache when he talked. He sat down next to Heck and tilted his cowboy hat to rest at a nearly vertical angle on the back of his head. "Good to see ya out and about. Edna let you out of the house again?" Ray gave a high, wheezing laugh. "Just pulling your leg, just pulling your leg."

He readjusted the giant holster that sagged at his right hip. It held a massive Ruger Super Redhawk .480 revolver, over a third more powerful

39

than a .44 Magnum. I guess Ray wanted to prove that he was more of a man than Dirty Harry. Each shell held at least 240 grains of powder and cost nearly two bucks. The gun was usually used for killing big game, some almost as big as rhinos. I never did understand why the department would let Ray carry a cannon like that. Maybe they figured he'd never actually use it.

I shook my head and moved to the tables, trying to ignore Ray.

"It ain't gonna flood." Fat Ernst rolled the cigar around in his mouth once, took a deep breath, grabbed the edge of the bar, and heaved himself to his feet. His round face turned red from the exertion. "Figured you might be around sometime, after that mess this morning."

"Shit. Don't remind me. Slim's been calling all day. Wants them Sawyer brothers shot on sight. I'll get around to getting a statement here soon. It's always some damn thing with that man."

Fat Ernst poured two shots of Wild Turkey. "Well, I can almost understand him being upset. Earl wasn't exactly in the best shape after going for a swim in the ditch and all." He slid one of the shot glasses across the bar to Ray.

"Hell, you don't know the half of it." Ray downed the shot, straightened up, and said, "I got the real story from a buddy a mine; he's in the Coast Guard." Ray nodded importantly. "Earl and these two other rich old boys, buddies of his in the CCA, rented a fourteen-footer out of Noyo Harbor."

The CCA was the California Cattleman's Association, referred to by most of the customers of Fat Ernst's bar as "those pricks from downstate," because the CCA was an exclusive club, reserved for the twenty-five richest ranchers in the state.

"That's some heavy inside dope you got there, Ray," Fat Ernst said, sarcasm falling to the bar between them in fat, quivering drops. "Hell, I already seen that on the news." He hooked the naked dentures over Heck's shot glass.

"Yeah, well, like I said, you don't know the half of it," Ray said quickly, smoothing out his pathetically thin mustache with his thumb and forefinger as if to reassure himself. I stopped moving the mop around for a moment and listened.

"These guys are fishing for steelhead, right at the mouth of the Klamath River. Maybe twenty, thirty yards out. You've been fishin' there, right?"

Fat Ernst nodded vaguely. Ray spit his words out in an excited rush. "They're right at the mouth out there, where the waves are surging around in every fucking direction, and the water's so churned up you can't see jack shit."

"Yeah, I been there," Fat Ernst said.

"'Course, it's too damn early for steelhead fishing, season don't open for another two months at least. But these boys"—Ray lowered his thin, reedy voice in a conspiratorial tone—"now, these boys are doing some serious drinking. Shit, Coast Guard found four empty bottles of tequila, and that's not counting the beer cans that washed away."

Fat Ernst yawned. Personally, I didn't give a damn one way or the other how Earl had died. Like I said, part of me was glad he was dead. I was about to hurry up and finish slathering dirty water on the floor and go home when Deputy Ray spoke up.

"So they're out there, okay, fishing and doing some serious drinking. And then one of 'em hooks a shark."

I let the mop drift around in small circles, almost by itself, and turned to the bar. Fat Ernst had actually turned away from the television set up in the corner and was now facing Ray, who was perched on the bar stool, leaning into the wood as if someone had propped a fence post up against the bar. There's something about sharks that grabs folks' attention.

"I guess it was just a blue shark, nothin' special, maybe eight, nine feet long. Sounded like the fella had a salmon on first, and the shark must've gone after that fish, just swallowed it whole, salmon, hook, and everything. Pure dumb luck it got hooked. Now, if it was any other line, a shark that size would've—"

"It woulda snapped," Fat Ernst broke in. When it came to catching and killing things, Fat Ernst considered himself an expert.

"Exactly. But these guys . . ." Deputy Ray pointed at Fat Ernst with his shot glass for emphasis. "These guys were using eighty-pound test, something like that. So they manage to haul it up to the surface, all fired up about taking those teeth. But the thing ain't dead, and it's thrashing around, right off the stern, and these dumb bastards don't know what the hell to do about it."

Fat Ernst filled the shot glass and said, "You put a bullet in its head, that's what you do." He gave a slow chuckle filled with phlegm, experienced beyond his years as a rough-and-tumble shark killer.

"Exactly," Deputy Ray repeated. "So while the fella that had hooked the thing, he's hanging on to that fishing pole, screaming about how he's gonna put them jaws above the fireplace, Earl is digging around for that old Army Colt .45. Meanwhile, his other buddy found a two-by-four somewhere, and he's trying to bash the shark's head in, but he's just pissing it off. So, I guess Earl stumbled to the back of the boat, and here's where the accounts start to differ. One fella said that the boat lurched sideways all of a sudden, from a wave, I guess, and the other fella, the one with the fishing pole, said the shark tried to attack the boat or some damn thing. Doesn't matter much, though."

Unable to help himself, Deputy Ray grinned. "Well, that .45 went off and Earl put a bullet right through his own fucking foot."

Fat Ernst wobbled and gave a wheezing laugh that sounded like gravel falling off a truck.

"That bullet went right through his foot and on through the bottom of the boat. But a course, they wouldn't of known that at the time, 'cause somehow Earl fell into that eighty-pound test line, and the fella dropped the pole to help. Well, the line got all wrapped around Earl's neck and I'll be damned if that shark didn't pull him right out of the fucking boat." Deputy Ray downed his shot but started to giggle, holding his hand up to his mouth to stop Wild Turkey from dribbling out. After a moment, he got himself under control and continued.

"I guess the shark went after that bloody foot for a while, chewed it pretty much right off from what I hear, and old Earl, drunk as hell, he just sank like a rock, and that was that. His friends couldn't help much 'cause they were trying to stop the boat from being tossed into the rocks. And that was the last they saw of him, until the Coast Guard found him a week later, all tangled up in those Indians' nets." He paused. "And that ain't all."

Fat Ernst poured another shot.

Ray whispered, "I guess when they brought him back up to the surface, things had been chewing on him. Things had been eating him *from the inside*. Didn't find no holes though. So that meant that these ocean critters, they crawled into his insides through his . . . his *orifices*, and I ain't talking about his goddamn mouth, neither."

And right then the front door bounced off the wall and Slim walked in, wearing his cowboy hat and a soaking wet oiled-canvas duster. He looked like someone had spit in his socks and he'd been wearing them for a few days now. He pointed at Deputy Ray. "Been looking for you. Where the hell have you been?"

"Sheriff's got me running around all over the place. I haven't—"

Slim shook his head, stalking across the floor, leaving another trail of mud where I had just finished mopping. "Don't give me any of that horseshit. This is serious. I'm talking about a goddamn hit and run." He shoved his finger into Ray's narrow chest and pushed the deputy back against the bar.

"Now you go out there and arrest them Sawyer brothers. I don't care how you do it, but I want them in jail by tomorrow morning, or I swear to God I will have your fucking badge." Slim looked like he'd not only rip the badge off of Ray's chest; he'd cheerfully eat it as well. "When I'm through with you, you won't be able to get a job guarding a goddamn garbage can, you got that?"

Ray swallowed, and that Adam's apple bounced up and down like a punching bag. "Yessir, sure. I'll go talk to 'em. Don't you worry."

"I don't want you to talk to 'em. I want 'em in jail or dead." Slim straightened and took off his plastic-covered cowboy hat. He pointed it at Ray, shaking little drops of rainwater onto the floor. "Hell, I'd prefer dead."

Ray nodded vigorously, as if he might just decide to drive out to the Sawyer brothers' house right now and start shooting.

Slim turned to Fat Ernst. "And if you see those punks—seems like they're here every goddamn time I drive by—you'll let me know, right?"

"Of course. We're friends, aren't we?" Fat Ernst mumbled around his half-chewed cigar, then grinned. "How about a beer?"

"Can't tonight. I have to go pick up the new casket myself 'cause Hutson's still in the hospital. Besides that, the whole goddamn back fifty acres is underwater, and on top of everything else, I got two dead steers I got to take care of."

Slim pulled a well-used handkerchief out of his back pocket and blew his nose forcefully, his entire body shaking with effort. I figured that snot must have been buried deep, like in his intestines. After briefly and automatically checking the contents, he stowed the piece of cloth safely back into his pocket. Then he jammed his cowboy hat back on and pointed at Ray again. "I ain't kidding about those goddamn Sawyers. They best be in jail tomorrow or, so help me God, you'll live to regret it."

Ray nodded again. "Yessir. You got it."

As Slim took a step toward the door, Fat Ernst lurched to his feet and raised his hand. "Hang on, hang on. Before you go rushing off, I got a . . . a business proposition for you." Fat Ernst broke off and looked at his hand, like he wasn't sure how it got there and now he didn't know what to do with it. He casually let it drift down to scratch his belly, pretending to ignore it.

Slim merely crossed his arms and waited, rain dripping from his cowboy hat.

"See, I've got a little supply problem . . ." Fat Ernst eased around the bar and approached Slim. His voice dropped to a murmur. "I'm almost out of meat here."

Slim began to answer, but Fat Ernst kept going, saying, "It's those goddamn bastards over at Costco. They got the orders screwed up again. Of course, I already paid 'em."

I knew for a fact that Costco refused to sell Fat Ernst anything until he paid off what he already owed them.

Slim said, "So?"

"Well, I was thinking we could maybe, you know, cut some sort of a deal. Something a little better than what Harris is paying."

Slim shook his head and cleaned out the inside of his nose with his thumb. "Sorry. Ninety-five cents a pound. Same as always."

"Okay, okay. But I'm thinking I could maybe, you know, pay you back a little later . . ." He grinned widely at Slim. Slim grinned right back. Both of them stood there, grinning away and showing lots of teeth. I felt like somebody ought to take a picture.

"I'm afraid I can't do it. I got expenses," Slim said finally.

The grin never left Fat Ernst's face, but I could hear air faintly hissing out from between his clenched teeth. "Aw, hell, that's okay. I understand. We all got expenses." He stuck out a beefy hand. "Maybe next time we can do some business."

Slim took the hand and shook it twice, and that should have been that, but I got a bad feeling it was just getting started.

CHAPTER 8

Around ten, Junior kicked the front door hard enough that the needle tracing its way over "Ghost Riders In the Sky" jumped and played the chorus twice. He stood in the doorway, grinning fiercely, and shouted, "Freeze, cocksuckers. This is a stickup."

Nobody moved except me. I had been wiping down the tables, trying hard to look busy. Actually, I was just killing time. When the door slammed into the wall and Junior appeared there like some sadistic jack-in-the-box, I put the pool table between me and Junior.

I know it wasn't the cool thing to do, to run like a frightened rabbit, but I couldn't help myself. I never knew what to think when it came to the Sawyer brothers. Hell, I wouldn't put it past them to try and hold up Fat Ernst. But Junior just laughed and grabbed a stool at the bar. His pompadour looked solid, as if he'd used about a gallon of hairspray along with some motor oil and industrial glue. I tried to act casual and started wiping down the nearest table.

Fat Ernst finally tore his gaze away from a fishing show on the television and shouted, "Close the door! You born in a barn?"

"Nope. I was born in the kitchen. Bert was the one born in the barn."

wormfood

As if summoned by the mention of his name, Bert staggered through the front door. His entire right arm was encased in a crude plaster cast. He was grinning too, but his eyes rolled loosely around in their sockets as if they weren't attached to anything. He raised his left arm in greeting and lost his balance in the process, nearly falling onto the pool table.

"What the hell happened to you?" Fat Ernst asked.

"Broke my arm!" Bert said proudly, brandishing his cast.

"No shit? Figured it was your leg."

"Aw, don't mind him," Junior said, making himself at home at the bar. "He was bitchin' and moanin' all day, so we swung by the vet's, and he set that sucker real good and gave Bert some horse tranquilizers." He looked over at Bert, still leaning against the pool table. "He's as right as rain now. Ain't that right, Bert?"

"You goddamn got that right," Bert said in a matter-of-fact tone. He managed to stagger toward the bar and drop onto a stool.

"You fellas fucked up my deal with Slim today," Fat Ernst said tiredly. "He was too damn pissed for business."

"Slim's always pissed about something."

Ray pulled himself to his feet and stuck his chest out. "Been meaning to talk to you boys about this morning."

"Shut your hole, Ray," Fat Ernst snapped. "Better yet, get the fuck out. We're closed. You too, Heck. Out."

Ray turned to the bar. "Hell, Ernst, it ain't even eleven yet. I got another three hours left on duty. And I'm supposed to interrogate these boys."

"Don't make me ask you twice."

Ray put on his hat and stood up. He tossed down another shot of Wild Turkey and readjusted his belt and cowboy hat. "Fine. Fine. I'll talk to you fellas later. Don't make me come looking for you."

"Shit, Ray, this morning, that wasn't our fault. Slim knows it. Talk to dipshit here," he said, and pointed at me. "And if Slim's still pissed off, you tell him he can kiss my sweet hairy ass."

Ray started to say something else, but Fat Ernst barked, "Pay up and get out. Now. And take Heck with you. Looks like he's passed out again."

"C'mon Heck. Let's go home," Ray grumbled. "Don't see why I always have to be the babysitter."

Heck whimpered something about his wife as Deputy Ray half carried, half dragged the old man toward the open door. Fat Ernst shouted after them, "And close that fucking door. Every goddamn mosquito in the county is just waltzing right in."

"You want us out too?" Junior asked.

Fat Ernst rubbed his eyes with his fists, making him look oddly childlike. A fat three-year-old with a crew cut. "Not yet. I got a little job for you." He sighed. "But since the rocket scientist here went and broke his arm, it looks like you're gonna need a little help."

Fat Ernst turned and stared at me. "Considering how you stepped into that pile of shit this morning, you just volunteered to help these fellas out. They're gonna run a little errand for me, and you're gonna go along for the ride. Maybe I'll even throw in a little extra cash. Fair enough?"

"Well . . . depends," I said, surprising myself.

Fat Ernst's thick features scrunched up together as if the fat rolls were trying to touch each other in the middle of his face. He turned to Bert and Junior and said, "You fellas sit tight. Got me a little attitude adjustment to make on an employee. Be right back."

He waddled down the length of the bar with surprising speed and grace, then grabbed me just above my elbow and nearly pulled me off my feet, shoving me through the swinging doors. I stumbled against the stove, sharp fear sparking and flaring in the pit of my stomach.

His thick, stubby thumb and fingers dug into the flesh on either side of my jaw, forcing my head up until I was looking directly into his big face. For a long, uncomfortable moment, he just stared at me and I realized that this was the first time I had ever met Fat Ernst's eyes. They were sunk deep into his pockmarked cheeks like two olives in a bowl of cottage cheese that had been left out too long.

wormfood

Fat Ernst swiveled his blunt head to the side and spat on the stove, then turned up the heat with his free hand. "Seems to me, boy, we got ourselves a little problem here. You been forgetting your place in the food chain." The spit started to sizzle and dance on the griddle.

My eyes never left the boiling spit. Thick grease began to pop on the black iron.

"I still own that shithole trailer and the land. So unless you and that old bitch want to find a new place to live, you best straighten up and fly right." He grabbed my left wrist and jerked my hand out over the griddle.

"When I say jump, you jump," he whispered into my right ear. "No questions. No back talk. No nothing. You got that?"

He forced my hand closer to the black iron. The heat started to sear my palm, just five inches over the stove. Liquid pain curled around my hand and raced up my arm. I sucked in a ragged breath.

"You hearing me, you little shit?" Fat Ernst hissed into my ear.

I tried to nod.

"So you're gonna help the fellas out tonight, that's all there is to it. You understand what I'm saying here?"

I kept nodding, unable to look away from what was left of the sizzling spit.

And suddenly, as quickly as he had grabbed me, he released my wrist and neck at the same time. I cringed back against the sink.

Fat Ernst took out a fresh cigar, bit the end off, and swallowed it. He shifted his center of gravity, rolling back on his heels. "Hell, son, I'm just trying to look out for your best interests. I know that you don't have a father around anymore to teach you things. I'm just trying to help you here. Life ain't a bunch of goddamn roses. You gotta work for things, get in there, spread a little manure around. Life don't just step up and spread her legs for you. You understand what I'm saying?"

"I . . . I think so." I didn't have a goddamn clue what the hell he was talking about.

"You're too damn soft, boy. Too much of a pansy. Life is gonna kick your ass and stomp you into the dirt unless you get yourself a little backbone."

I nodded and let my gaze fall to the floor.

"You look at me when I'm talking." I jerked my head back up and stared at his face. But I couldn't look into his eyes. I focused on his squat nose instead.

He continued. "Like I said, I figure since you ain't got a father around, I guess it's my place to step in and help you out a little. Give to the world and the world gives back, you know? Now . . ." He paused, pulling the unlit cigar out of his mouth and sucking the flecks of tobacco out of his teeth. "You ain't afraid of a little hard work, are you?"

I shook my head, still watching his nose.

He nodded, "Good, good. You're gonna go help these boys out tonight. You do a good job and don't bitch and whine too much and give 'em too much trouble, I'll have maybe, something like twenty bucks waiting for you tomorrow."

I got brave for a moment and spoke up. "What do I have to do?"

Fat Ernst's eyes folded into slits and I could tell he didn't like the question. "It's a job, that's all. If I want any shit out of you, I'll kick it. Now get this stove cleaned up and finish those glasses in the sink." He turned and walked back through the swinging door.

As it swung back, I took two quick steps and pressed my right cheek to the door, watching through the crack.

Junior asked, "What do we need him for?"

Fat Ernst lowered his voice. "Remember back, 'bout two years ago? I ran out of meat?"

Bert shook his head.

Junior said, "Yeah. You want us to do the same thing?"

Fat Ernst nodded.

Junior asked, "Same place?"

"Yep. Two fresh ones today."

"So why do we need the kid?"

"Dickhead here's got a broken arm. You gonna handle them things by yourself?"

Junior thought for a moment, then nodded.

Fat Ernst turned back toward the kitchen and shouted, "Boy! Time to go."

I stepped away from the door, then slowly untied my apron, taking a deep breath. "Let's go!" Fat Ernst barked again. I pushed through the doors.

A deep, cracking belch erupted out of Junior, lasting nearly ten seconds. He grinned at me. "Get your waders on, Archie."

Fat Ernst thumped a bottle of Old Grandad on the bar to get Junior's attention. "You just see that the job gets done right."

Junior grabbed for the bottle, but Fat Ernst wouldn't let go, staring into Junior's eyes. "And keep it quiet, you understand?"

"You bet."

I spoke quickly. "I'll get paid tomorrow, right?"

Fat Ernst turned his attention back to the television. "Tomorrow," he said simply and released the bottle.

"Giddyup," Bert said and started giggling.

CHAPTER 9

The Sawyer Hide and Tallow truck flew east down Highway 200 under a starless sky, heading for the foothills. Sickly twin cones of urine-colored light lit up the dark asphalt, but just barely. Not that anybody could see much out of the windshield. It was a regular bug graveyard out there.

I checked my watch. 11:23. I hoped Grandma wasn't too pissed off. Fat Ernst hadn't let me call her before the Sawyer brothers had dragged me out to their truck.

The silence made me uncomfortable. It meant that the Sawyers were thinking. I was afraid that Junior might bring up the crash this morning. So I asked suddenly, "How'd you guys end up picking up roadkill and dead farm animals for the county?" Anything to break the silence. "Sounds like a helluva job."

"Hey, smartass, we provide a pretty goddamn valuable service here," Junior said defensively, pointing at the grimy glass and the highway beyond for emphasis. "Shit, if it weren't for us, folks'd be up to their eyeballs in these dead things. You couldn't hardly drive down the highway with all the dead animals. I mean, do you have any fucking idea how long it takes for a horse to rot?"

"Long time, I guess."

"You goddamn got that right," Bert agreed, sniffing his finger.

"It takes fucking forever, let me tell you," Junior nearly shouted. "Did I mention the flies? You better be on that shit quick."

I whistled low. "I didn't realize picking up dead animals was so complicated."

"You better believe it."

"And these ranchers around here, they pay you to come pick up dead livestock?"

"Most of 'em. 'Cept for that sonofabitch Slim Johnson."

"What's he do?"

"He just puts 'em in his dump, way out in back of his place so he don't have to smell nothing. Lets 'em rot. Too goddamn cheap to even pay us, and we come goddamn cheap."

"Oh. So, uh, why do you pick them up at all? I mean, what can you do with them? What do you do with the meat?"

"Hell, all kinds of things. Dog food, fertilizer, glue . . . Shit, all kinds of things." Silence filled the cab for a few moments. Junior handed the bottle back to Bert.

I asked, "Hey, how'd you guys get that bull skull in the first place, anyways?" The skull itself was back on the front of the hood. The broken horn had been reattached with a combination of duct tape, bailing wire, and probably the same glue that held Junior's pompadour in place.

"Now that, that is a funny fucking story," Junior cried, slapping the steering wheel.

"You goddamn got that right," Bert said.

"You wanna tell the story? Huh? Then shut your hole," Junior barked.

Bert stuck his finger back in his ear.

Junior continued. "It happened like this. You remember that bull of Slim's? You know, named it King Solomon, some kind of goddamn Bible name, but you know the bull, right?"

I shrugged. "Yeah, I think so."

"Slim's prize fucking bull stud. Cheap bastard made a fortune off of selling the semen. Sent it all over the country." He reached across me and grabbed the bottle of whiskey out of Bert's limp hand. The truck drifted across the yellow line down the center of the highway and swung back.

"This one night, Ma decided she wanted some fried chicken for dinner. She gave us some money and sent us off to Ketchum's Feed and Grain. Well, hell, I figured we'd just save that money, get us a few tiddlies at Fat Ernst's instead." Junior jerked his head back and poured a generous amount of Old Grandad down his throat.

I wondered where we were going.

Junior swallowed and exhaled slowly, a foul, dark mist spewing from his lips. "I figured, what the hell? Slim's got a shitload of chickens. And his stupid fat cow of a wife, she don't know how many goddamn chickens she got. They're everywhere. So me and Bert, we're feeling downright tuned up, so's I said to Bert, fuck it. Let's go hunt us some chickens. I grabbed Mr. Eliminator, my bow, this badass big boy right here," he said, jabbing his thumb with drunken importance at the black compound bow hanging in the back window. "So we snuck over to Slim's, found the chickens out back, by the barn. I gotta tell ya, it was so goddamn easy I can't believe we hadn't been doing it all the time. Them chickens are downright stupid. I got two or three, and decided I needed one more. Make Ma happy. So I'm ready, got a razor-tipped arrow, locked and loaded, and goddamned if I didn't miss that chicken."

"Missed that chicken," Bert agreed.

"But I nailed ol' King Solomon right in those precious balls of his. Razors went right through those fuckers like shit through a goose. Funniest damn thing I ever seen. Holy Jesus. Shoulda seen that bull take off, jumpin' and buckin' around. I 'bout pissed myself."

Smells like you did, I thought.

"You goddamn got that right." Bert giggled.

54

"Yeah, I heard Slim was so goddamn mad when he realized ol' King Solomon's balls was useless, he stomped out into the corral with his .30-.30, and *blam*! Shot that fucker right between the eyes. Then just let it rot, right there in the corral. And shit, if you thought he was pissed then, holy Jesus you shoulda seen his face when he found out me and Bert had stolen the skull and put it on the front of our truck. Now that, that was funny." Junior and Bert both laughed.

"So, uh, what's this job we're doing tonight?" I asked.

Bert started to speak, but Junior cut him off. "We're picking up something," he said and left it at that.

"Gate's coming up," Bert said.

Junior started downshifting. I leaned forward, trying to see out of the windshield. I couldn't see anything except miles and miles of dark, rolling foothills. "Where are we?" I asked as the truck rolled to a stop.

Bert kicked open his door and jumped out into the darkness. A moment later, I could see him in the headlights, holding a large pair of bolt cutters. Bert grabbed a chain that locked a small gate to the barbed wire fence.

"Back end of Slim's place," Junior said.

Bert wedged the top handle of the bolt cutters in his right armpit, between the cast and his chest. With his left hand, he grabbed the bottom handle and jerked it upward. The chain split easily. Bert pushed the aluminum gate into the field and Junior drove slowly through and stopped, switching off the headlights.

"We're not gonna kill a cow, are we?" I asked.

"Nope," Junior said flatly, taking another gulp of Old Grandad. "Just picking up one that's already dead."

CHAPTER 10

Bert stepped onto the running board on the passenger side and stuck his head through the window. Junior popped the clutch and the truck surged forward into the hills. Bert held out his good hand and Junior gave him the bottle.

"You see it yet?" Junior asked.

"Nope. Not yet. More to the left," Bert said between sips. "Wait, slow down."

The truck rumbled slowly across the foothills. Bert nodded. "We're close. Close. I can smell it."

"Smell what?" I asked, wondering how Bert could smell anything but his own body. Panic started to worm its way into my brain like a fat, sluggish tumor.

"There." Bert gestured with the bottle. "There it is."

"There what is?" I asked, trying not to breathe too fast.

"Slim's dump," Junior answered, swinging the truck around on the side of a hill.

The cab tilted to the left and I tried to hang onto the seat so I didn't slide into Junior, as he shifted into reverse, watching his side mirror.

﹌wormfood

Bert leaned out, hanging onto the door, and watched the back of the truck while Junior eased down the hill.

"Keep going . . ." Bert nodded, giving directions. "Easy . . . easy . . . Three feet and . . . stop. Right here. Stop."

Junior stomped on the brake and, just to be on the safe side, pushed down on the parking brake and locked it with his foot. Then he twisted the key and killed the engine.

We sat in silence for a moment, listening to the engine tick. Bert passed the bottle back to his brother, who tilted it to the ceiling. He swallowed and burped, filling the cab with the stench of Old Grandad and strong chili. He grinned and shoved the bottle at me. "Snort?"

I shook my head.

"You're gonna need it." The grin got wider.

I took a deep breath and grabbed the bottle, taking a tiny sip before I could stop myself. It tasted like wet leaves soaked in kerosene. "Jesus," I whispered. My eyes were watering. Bert giggled and grabbed the bottle. Then something else caught my attention.

I turned to Junior. "What's that smell?"

Junior winked and hopped out.

I whispered, "Shit," to no one in particular and slid across the seat then cautiously stepped out onto the wet grass. Bert clambered up the wooden slats of the truck like a monkey with one arm and bent down, disappearing in the darkness. He reappeared suddenly, swinging his Maglite around and stabbing it into my eyes.

I squinted into the glare and asked again, "What's that smell?"

It didn't just smell like something had died and been rotting slowly. No, this was something much, much worse. It was the kind of smell that seeped into your skin, your hair, your soul.

The light bounced around for a moment, vaguely illuminating the edges of a large pit near the back of the truck. It looked like it had been dug in the middle of a deep, wide ravine. The sharp edges of the hole were about fifteen feet in diameter and the bottom was shrouded in darkness. I leaned forward, one hand on the truck, desperately trying to breathe through my mouth.

Junior joined me on the other side of the truck and finished the Old Grandad with a satisfied gasp. "Makes life worth living," he breathed, indicating the bottle, and then tossed it into the darkness. It landed with a loud splash. "Sounds full," he said.

"What is this?" I whispered.

"Our hot tub," Junior whispered back and the flashlight found his grinning face, filled with deep, black hollows.

A low whine split the darkness. I looked up to find a large meat hook welded to a cable dangling in front of me. It hung from the thick steel arm that jutted out from the back of the truck. The cable was attached to the winch near the cab. Bert moved to the back of the truck, waving the flashlight in front of him. The mud in front of me and Junior suddenly leapt into sharp focus, and the light spilled into the pit.

Ten or twelve dead cows and several dead sheep floated lifelessly in the rancid rainwater.

"Told you it was full," Junior said.

Some of the livestock had been there a long time. The water in the pit looked thick, like some sort of tomato and meat soup that had gone bad. "Holy shit," I repeated to no one in particular.

"Me 'n' Bert like to come out here and soak in it. Makes our skin all soft and snuggly," Junior said. "Toss me that hook, Bert."

He grabbed the swinging hook and turned to me. "Get a fresh one, okay?"

I took a step backward. "What?"

"I can see two new ones down there. We only need one, although both would be fucking great."

"Wait, hold on just a minute. You . . . you want me to go down there?"

"You catch on pretty quick for a fucking idiot."

"You gotta be kidding," I hissed. "No way. No." My voice rose to a shout. "Ernst ain't paying me enough for this shit!" I started to say something else but caught a flash of Bert's cast out of the corner of my eye, and suddenly a sharp explosion went off inside my skull. I collapsed into the mud.

The darkness was soft and quiet. It felt almost comfortable, but then I heard someone say, "Pussy." I wanted to say something, to shout, scream, something, but nothing seemed to be working right. Something cold slapped my face and just as I realized it was mud, something tugged at the back of my shorts. I had a strange sensation of being lifted. My fingers brushed against something that felt vaguely familiar. Shoelaces. Shoelaces with knots tied in them. My own shoelaces. I figured out that I was somehow bent nearly double, suspended in midair by the back of my shorts.

I blinked furiously and shook my head. Synapses fired at random in my brain, misfiring and sparking in strange patterns. I kept shaking my head and, suddenly, my vision popped back into place, except that it was rolling back and forth as if something were wrong with the vertical control.

I realized I was looking at the pit as it slid to and fro underneath me. *It's just a dream, this is just a dream*, I decided. Some sort of panic attack. I just gotta get control of myself. Everything's gonna be okay. Everything's just—

Something at the back of my shorts popped, and I dropped eight feet into the water.

Right before I hit, I could hear Junior and Bert laughing hysterically.

I landed on my side with a flat slapping sound, dropping into a space between two dead cows. It was almost warm, like a bath that's been waiting a little too long. I fought my way to the surface of the rancid soup, gagging and thrashing. The greasy water was in my eyes, my ears, my nose, and even, oh, Jesus, my mouth.

It didn't taste dead, like I expected, but horribly, horribly alive, as if I could actually feel the bacteria and viruses and germs and God knows whatever else in that toxic soup swim and flit about across my tongue. The panic tumor in my brain burst, sending adrenaline shooting throughout my body, and I kicked and flailed, feet and hands slamming against soft, rotting meat.

Fibrous chunks of flesh disintegrated under my fingers, floating away from the rolling carcasses. Shadows danced wildly across the cows, making them look as if they were surging around the pit, fighting not to drown.

"Oh God, oh fuck." I gagged.

The meat hook sunk slowly into the liquid muck to my left.

"Let's go! We don't have all night!" Junior shouted hoarsely, cupping his hands over his mouth.

I thrust my chin toward the sky, anything to keep the thick water out of my mouth. My arms thrashed desperately at the hook, managing to wrap my fingers around the smooth, curved metal. I grabbed the cable with my other hand and pulled myself somewhat out of the water.

Things twisted and squirmed all around me. I felt something moving in my right nostril and forced myself to stick a finger in there and dig out whatever it was. I pried it out and caught a quick glimpse in the erratic light of a squirming maggot on the end of my finger.

"Let's go!" Junior hissed.

I took several quick, shallow breaths, and flicked the maggot away into the darkness, then locked my lips together and rolled the nearest steer over. I gritted my teeth and sunk the hook into a meaty shoulder of the carcass.

"Get out of the way!" Junior shouted through his cupped hands.

I reluctantly let go of the cable and paddled backward. Bert reversed the winch and the generator began reeling the steel cable toward the back of the truck. The dead steer was slowly lifted out of the water, its neck hanging at an odd angle and its eyes staring blankly at me. Streams of dark water ran off the matted hair as the light followed it up.

I clung to a basketball-sized rock sunk in the wall and kicked away another carcass, rotten to the bone.

I looked up just in time to see the steer's shoulder muscle split in half with a wet, ripping sound. The carcass dropped back into the pit, landing on me like a freight train and driving me under the surface.

wormfood

This time, panic took over completely. My world got as dark and muffled as a nightmare; I could hear only thick, liquid sounds and my own frantic heartbeat. I fought my way to the surface, twisting, clawing, and kicking at the water and the soft meat.

My hands found the rock again and I managed to pull my head out of the water.

Junior hollered through cupped hands, "I said a *fresh* one, dumbshit!"

Bert giggled and lowered the hook once again. Pushing away from the rock I grabbed the hook, then lifted my head and shoulders out of the water, kicking away some of the more rotten cows. *There. There's one.*

I half kneeled on one of the carcasses and raised the hook above my head. Thick warm water trickled down my neck. Then I brought that sucker down with all the strength I had, sinking the hook, deep this time, into the neck of the dead steer.

I heard the winch begin to whine above me. The steel cable grew taut and began to lift the second steer out of the water. Junior followed the carcass with the flashlight. It spun slowly in midair, front legs jutting stiffly away from the body. I hung onto the rock in the pit wall, watching the splayed rear legs being pulled from the water. Then the light was gone completely, leaving me in total darkness.

"Get the light down here!" I shrieked. "Please!"

Junior hissed down into the pit, "Quiet! Quiet!" I heard the winch's whine change pitch, then a dull thud as the steer landed in the back of the truck.

I kept kicking the rotten cow corpses away. Something brushed against my hand. Something that wasn't just floating along the surface. Something that moved on its own.

It wasn't a maggot; it felt too big. I shrieked and slapped at the water. "There's something down here!" I screamed.

"Shhhhhh!" Junior hissed. "Shut up!" He angled the light down into the pit, revealing the choppy surface of the water.

I felt a stabbing pain in my right palm and I screamed again, jerking my hand out of the muck. A thin, gray tube was attached to the webbing between my thumb and forefinger. As I watched, the thing undulated, like it was swallowing, and it slid a half inch deeper into my hand. I could feel it inside, squirming, chewing on muscles and tendons. Screaming, I ripped the thing away with my free hand.

"Shut the fuck up!" Junior shouted hoarsely.

The hook bumped my head. I grabbed it, shrieking, "Something bit me!" I wrenched my gaze toward the truck but could see only the dim sky, the flashlight, and Junior's silhouette. "Up, you stupid motherfucker!"

The hook started to rise. I clung grimly to it, pulling my knees up to my chest. It rotated slowly as it rose, and I was pulled sluggishly away from the surface of the pit, slowly spinning in midair. I blinked slime out of my eyes and glanced down.

The dead steers were gently rolling in the small waves I had created with my kicking. Long, gray things darted about, squirting across the surface between the carcasses.

"Oh, shit," Junior whispered. I hoped that he had seen whatever those gray things were, but his eyes were fixed on the horizon. "It's Slim." He killed the flashlight. "Let's go, let's go."

The hook finally reached the edge of the pit, but I was holding on with both hands so Junior grabbed the back of the truck to give himself some stability, then reached out with his other hand and grabbed the cable. He pulled me toward the edge.

I blindly shot my leg out, dug my shoe into the mud, and lurched toward the truck. I fell hard, gasping for breath. Junior immediately nudged me with the toe of his cowboy boot, keeping an eye on the distant light. "Let's go. We don't need Slim out here, nosir."

I grabbed the trailer hitch and rose to my knees. I looked down into the darkness of the pit and tried to flex my hand. A twisted hole bled slightly in the webbing by my thumb.

Junior kicked me in the butt. "C'mon. Let's go. Get in the back. Don't need you stinking up the cab." I felt myself lifted from behind and thrown into the truck, landing on top of the carcass with a wet, hollow thud. I rolled off the steer and pushed myself back against the cab with my feet. Junior slammed the door and started the truck. I drew my knees up to my chin and kept working at making a fist, over and over, making the wound bleed more and more and more.

The truck lurched up the hill and we rumbled off into the night.

CHAPTER 11

The truck bounced and swayed up the pitted gravel road that led over the low foothills. We were headed down the back end of Road E toward the Sawyer house. I'd never been there, but I knew where the house was. Everybody knew where the house was; everybody knew because it was a place that you stayed away from. Even the mailman refused to come all the way out here. Instead, he dumped the mail into a bucket out on the highway.

Thunder rumbled softly to the west, but the air was dry for the moment. A cool night wind had dried the thick, scummy water on my skin, leaving a filmy, greasy residue behind. The truck jerked violently to the left, plowing through a deep puddle, and I rolled with it, bracing my foot against the wet, matted hair of the carcass for support. The steer lay stiffly on its side, legs jutting straight out, and rocked slightly with the motion of the truck. Then we were over the top of the foothill and shuddering down the other side into the deep hollow where the Sawyer brothers lived. I pulled my eyes away from my bloody hand and twisted around so I could see through the two-inch gap in the wooden slats.

The weak headlights splashed over a tangle of old fig trees that had never been pruned. A quagmire of rotten figs blanketed the ground beneath the trees. As we got closer, I heard a low buzzing fade in and out. It took me a moment, but when a wasp landed on the steer and crawled around, I realized what was causing the buzzing. I had never heard or seen wasps out at night before, and it made my skin crawl.

A large, two-story farmhouse loomed up at odd angles into the circle of fig trees. It almost looked like the trees and the house were resting on each other for support. Faded white paint peeled away from the wooden sides in long, ragged strips. The gutters, filled with dirt and leaves and rainwater, had been partially torn away from the house by the summer storms. The whole place reminded me of some blocky gray spider with broken legs, waiting patiently for unsuspecting prey in a half-finished web. The truck bounced past the house and the headlights found the barn.

It squatted on a low hill to the right of the house. Junior swung the truck in a tight circle, oversized tires crunching against the irregular patches of gravel, reversed with a jolt, and backed toward the large sliding doors in the center of the barn. As we swung around I caught a glimpse of the backyard.

Here, the fig trees separated almost reluctantly away from the house and circled around a forest of giant weeds that filled the open space like rioting green wildfire. I could just make out the vague shapes of the corpses of five or six lawnmowers lurking in the tall Johnsongrass. I wondered if they'd died while valiantly trying to cut those weeds, killed in action. Strange plants in cracked ceramic pots hung haphazardly from the wooden beams, spaced unevenly along the sagging eve.

Something was burning in the middle of the backyard. Thick, dark smoke billowed from what looked like a burn barrel. As my eyes adjusted to the darkness, I saw a small figure next to the barrel, a woman maybe, hunched over a large metal tub. It kind of looked like she was washing clothes or something. The fire sent flickering, leaping shadows against the house and I couldn't see clearly.

But I knew it was Pearl.

The headlights spilled over onto the fig trees. I kept watching the gaunt, dark figure. The tub looked like it was full of water or some other liquid, and Pearl was holding something under the water with her good arm. The other one, the one that I heard had gotten caught and chewed on by the lawn mower, she kept close to her body, curled around her torso. She wore a shapeless house dress, but I could tell she was thin, I mean, real thin. Her body looked like nothing more than a skeleton loosely wrapped in shredded newspaper. Long, stringy hair hung over her head, obscuring her face.

I was glad, but a little disappointed too, because I had also heard that the lawn mower had gotten hold of her face as well when it jerked her arm into the spinning blade.

Every once in a while her good arm, the one holding whatever it was in the tub, would give a little shiver. Then, finally, she lifted the thing out of the tub. It was some sort of lumpy cloth sack; a white pillowcase trapping a small, dense object. She turned away from me and twisted around to the burn barrel.

The truck stopped with a jerk and as the engine rumbled softly I heard a little moaning kind of chant from the backyard. No real words that I could tell, just a lot of mumbled babbling, but uttered in a low, kind of singsong way. It almost sounded like she wanted to sing louder, but her lungs wouldn't let her. She reached into the sack and lifted out a dead, wet kitten.

I don't know if I gasped or swallowed too loud or what. Pearl jerked up her head and stared right at me with her wide right eye. I was still hunched deep in the shadows in the back of the truck and I'm dead certain there's no way she could have seen me, but, I swear, her eye found mine.

She dropped that kitten in the burn barrel.

I flinched, jerking back against the dead steer. The dampness from the wet hide started soaking my T-shirt again, but I didn't care. Compared to that woman, I'd hug a dead steer any day.

♪ wormfood

Junior shouted something and Bert gave a high, ragged cackle The passenger door opened. Bert jumped out, half humming, half breathing the theme to *Hawaii Five-O*, and opened the barn's sliding doors.

The large slabs of warped and buckled wooden planks rolled away from each other in a grinding squeal of protest, revealing total darkness. It looked like a deep, gaping maw had suddenly opened in the wall and was about to swallow the truck whole.

As the truck backed into the darkness, the fear tumor reemerged, slithering sluggishly up my spine. Junior hit the brakes and the inside of the barn was bathed in a dim, red light. Five bare lightbulbs, unevenly spaced along a frayed cord that stretched the length of the barn, flickered to life. The light forced the darkness back into the crevices and corners of the yawning space, where it waited impatiently in deep shadows.

The first thing I noticed was the meat hooks. Two rows of them. They hung from a series of rafters, dangling just above a huge, thick wooden table. The truck backed into the barn until the trailer hitch disappeared under the table and the engine died.

I dropped my gaze from the hooks and let it roam around the mountains of junk that filled the barn. Off to my right were mounds of thrift store clothing, piled haphazardly on several old couches. The couches looked wounded, hemorrhaging white stuffing. There was junk everywhere—heaps of dining tables and chairs, at least two dismantled motorcycles, mountains of firewood, a thirteen-foot aluminum boat, cardboard boxes, camping gear, toys, crumbling bricks, sacks of cement mix—and sprinkled over everything like confetti were beer cans and empty whiskey bottles.

I heard Bert rummaging around through several piles of cardboard boxes at the far end of the barn, and listened as Junior climbed out of the truck, but it all sounded hollow and faint, like the sounds were coming out of a cheap AM radio. A terrible weight settled across my limbs, as if gravity had increased and was anchoring me to the bed of the truck.

Although I felt my body slowly crumbling into total exhaustion, I didn't have to be asked twice when Junior jumped into the back of the truck with a chainsaw and yelled, "Move it or lose it, fuckhead."

He yanked the starter cord and a high-pitched, chittering whine chewed through the quiet of the barn. A noxious cloud of exhaust, a mixture of gasoline and motor oil from the two-stroke engine, filled the air.

I pushed myself to my feet with my good hand and edged around the other side of the carcass. Junior grabbed the steel hook in the steer's neck. I heard the hook come free even over the roar of the chainsaw; a wet, squelching sound that reminded me of when I yanked my shoes out of the mud in Fat Ernst's parking lot.

Junior slung the hook and the cable over the wooden slats on the side of the truck. Wielding the chainsaw in one hand, he casually lopped off the steer's back legs at the knees. The engine barely changed pitch as the spinning teeth easily chewed through the thin muscles and bone. The two severed legs, each about a foot in length, clattered to the truck bed like a couple of small chunks of firewood. I turned away, fighting the nausea that suddenly filled my body as if something inside had broken open and the contents were leaking out.

I ignored the hole in my hand for a moment and grabbed the side of the truck, jumping to the cement floor. It was covered in some sort of black, gummy substance that made my shoes stick to the cement. Bert was still at the other end of the barn, digging through boxes and bobbing his head in time to the music only he could hear.

Junior rested the chainsaw on his left hip. He shouted at me over the roar of the chainsaw, "Hey, zipperhead."

I didn't look up. I placed both palms flat on the table and leaned over, fighting to breathe evenly though my mouth. If I threw up in the Sawyer brothers' barn there was no telling what they might do.

"Hey!" Junior shouted again, then revved the saw three quick times to get my attention. "It ain't break time, Archie. We got some butcherin' to get to, you hear me?"

I nodded and finally looked up.

wormfood

"Drag that old tub over here," he yelled, pointing the chainsaw at an ancient bathtub with claw feet. It was wedged between a stack of bald tires and a tangled mound of barbed wire. "Toss them forelegs in there. We'll dump everything else in there, too." He killed the saw, and in the sudden silence I could hear Bert still half singing the tune from *Hawaii Five-O*. Junior continued, "No sense in letting good meat go to waste. The hogs are gonna think Christmas came early this year."

I walked slowly to the bathtub. The bare bulbs behind me sent a long, distorted shadow across the tub and I couldn't see what was inside. I didn't care what the hell was inside of it; all I wanted was to get home, to get to the shower, to scrub the slime of the pit off, to boil my skin until I felt clean, and then to sleep for a week. I didn't want to think about what the Sawyer brothers were going to do with the meat. It didn't matter. Getting away from these lunatics was the only thing that did matter. And that meant the faster they finished with the steer, the faster I could get home.

So I grabbed the cold, pitted edge without looking inside and pulled. The tub jerked forward, claws scraping the grime on the cement floor. An angry explosion of flies rose into the air from the tub, swarming about my head, and crawled through my hair, across my face, into my ears. I jumped back, swinging wildly at the buzzing black static that surrounded me.

When the cloud of flies had settled back into the tub, I took two careful steps forward and peered inside. The porcelain was covered with a thick coat of what looked like dark rust, and I realized with a fresh surge of nausea that it was dried blood. I swallowed, waved away several flies, and grabbed the tub again.

As I dragged it toward the table, Junior forced the steel hook with the cable through the two narrow bones in each of the steer's back legs. He had looped the cable through a series of pulleys hanging from the ceiling near the rest of the dangling meat hooks, and in this way could hoist the thousand-pound steer up over the table. He yanked on the hook, grunting with the effort, testing the strength of the tendons.

But the hook held and Junior seemed satisfied. He started the winch and we watched as the carcass, lifted by the hook pinning both of the back legs together, slowly rose off the truck's bed. The front hooves slid back off the truck and onto the table, leaving trails of mud and slime. The bones in the hips popped and snapped as the full weight of the body hung from the hook, but the tendons and muscles held. Junior smiled and patted the ribs affectionately as he followed the steer off the truck and onto the table. "Good steer," he said and shifted his snuff from one cheek to the other. "Good strong steer." He nodded at me, "You got us a good one." I almost felt proud.

The steer dangled stiffly. Junior circled the carcass and patted it affectionately, like it was a big, sleeping dog. "Bert," he said, "you gonna get those knives out or you just gonna keep jerkin' off all night?"

"Holy shit!" Bert exclaimed, freezing with a sudden, electrifying realization. "I broke my arm," he said as if he had just noticed. "How'm I gonna . . . What . . ." He let his voice trail off, horrified at the thought of life without masturbation. He tilted his head to the side, almost resting it on his right shoulder, considering other possibilities. "You ever try it with your left hand?" he asked Junior.

Junior ignored him, concentrating on the steer. He smoothed out his pompadour with both hands, rotating his hips ever so slightly, dancing in slow motion with the carcass, seducing it. He pulled off his shirt and tossed it into the back of the truck. The center of his chest was full of scars; the pattern almost looked like the design of a star or sun, but I couldn't figure out what kind of injury could have caused them.

Bert wouldn't give up. "You ever try with your left hand, Archie?" he asked, shoving his left hand down the front of his pants and trying it out.

I shoved the bathtub closer to the table.

Junior shuffled around the steer and caressed it. He said very evenly, almost quietly to his brother, "Quit fucking around and get those knives over here. It's time to get down to business." He patted the carcass one

70

more time and bent down to grab the chainsaw. It started on the first pull.

I took a step back.

Junior looked up and grinned. "Wanna see something neat?" he shouted over the roar.

I shook my head.

Junior solidly planted his feet shoulder-width apart, one foot on the table, one foot on the back of the truck. He raised the saw, right hand on the handle, finger on the trigger. His left hand gripped on the cross bar and turned the saw sideways. He hit the trigger once. Twice.

I took another step backward.

Junior sank the screaming teeth into the steer's neck, just above the ears. The high-pitched whine dropped into a growl. A fine mist of blood and tissue sprayed straight out from the saw. The steer's head began to slowly separate from the neck, splitting a deep valley into the flesh.

The head hit the table at the exact same time Bert dumped the contents of a small cardboard box onto the table. Long butcher knives, hammers, chisels, and meat cleavers clattered across the dark wood as the steer's head bounced off the table and landed on the floor next to the bathtub.

Junior nodded at the severed head and shouted at me, "Grab it. Toss it in the tub. We'll boil it down later." He squeezed the saw's trigger, sending another spray of bloody mist into the air.

I kept a close eye on the chainsaw and scurried forward, grabbed the steer's ear, and dragged the head back to a safe distance. The ear felt surprisingly soft and smooth. Without looking at the head, I tried to lift it, but was unprepared for the weight. It must have weighed at least thirty pounds, and the ear slipped through my fingers causing the head to land with a dull thud on the cement floor.

I got a better grip on the ear and dropped the whole thing into the bathtub. Another black explosion of flies burst out of the tub, but they quickly settled back, covering the head. I turned away, not wanting to watch the flies begin their feast.

Bert suddenly shouted, "Think fast, Archie," and a meat cleaver came shooting across the table toward me.

I jumped out of the way as the cleaver sailed off the table and landed in the coils of barbed wire. Bert giggled. Junior stood back and eyed the steer's stomach. He hollered at Bert, "Grab that push broom. When I open him up, we can just push all the innards off the table here into the tub."

I bent down and carefully plucked the cleaver from the barbed wire, turning back just in time to see Junior splitting the steer's abdomen open. The results were instantaneous.

An ocean of blood and miles of grayish-blue, ropy intestines spilled out onto the table. A surging flood of rotting meat and fluids washed over Junior's cowboy boots. "Goddamnit," Junior said. "Shouldn't have worn my good boots."

The stench of spoiled flesh and fecal matter slithered up into my nostrils and nested there. *Jesus*, I thought, trying not to gag. *Just when I thought things couldn't get any worse.*

And then things got worse.

CHAPTER 12

In the swamp of blood and intestines, something moved.

Several somethings moved.

"What the hell!" Junior shouted, jerked his bloody cowboy boot out of the mess and brought it down hard, grinding meat into the table. Ripples in the blood caught my eye, flashes of a pale gray amidst the darker gray of the intestines.

The worms. They twisted and squirmed through the wet meat lying on the table. Flattened gray tubes almost a foot long, covered in a viscous white slime, slid across the table in an eruption of obscene movement. Six short tendrils, or barbels, looking like the fluid antennae of a slug, surrounded the mouth on the bottom of the worm and tested the air. It didn't look like the worms had eyes, just round lighter patches on either side of their heads.

Junior kept screaming and stomping on the worms in a sort of deranged hillbilly tap dance with a dead steer for a dancing partner. His cowboy boots stuttered and pounded the table in a frantic rhythm. And still the worms kept coming, dozens of them, spilling, squirming, oozing out of the spilled guts.

I gripped the cleaver tightly in my right fist, raised it high, and rushed toward the table. Screaming, I brought it down in a slicing arc, twisting my upper body in the effort. The rusted cleaver easily split one of the closest worms in half and sank into the table.

The slimy gray flesh came apart like wet cardboard. Blood oozed out of the severed ends in slow motion. I yanked on the handle, but the blade stuck fast in the wood. Another worm slid closer and its barbels stretched out, tasted the blade.

"Oh, shit. Shit!" I breathed and yanked again, but the cleaver remained anchored in the table. Then, as if responding to the warmth of living flesh, the worm slid closer to the handle, closer to my hand.

"Shit," I hissed, grabbed the handle with both hands and wrenched it free. I brought the cleaver down again and again, viciously chopping the worm into three ragged pieces. The severed chunks twitched and undulated slowly, dying reluctantly, like a lizard's tail.

Bert brought his short-handled sledgehammer to the party and smashed at the worms. Every blow sent a moist cloud of blood into the air. The sounds of harsh grunts, wet *thwacks*, and the idling chainsaw echoed through the barn. I kept hacking away at the worms and the meat, bringing my cleaver down on anything that moved. Junior had taken to holding the chainsaw above his head and jumping on the worms with both feet.

Finally, after several frantic minutes of hacking, stomping, and pounding, it was over. I sucked in great ragged breaths while scanning the finely chopped meat in front of me for any signs of life. I couldn't tell where the chunks of worms ended and the chunks of intestines began.

"C'mon you little fuckin' wrigglers," Bert said in a high, strangled voice and brought his hammer down at random. His pounding rhythm faltered, slowed, and stopped. Junior shut the saw off and in the sudden silence I could hear only the whispering rain hitting the tin roof. Junior nudged the dangling carcass with the tip of the chainsaw, making the steer sway slightly. Nothing else, no other worms, came out of the long,

74

jagged slit. He shoved the steer again. Still nothing.

"See? See?" I asked, still breathing fast. "I told you there was something down there in that pit. I told you."

Junior ignored me and gingerly pushed the sharp, blood-soaked toe of his cowboy boot through the crushed intestines. "Huh," he said finally. It wasn't a question, or even an acknowledgment of me.

"I told you," I repeated.

"Shut up," Junior said tiredly, and hawked a thick, wet ball of chewing tobacco into the tub. It didn't bother the flies much. He dropped the chainsaw into the meat on the table and smoothed out his pompadour with both hands.

I turned my blade sideways, so it was parallel to the surface of the table, and gently slid the edge under a worm. It was dead, but wasn't as severely sliced and diced as some of the other worms nearby. This one had only been cut in half. I eased the flat cleaver under the worm's head but couldn't find the other half. The elastic barbels had shrunk to short nubs in death.

"What are these things?" I asked, more to myself than expecting any answer from the Sawyer brothers.

Junior stared hard at me for a moment, like the way an amused cat might watch a mouse with a broken back struggle across the floor. "Who cares?" He shrugged. "Steer had worms. Big fucking deal." He half snorted, half chuckled, and spit into the tub again, then squatted on his haunches. He looked me dead in the eye. "Welcome to the farm, city-boy."

Bert cracked up, his high-pitched hyena laugh bouncing off the tin roof.

Junior smiled. "I bet you think all them hamburgers just come out of a factory someplace far away." He snapped his fingers. "Something clean like that. Or maybe you just thought there was this magical hamburger tree out there under a sparkling rainbow somewhere. No muss, no fuss."

I dropped my eyes to the worm and carefully rolled it back and forth on the blade. The mouth was sunk into the flesh under the head; twin rows of tiny, curved teeth came together at the back of the mouth in a *V* shape. I couldn't figure out how the teeth worked. I looked back up, met Junior's stare and said, "Yeah, but have you ever seen anything like this?" I held up the cleaver.

Junior never took his eyes off me. "Shit. I've seen lots of worms. Worms ain't nothing."

I thrust the cleaver closer to Junior's face, pushing my luck. Then I flashed back to my biology class, trying desperately to remember when we dissected earthworms. "These things aren't your regular parasites. These things aren't heartworms, or blood flukes, or goddamn tapeworms, night crawlers, or . . . or . . . These things are different!"

Junior still wouldn't look at the worm. "So what? They might be a little bigger maybe, but so what? It's not like they're gonna hurt anything now." He stood suddenly, looking back to his brother.

"Hey, Bert, you remember that time you had worms? Back when you was in junior high? 'Member? Ma kept telling you, but you just wouldn't stop playing with the dog shit. You couldn't keep your hands out of it."

"Yeah, yeah, I remember." Bert nodded, grinning hugely in the cold glare of the bare white bulbs. Flecks of fresh blood were drying on his yellow teeth.

"So you got worms. They bother you any? I mean, did they hurt?" Junior asked.

"Nope. Can't say they did much of anything. The only time I noticed 'em was when I got all cramped up and, boy"—Bert gave a warbling low whistle—"you shoulda seen the toilet. They were everywhere."

I tipped the cleaver sideways, dumping the severed worm head back onto the table.

"So what happened? How'd you get rid of 'em?" Junior asked.

"Ma took me to the vet. He gave me some pills." Bert shrugged. "And that was it. They all came out dead."

"Yeah, you showed me." Junior turned back to me and grinned triumphantly.

A few quiet seconds crawled by.

"What are you gonna do with this meat?" I asked quietly, not meeting Junior's eyes.

But Junior ignored me and asked Bert. "So it wasn't no big deal, right? I mean, the worms didn't affect you permanently or nothing."

Bert thought hard for a moment, wrinkling the flaking, spotted skin on his forehead. He finally shook his head spastically, like a dog trying to shake water out of its ears. "Nope."

Junior stepped back and kicked the steer, a solid kick that made the thousand pound carcass jump slightly. It gently swayed back and forth. "I dunno. I figure we got two choices here. We can go all pussy and act like a bunch of scared old ladies, and just feed this big bitch here to the hogs. But then . . ." He swept his gaze back down to me and slowly advanced across the table. "Then we don't get paid. We don't get nothin'. On the other hand, we just make sure we kill all these goddamn worms and we keep our mouths shut."

I tried again. "Where's this meat going?"

Junior turned back around and kicked the carcass again, harder this time, asking Bert, "You think there's any more of them in here?"

I raised my voice. "Where's this meat going?"

"Nah. I'd say we got 'em all," Bert said.

"That's what I figure too."

"What the hell is wrong with you?" I shouted, and slammed the cleaver down on the table. "That steer was sick! There's something wrong with it! These worms, they—"

"Easy, Archie. Don't forget, you're the dog around here."

I backed away from the table, still clutching the cleaver tightly. "Where's that meat going?"

Junior sighed, rolled his eyes. "Okay. Okay. If I tell you, you gotta promise not to say nothin' to nobody. If Fat Ernst found out, hell, he'd have my balls for breakfast." He lowered his voice.

"Fat Ernst has got some deal where he supplies a little meat to this small outfit that makes cheap, generic dog food. He only does it once in a while. And only when he's got some extra meat that he can't sell to customers anymore, 'cause the meat has gone past the . . . whaddya call it? The expiration date or something. Better than throwing it away, right?"

I wasn't sure if I had ever seen Fat Ernst getting rid of anything that happened to age past its expiration date, but I had to admit, it did make sense. It fit Fat Ernst's do-anything-for-a-buck attitude.

Junior continued. "He wasn't planning on doing it again for a while, seeing how he was getting low on meat. But since he needs some quick cash, he figured it wouldn't hurt nobody if me and Bert just picked up a dead steer from Slim. It's not like that cheap bastard was going to use the meat or anything. So you see? Fat Ernst told us to do it so he could snag a little cash, pay for some booze and better meat and so he could pay you. That's the only reason, I swear. But don't tell him I told you, okay?" Junior spread his arms and shrugged.

"It's up to you. You can either stay all squeamish like some little crybaby and me and Bert, we'll do the work and get paid, or you can grow some balls and stay with us, get the job done. It's that simple. Either way, this steer is gonna get butchered. Me and Bert are gonna get paid. That's all there is to it." Bert nodded, scrubbing the dried blood off his teeth with his tongue.

Junior looked down at me. "The question is, do you wanna get paid?"

I swallowed, keeping the cleaver tight in my fist. I wanted to tell the Sawyer brothers to go to hell. I wanted to send the cleaver sailing back across the table at Bert. I wanted to walk out of the barn. I wanted to call the police. I wanted to call the health inspectors. I wanted to call somebody, anybody.

But then I remembered Grandma.

If I left now, not only would I not get paid for this job, I probably wouldn't get any wages at all for the past two weeks. But that wasn't

wormfood

the worst that could happen. The worst was that Fat Ernst would happily kick Grandma and me out of the trailer. And then what? Where would we go? Grandma didn't have the money to move anywhere. Neither one of us had enough money for much of anything.

So I finally looked up, found Junior's eyes. "Let's get it over with."

I tried to tell myself that it didn't matter if I was there or not. The steer was going to get chopped up for dog food, one way or another.

Junior grinned. "Hell, that's the spirit." He ran his hands through his hair again. "Sharpen those knives, Bert. We got us a steer to butcher."

I closed my eyes. Now that the decision had been made, I felt my mind going numb. I couldn't feel my fingers curled around the cleaver, couldn't feel my legs. I just let myself drift somewhere else and turn things over to my body, let it take care of things for a while on autopilot. It was easy.

The night slipped into a soft haze of brief, frozen images. Pushing the mangled intestines and dead worms into the bathtub. Junior jaggedly slicing the thick hide of the steer, splitting it straight down the back. Peeling the hide, exposing the muscles. Blood pooling on the table. The cloying, sickly sweet smell of blood and fresh meat and death. The guttural sound of the chainsaw, engine straining as it chewed through dense meat. One of the thick back legs, severed at the hip, being slammed onto the sticky table in front of me. Raising the cleaver . . .

And eventually everything, the sight of raw meat, the sounds, the smells, everything, faded away into a fine red mist.

CHAPTER 13

I rode in the back of the truck again, braced up near the cab, wedged in between two large coolers that held the meat, because Junior was worried that I might get the cab dirty. My clothes were still wet, and my arms were covered in dried, sticky blood up to my elbows.

I grabbed my tacky elbows and held my arms close, ignoring the blood. I didn't want to think about the meat in those coolers. Not tonight, not tomorrow night, not ever. I wasn't paying attention to where we were, and wasn't prepared when the truck slid to a stop on the rain-slicked pavement. The coolers slammed into the cab.

Junior started pounding on the back window. "Let's go, dickhead. This ain't a goddamn taxi."

I pushed myself awkwardly to my feet, using the coolers for support and gingerly inched toward the back of the truck, joints stiff and aching from the cool night wind. Suddenly, the truck lurched forward a couple of feet and I stumbled forward, almost going to my knees. The engine sounded like a pit bull strangling itself on a fraying leash. I could hear Bert cackle and Junior pounded on the back window again. I grabbed the steel bar and jumped out.

wormfood

The truck pulled away immediately. Bert stuck his upper body out of the passenger window, waving his cast wildly. "See ya tomorrow, Archie!" *I hope not*, I thought. As the night swallowed the red taillights, I headed up the driveway.

The clouds had rolled on and the rain had finally died, leaving lakes of shallow, wide puddles that filled the long driveway. I walked out across a sea of stars, heading for Grandma's trailer, each footstep shattering the sky and sending expanding ripples of rolling stars into the darkness.

And before I realized it, I was home.

A faint blue light flickered in the windows. Grandma must be still up, watching television. I hoped she wasn't waiting on me. I didn't know what time it was, only that it was late, real late.

I crouched at the end of the driveway, near a corner of the garden, and plunged my arms into one of the puddles. I scraped most of the blood off my arms, but I wondered how I was going to get cleaned up enough to even go inside so I could take a shower.

When I got closer to the trailer, a match flared in the darkness near the back door. The orange flicker illuminated Grandma's face, sending tiny brown shadows dancing across her wrinkles. She was sitting on the top step, lighting her pipe.

"Howdy, pilgrim." She smiled, gray smoke curling out of the upraised corners of her mouth. It was an old joke. The Duke had been Grandpa's favorite.

"Hey, Grandma." I sat heavily on the bottom step, rested my arms across my knees and let my head fall on my forearms. The exhaustion suddenly caught up with me, making my muscles feel like they were filled with the little steel pellets that Grandma loaded into her shotgun shells, and I seriously considered sleeping out on the wooden stairs.

Grandma spoke, her voice low and solid behind me. "I've been wondering about you. Sounded like them Sawyers."

I took a long, deep breath and let it out slowly through my nose. I didn't know what to say. Where could I start? I felt ashamed, for some reason I couldn't put my finger on.

I could smell the pipe smoke before she spoke again. "I'm just gonna say this once. That family, them Sawyers, they're about the worst bunch of inbred mistakes this town's ever seen."

Grandma was silent for a moment, then said almost too quietly for me to hear, "I used to know the mother. Pearl Sawyer. We went to high school together. We, ah . . . Well, see, your granddad, he was quite the ladies' man back then. He saw a lot of girls, including me and Pearl. She fell for him just as hard as I did. And she was awful good-looking back in them days and wasn't shy about getting to know a boy up close and personal, if you know what I mean."

I twisted around and sat sideways on the steps, watching Grandma. She stared out above my head at the dark patch of garden, a midnight sentinel standing guard over her beloved tomatoes. "Never held it against him, though. I guess he had his fling with Pearl before he started coming around to see me. But when he broke it off with her to get serious with me, Pearl took it kind of hard. She was downright pissed, you could say. But she left us alone for the most part, and I thought that was that. But not too long after me and your grandfather got married, he found a dead hog on our front lawn one morning. Some sort of message had been written on the front door in the hog's blood. I never could understand what it said, but your grandfather just laughed, said Pearl was trying to scare him with some kind of a curse. Said she was just jealous, nothing to worry about. It worked kind of, I guess, scared me a little, but he told me not to worry, and as the years went by, I had other things to worry about, like the Depression and him going off to war, and eventually I just forgot about the whole thing."

Grandma struck another match and relit her pipe. Then she shook out the match and carefully placed it on the splintered step beside her. "Never thought about it again until he died. I never told you the truth, Arch, about how your grandfather died. You were just too young, and

I didn't think it would do any good."

I waited, afraid that if I said anything, Grandma might stop talking.

She sniffed once and wiped at her nose quickly, saying, "You know how we used to have around twenty pigs back then, along with the goats, right?" I nodded. Grandma looked up at the brilliant stars. "Well, your grandfather, ah, he had a heart attack. That part was true. The thing I didn't tell you was that it hit him when he was feeding the hogs one day. He collapsed, and . . . well, the hogs ate most of him before I found him." She swallowed, and when she continued her voice was thick.

"And the strangest thing was, was the first thing that popped into my head when I saw what was left of him, lying in the mud, all tore up like that, was that dead hog and the blood on the front door all those years ago."

Grandma coughed a little, a dry, rasping sound that sent a small cloud of sweet-smelling smoke into the still night air. I sat perfectly still, still trying to process the story somehow. It didn't seem real. The man I had thought was my father for a long time, the man who had taught me everything about guns and shooting, the man I had thought was the toughest man in the world, that man, dead in the mud, ripped open by pigs. It was too much to take in. I couldn't get my head around it, couldn't even begin to accept it.

Grandma spoke again, her voice dry as smoke. "So I don't know if it was her or not, and I don't know if I ever want to know. But I don't want you getting anywhere near that family. They're dangerous. And that Pearl, she's the most . . . most evil human being I've ever come across. I don't even know if I'd call her human. I ain't ashamed to admit that she scares the hell out of me."

I wanted to say, *You're goddamn right. She scares the hell out of me too. I saw her kill a kitten tonight and stare right at me in total darkness, and she scared me bad enough I almost pissed my pants*, but instead I just mumbled, "Okay, Grandma, okay. I'll stay far away from them, I promise."

We sat in silence for a few moments, watching the stars. I had heard on the news at the bar that another storm front was rolling up the valley, and I wasn't sure when we might get to see clear skies again.

Finally Grandma spoke up, softer, more gentle this time. "If you don't mind me saying so, Arch, it smells like you got sidetracked on your way home."

I shrugged. The last thing I wanted to tell her was about the pit and that I had been at the Sawyer place. "It's . . . it's been a long day," I said finally.

She tapped her pipe against the steps, knocking the ashes into the wet weeds. "Then why don't we get you cleaned up a little?" She shook her head, dropping the pipe into a large pocket in her dress. "You sure aren't going inside smelling like that."

My knees popped as I found my feet. I reached out to help Grandma stand, but she waved me away.

"Bring that hose over here," she said. "And while you're at it, take off those damn shoes. They ain't fit to scrub out a septic tank. I'll put 'em out of their misery tomorrow and burn them."

That sent a tiny, scrabbling shiver up my spine when I thought about the kitten and the burn barrel. But I shoved the image aside, buried it deep as I grabbed the hose and turned the spigot on. The water coming out was cold, but clean. That's all I cared about. I dragged the hose back over to the steps and handed it to her, keeping the stream aimed at the lawn.

"Now hold still," Grandma said.

The spray hit my chest and my breath caught in my throat from the sudden shock of the cold water. I pulled off my shirt and flung it to the side. Then I bent down to rip off my shoes. Grandma aimed the spray at the top of my head and for a moment all I could hear was the water hitting my scalp. It didn't feel so cold anymore.

Later, as I stood dripping on the top steps, Grandma affectionately wrapped a towel around my shoulders. I pulled it together across my chest and met her gaze. "I . . . I'm just trying to do the right thing," I said.

She nodded, taking a smaller towel and vigorously drying my hair. "That's all you can do. And if you ever need any help, you just holler."

"Thanks, Grandma."

"Now get in there and take a shower. You need it."

SATURDAY

CHAPTER 14

I wanted to say to hell with it and sleep in a little the next morning, but Grandma knocked softly on the bedroom door around seven and said quietly, "Arch? You up?"

"I'm up, I'm moving," I said thickly. For a moment, I thought I'd overslept again and was late for work. And right around then everything from the night before came flooding back, collecting into seared images behind my eyes. The pit. Rotting steers. The worm thing trying to eat into my hand. Junior and his chainsaw. Intestines and worms spilling out all over the table. After all that, I wasn't exactly in a rush to get to work.

"Yeah, I'm up."

"You think you could thin out the squirrels a little? Little bastards have damn near eaten all of my squash and since the corn's getting ripe, they're just going to get worse. I'd keep an eye on things, but I promised Peg I'd take her some tomatoes."

Peg was Grandma's closest, well, her only friend really. She lived down the road about a mile and a half, and scratched out a living by raising mean, thin chickens. Once, when Peg chopped the head off of one of the chickens with a wood axe, I swear that headless chicken ran around for a full five minutes before the body realized that the head wasn't attached and it was supposed to be dead. Even when it finally toppled over, it fought death the whole way, flapping its wings and kicking up a cloud of blood and dust. Grandma was always trading vegetables for eggs and headless, plucked chickens. I figured that half the time, the trading was just an excuse to get together and puff on their dead husbands' pipes, filling the chicken yard with sweet-smelling blue smoke. Peg couldn't walk too well, even worse than Grandma, so they always met at her house.

"Sure, Grandma. I got the time."

"You still going into work?"

"I gotta, Grandma."

She nodded and gave me a glimmer of a smile. "You take care of yourself."

"I will."

Grandma nodded and shut the door.

I slipped out of bed and took another long, hot shower, scrubbing my skin until it was a bright shade of pink. I stayed in there until the water had gone cold, and only then reluctantly climbed out.

Grandma had dug a pair of Grandpa's old black boots out from somewhere and set them in the hall. There was no sign of my tennis shoes, and I figured it was for the best. Grandpa's boots were a little big, but with two pairs of socks, the creased leather molded around my feet just fine.

A giant tomato and onion omelet was waiting for me on the counter in the kitchen. After last night, I wasn't sure if I'd ever be hungry again, but I surprised myself and inhaled the breakfast.

I checked the clock. Seven-thirty. It was time for a few squirrels to meet their maker. I opened the front hall closet. More than two dozen boxes of shells were stacked neatly on the floor next to the encyclopedias. I could remember when the closet was full of Grandpa's guns:

∫ wormfood

Winchesters, Rugers, Remingtons, a couple of Browning shotguns, a Colt 1911 .45, and even an ancient Model 1885 High Wall single shot. They were all gone, all sold to pay for rent and food. Grandma cried when she had to sell the Highwall rifle, Grandpa's favorite. That was the only time I ever saw Grandma cry.

All that remained was the Browning .10 gauge shotgun and Grandpa's Springfield 30.06, the two guns Grandma refused to sell. I grabbed a box of shells and the rifle case. Nestled in threadbare red imitation velvet waited my grandfather's 30.06. Bolt action, with a five-round clip. Walnut stock. Iron sights, grooved slots of metal at the end of the barrel.

I never liked using scopes. Looking through a scope always made me feel sort of disconnected from the rifle somehow. I felt much more comfortable sighting down the barrel, through the iron sights. It felt as if the rifle and I were working together, instead of screwing a chunk of glass on the top and using that to find your target. You never knew where the scope was aiming; if it was off just a little, you wouldn't know it, you couldn't feel it, but by sighting down the barrel, you knew roughly where you were putting the bullet. For long-distance shots, I used a pair of binoculars, just to double-check that the tiny brown blur in the distance was, in fact, a squirrel and not just a knotted root. Shells were too expensive to waste on killing a piece of wood.

The second reason was that using a scope felt too much like cheating.

The term "thirty-aught-six" simply meant that the rifle was a thirty caliber, that is, 308 thousandths of an inch wide, and the aught-six signified the year it was invented—1906. Besides loading her own shotgun shells, Grandma also kept me supplied with plenty of shells for the 30.06, using a 150-grain bullet, propelled by 52 grains of 4064 Dupont powder. This was a deer-hunting load, a huge load to inflict on the squirrels, but Grandma never changed or reduced it. For one thing, that was how Grandpa had set up his loading bench and dies, and Grandma got nostalgic about things like that.

The other was that she felt kind of sorry for the squirrels, even though they weren't anything but country rats—these weren't cute, fluffy gray tree squirrels, just disease-ridden rodents that lived in giant colonies of tunnels in the dirt.

"I won't let them eat my garden, but I don't see any need making 'em suffer either," Grandma said.

Well, the squirrels sure didn't suffer much when hit by a 150-grain bullet. They never even knew what hit them; the bullet usually just turned them inside out instantly. One second, they're sniffing around in dust, and the next, they're climbing that great oak tree up into the sky. They never felt much of anything.

Still, I can't say I enjoyed killing them. I liked shooting, loved it, *lived* for it most days, but I never thought drawing blood when you pulled the trigger was much of a sport. It was too easy. I'd rather just throw some old golf ball as far as I could toward the foothills and shoot at that for a while. But we had to protect our food.

Grandma's garden came first. And so, every month or so, I'd grab the Springfield and a box of shells and head into the knee-high Johnson grass beyond the garden to a level spot under the dead oak tree out in the middle of the field.

The tree was a monster; it had been out there forever. Lightning had struck it once or twice, and the branches grew out into the clouds in dizzying, twisted patterns because of the jolt. I don't know what finally killed it. I like to think it was old age. It had been dead a couple of years now. The tree had also survived a few grass fires, and I could just make out the dim lines at various points along the thick trunk that spoke of floods in years past. Some of these lines were above my head.

About sixty yards past the tree to the north, the field dropped into a dry creek bed, nothing more than gray gravel and red mud. I'd never seen any water come down the creek, just puddles that collected after heavy rains. The foothills rose on the other side of the creek bed. This was where the squirrels lived. Over the years, before they built the dam and created the Stony Gorge reservoir, the creek had sliced chunks of the hills away, and now crumbling dirt cliffs rose out of the gravel, some nearly twenty to thirty feet high. Giant colonies of squirrels, some numbering into the hundreds, maybe even thousands, lived in there, in complicated mazes of holes that periodically opened out into the dirt face of the cliff. And there, when I walked out to the old oak tree, was where they died.

I leaned the rifle against the tree and studied the sky. No rain yet, but plenty of fat, angry clouds rolled across the low sky. I squatted down and got comfortable, mashing the tall grass down to form a cushion, my back to the tree, dirt cliff slightly off to my left. Sometimes, just to make things interesting and give the squirrels a sporting chance, I'd shoot standing, or off-hand as the old-timers called it, but today I was too damn tired and in too much of a hurry. I just wanted to kill a few squirrels and get to work before Fat Ernst got mad. Again.

I settled into the grass, feet planted firmly, knees bent at a 45-degree angle. If the holes in the cliff were at twelve o'clock, then I faced more or less toward the two o'clock mark. You always turn a little sideways to what you're shooting so you can support the gun easier. If you face the target head on, then your left arm has to hang way out there, holding on to the end of the forestock, supporting the barrel. You can't keep it steady. But if you turn sideways a little, then the rifle is resting across your chest, allowing you to draw your left arm in a little, so you can brace that elbow on something like, say, your knee if you're sitting.

The key to holding any gun steady is in your posture. The idea is to build a series of solid supports, using your bones, locking them into place, from the ground up to the gun. I don't care how strong you are, holding a rifle steady only using your muscles while firing at a target a hundred yards out is damn near impossible. You'll shake too much. You need to relax those muscles, you need to be calm, breathing nice and slow and relaxed. Even your pulse can throw off your aim. It doesn't have to be much. Moving the barrel a fraction of an inch could translate into missing the target by nearly a foot at a hundred yards.

My grandfather taught me everything about shooting. I can re-member starting with a .22 when I was six, shooting at paper plates nailed to fence posts, then moving on up through .410 shotguns, and finally into larger rifles and shotguns like his 12 gauge pump Winchester and a .484 Remington. One summer evening, when the blazing sun had dropped halfway behind the coastal range to the west, when Grandpa and me were sitting under the same oak tree, watching for squirrels, he told me, "A gun is nothing more than a tool, but don't forget that it's nothing less than a tool either. Like any tool, a gun is only as smart as the person wielding it, but if you know what you're doing, then a tool can move mountains. Squeezing the trigger is nothing less than imposing your will on the universe."

I rested the rifle across my knees and fed five shells into the clip, loading them from the top, forcing them into the slot until I heard the click of the spring locking into place. When the clip was full, I took a deep breath, readjusted my knees slightly, and brought the binoculars up to my eyes, letting the air in my lungs out slowly and evenly.

The cliff face leapt into view with startling clarity. Sure enough, the squirrels were out and about, busily scurrying from one hole to the next in a flurry of motion one second, the next second freezing, watch-ing, and listening—then another blur of motion. The trick was to nail them when they stopped to listen for predators. I suppose that's kind of iron-ic, but they were just too damn hard to hit when they were moving. You had to factor in lead time and wind and all kinds of other damn things, and when I was pressed for time, I simply shot them when they were still.

The squirrels were all over the place. I could easily find them with my naked eyes, so I dropped the binoculars back to my chest, took another deep breath—settling in now, focusing my energy, quieting everything else down—and brought the rifle up to my shoulder. I pulled it in snug, because a 30.06 kicks like a mule that's just been blinded with a faceful of pepper spray. You don't really stop the recoil so much as ride it, guide it. I never braced myself against the tree, putting my shoulder between the stock and the trunk of the tree—I'd end up dislocating my shoulder or worse.

Grandpa used to tell me a story about this one time Earl Johnson came by the gun range. Earl was in his twenties. He was one tough customer, wearing brand-spanking-new hunting gear, boots, jeans, a giant cowboy hat. He wanted to sight in his new deer rifle, some ungodly huge .50 caliber Weatherby that had been built for the sole purpose of killing elephants. Grandpa strongly suggested that Earl might want to use a shooting bench, but the great white hunter knew what he was doing, dammit, he didn't need to be treated like some god-damn woman.

Earl eased into a prone position, took his time settling down, get-ting the rifle with its huge barrel into place, and finally pulled the trigger. After the smoke cleared and the echoing thunder died, Grandpa found Earl whimpering in pain. The recoil had been powerful enough to drive him backward nearly a foot. The toes of his cowboy boots had left two neat grooves in the dirt, and the stock had broken Earl's collar-bone in two places.

I wedged my elbows into the slight indentations in my knees, the shallow groove right between my kneecap and the muscle on the inside of my leg, so the rifle was supported on the tripod I'd made with my skeleton. Two knees up to two elbows, with my shoulder as the third point in the triangle. The rifle slipped easily, naturally into place as if it knew where to go, as if it belonged there all along, as if it had never left my shoulder and cheek.

I sighted down the barrel, staring down between the notches in the iron sights, and everything else in the world fell away. Nothing else existed except myself, the rifle, and the squirrels. My breathing got even slower, deeper. The index finger of my right hand gently, ever so gently came to rest on the smooth trigger, almost as if there were an extremely rotten egg between the trigger and the guard and I was afraid of breaking the fragile shell. Then my eyes focused somewhere beyond the tip of the barrel, rushing forward across the field and coming to rest on the cliff face, alive with the motion of squirrels dashing from one hole to another.

A blur of brown fur scurried into my line of sight and froze, becoming a statue of a scraggly adult squirrel, ears up, mangy tail held high, claws clutching at the solid dirt. I swung the barrel slightly, until the notches lined up just behind the squirrel's front shoulder. I held my breath, then let it out slow, slower still, until I wasn't really breathing at all, and squeezed the trigger.

The world jolted, winked out for an instant, and the squirrel was gone. No pieces, nothing. It was simply gone. The crack of the shot rolled out across the field and into the hills, bouncing back toward the tree. Strangely though, I only really heard it with my left ear.

Without moving my left arm, I reached up with my right, jerked the bolt up and back. The spent casing went flying toward an old coffee can I kept, about four feet off to my right. I collected the casings when I was finished, and took them back to the trailer so Grandma could reload them.

I slid the bolt forward and locked it down. My finger found the trigger all by itself as I scanned the cliff again. Everything was still. The squirrels understood that one of their own had been touched once again by God, but they weren't sure where His hand had come out of the sky. So they froze, listening, watching.

Another crack of thunder. This time, the bullet slammed into the squirrel's chest, near the ground. The thin body flew off the cliff in a spectacular cartwheel, sending drops of blood into an abstract, circular pattern into the dirt. It bounced once before falling out of sight into the gravel of the creek bed. The body wouldn't last long; the vultures would arrive as soon as I left. They were probably circling already.

In these hills, gunfire tended to attract scavengers.

I shot twenty-two more squirrels in fifteen minutes. That was enough. Only one shell was left in the breech. It took a while, but the squirrels finally realized that it didn't matter *where* the hand of God was coming from, only that it was coming out of the sky with a vengeance, and it was safer to hole up inside the burrows until God got bored and went somewhere else. I watched the cliff face for a moment through the binoculars, satisfying myself that there wasn't going to be any brave or just plain stupid squirrel trying to make a mad dash to another hole. There wasn't.

I was about to put the binoculars down and collect my spent casings when three quick puffs of dirt popped out of the cliff and an instant later three light cracks of another rifle echoed out across the field. I dropped the binoculars and scrabbled back against the dead tree, breathing hard. I waited a moment, watching the cliff, but the gunshots rolled away as if they had never happened.

After a full minute, I poked my head carefully around the tree, checking the field behind me. It was empty. But there, on the far edge of the field, a bright red Dodge pickup, sitting way up on some kind of lift kit, was parked on the side of Road E. I could just make out the shape of someone sitting in the driver's seat.

I brought the binoculars up and found someone with long blond hair pointing a rifle at me. I jerked back around the tree, breath trapped in my throat. It took a moment, but then I realized that the rifle had a scope on it, and the person was probably just watching me through the scope. That didn't make me feel any better. Only some kind of a moron would watch somebody else through a scope, not realizing that they were also aiming the rifle at the person. Or maybe they did realize it.

I took a chance and peered back around the tree. Now the person was leaning out of the window, waving at me. The rifle was gone. I glanced quickly through the binoculars again.

The red pickup sprang into view, in sharp focus, showing me everything. The person in the window was wearing a tight white blouse, and I couldn't help but notice the generous swell of breasts barely contained underneath. The waving wasn't helping me much either; the breasts shimmered slightly with every movement. I finally managed to tear my gaze away from the curves to see the face. But I knew who it was. Knew it before I even saw her face. I suppose I knew it when I saw the pickup, saw the blond hair.

It was Misty Johnson. And she was waving at *me*.

CHAPTER 15

I wasn't sure what to do, so I raised my right arm and kind of waved back. Actually, it took me a few seconds to figure out that she wasn't so much waving at me as she was waving me over to her, beckoning me.

For a moment, I couldn't move. The idea that someone like Misty Johnson was calling me over to her snapped something in my brain, disrupted the flow of thoughts, and so I stood rooted to my spot under the oak tree. She kept waving at me.

I left all the spent casings behind and didn't waste much time getting across the field.

She had the upper half of her body out of the driver's window, resting on her elbows, watching me get closer. Her arms pressed her breasts together, pushing them up and out. I think she knew what she was doing, knew exactly the kind of effect it was having on me. I stopped on my side of the old barbed wire fence, trying hard not to stare up at her.

"I was watching you shoot," she said. "You're pretty good. Never missed once."

I shrugged and stammered out something like, "I get a lot of practice."

"I'll bet. What's your name?"

"Arch Stanton."

"You live here?" Before I could answer, she said, "I've seen you at school, right?"

I shrugged again, trying to blurt out something, anything. "Ah . . . uh-huh." That's me—Mr. Smooth. I was just glad she didn't mention seeing me yesterday morning, when her dad went for a swim in the ditch.

"Wanna go for a ride?"

My heart stopped. "Uhh . . . A ride?"

She sat back, pulling her body into the truck, then held up a rifle. For the briefest second, I found that I could tear my eyes off her breasts and focus on the rifle. It looked expensive. But then she stuck her head back out the window and thrust that chest at me again, and I forgot all about the rifle. My gaze slid right back into place, like a couple magnets were pulling at my eyes.

"I just got this," she said, holding the rifle out to me, "but I can't figure out how to sight it in. I saw you shoot once before, out at my house, for my dad, and thought you could help me."

I bent over and slipped through the strands of barbed wire, and walked up to the truck, forcing myself to look only at the rifle. Like its owner, the weapon was beautiful.

It had the basic shape of an ordinary rifle, with a Mannlicher stock, meaning the forestock extended out to the end of the barrel, but I had never seen anything like it. It had a bolt action, with a painstakingly checkered stock, made from a kind of dark, almost black, hardwood that I couldn't place. Misty held the rifle out to me and I took it with a kind of holy reverence. I recognized only one of the words etched along the barrel. Anschütz.

"That's gorgeous," I whispered. "This is an Anschütz rifle." I didn't even know that they made hunting rifles. As far as I knew, they made the most accurate target rifles in the world. The name is known as The Rifle of Champions. I mean, if you cared about precision and accuracy at all, then these rifles were the absolute best. Damn near every Olympic shooter in the world used an Anschütz. It even had a Zeiss scope. Unbelievable. It was expensive, all right. "This is one hell of a rifle," I managed to mumble, handing it up to Misty. "It's beautiful."

She shrugged. "It's some German thing, the only thing Dad ever bought that wasn't American made. Said that since the caliber was small enough for me to handle, he wanted me to have it. But it needs to be sighted in. What do you say?"

I thought about it, wondering what the price would be for getting to work late once again. It didn't take long for me to decide that whatever the punishment was, it wasn't going to stop me from taking a ride with Misty and getting to shoot that rifle. It wasn't just a gun; that was a work of art. I nodded. "Sure. Let's do it."

She grinned at me and winked. Actually winked. My heart started hammering at my rib cage again and I walked around the front of the truck, praying that I wouldn't get a sudden, unmistakable hard-on, which is what happened most of the time when I thought about Misty.

I set my jaw tight, coming up with an emergency plan. If I felt any stirring down there, I would force myself to think about the toilet at Fat Ernst's. That would be enough to kill any desire in anybody.

Misty put my 30.06 into the gun rack in the back window with the Anschütz. As I lifted myself up and into the seat, she turned the engine over, saying, "I know just the place."

That got my attention, because I figured we'd simply go over to her father's ranch, out into the hills. But if we weren't going to her place . . . where could we go? Fat Ernst's toilet!—Fat Ernst's toilet, I reminded myself.

Misty cranked the radio dial up and some god-awful modern country music filled the cab. At least it wasn't "Sweet Home Alabama." She jerked the truck into gear and stomped on the gas. I held on to the armrest tight, trying not to make it look obvious.

She didn't say much during the ride, just bobbed her head along with the inane music, hair-sprayed blond hair jittering slightly. That was okay. I didn't know what the hell to say anyway. Instead, I tried to keep an eye on where we were, stealing sidelong glances at her tight jeans. After a while, I figured I'd better say something, and stammered out, "Sorry to hear about your dad." I winced, realizing I had just repeated the same goddamn thing that Fat Ernst had said. "I, uh, lost my dad too."

Misty shrugged. "Thanks. It's okay." She barely slowed down when she hit the highway and headed east, up into the hills toward the reservoir. She said, "I keep wondering if I'm supposed to feel worse. Dad wasn't . . . he had a good heart in there somewhere, maybe sometimes. But I didn't like how he treated Mom." She glanced sideways and gave me a cold smile. "And ever since I started seeing boys, me and Dad never got along at all."

The truck followed the highway farther up into the foothills, up past the long, straight bank the Army engineers had built to contain the Split Rock reservoir. Then she steered the Dodge onto a narrow dirt road that ran parallel to Stony Creek for a ways before it opened out into a huge gravel pit. I'd never been here, but I realized exactly where we were. The Quarry.

The Quarry was part of an abandoned sand and gravel plant that had stood at the edge of Stony Creek. When they had exhausted the supply, the company moved on, taking over a place farther downstream, leaving behind over three acres of wide, empty craters. This was where the juniors and seniors at the high school came to party every Friday and Saturday night, a place that was whispered about in the halls by the younger, less-than-cool kids. I'd heard a lot of stories about this place, exaggerated tales of drunken fights and urgent back-seat sex. The Quarry had seemed, to me at least, about as far away as the surface of the moon.

And here I was. With the one and only Misty Johnson, no less. Misty had been the star of many of the stories, but I couldn't think about that now. I'd save those thoughts for later.

The Dodge slid to a stop in a surge of gravel near the entrance and Misty killed the engine. She pointed at a pile of rusted oil barrels at the far end of the crater, over a hundred yards away. "Go set up some beer cans on those. We'll use 'em for targets."

I was about to ask where the beer cans were when I looked down. Dozens of empty beer cans and bottles lay scattered across the gravel like wounded soldiers after a terrible battle. I climbed out and had a sudden flash of irritation at being ordered around like a servant, but what was I going to do about it? Absolutely nothing. I collected five empty, sticky Budweiser cans and held them against my chest as I jogged through the puddles and mud toward the pile of barrels like an obedient puppy.

I pulled one of the barrels down, rolling it against several that were standing upright. Then I set the cans up, propping them one by one up against the barrels behind the barrel lying on its side. This way, I could track the path of the bullets by wherever they left holes in the barrels around the cans.

When I got back, Misty already had the rifle loaded, bracing it casually on her hip.

I skirted around a blackened fire pit and felt something stick to the bottom of Grandpa's boot. I twisted my ankle around and reached down to pull off whatever it was, when I saw it, twisted and semitransparent, wedged into the waffled sole. I flinched, jerking my hand away.

For a heart-stopping second, I thought it was one of the worms. Then I figured out what it was, even though I'd never seen one before. A condom. Used, by the look of it. My stomach rolled and dropped somewhere down between my feet. A hot, tight feeling crawled over me, scary and exciting at the same time. I looked up and Misty winked at me again. I shrugged and tried to grin back, scraping off the condom on the gravel.

"So, what do we do first?" she asked.

"Well, we need to brace the rifle, get it steady, find out where it's shooting." I looked at the truck. It was too high; we couldn't brace the rifle across the hood. "You got a blanket, or something like that?" I asked. "We're gonna have to lie down."

Misty gave me an amused look and I suddenly realized what that had sounded like. I giggled nervously. "I mean, you need a pad . . . or something . . . to, uh, put on the ground," I finished lamely, sweeping my hand out to indicate the rough gravel.

She handed the rifle to me. I carefully laid it out on the tailgate, examining the scope as she opened the door. Misty came back and set a balled-up blanket next to the gun, saying, "Will this work?"

"That'll work, uh, just fine." I shook out the blanket, trying to ignore the slightly musky smell, and it fluttered out to the ground. I smoothed it down and grabbed the rifle, kneeling on the blanket. Misty dropped to her knees next to me, close enough that I could smell her perfume. *Fat Ernst's toilet,* I kept reminding myself, and managed to focus on the rifle instead.

"Okay. Go ahead and lie down," I told Misty. She gave me another bemused snicker and leaned forward until she was on her stomach. "Get into, uh, a prone position. Okay, good. Prop yourself up on your elbows there, at an angle, and"—I almost said *and spread your legs a little,* but caught it just in time, choking out—"and, and there you go." I handed the rifle to Misty, desperately trying not to look at how the fabric of her jeans clung to the ripe, curving cheeks of her ass. *Fat Ernst's toilet . . .*

She settled into position, left elbow forward just a little, right arm out to the side.

"Okay good, good. Now, when it feels right, go ahead and take a shot." I had barely finished the sentence when she pulled the trigger. A distant puff of dust, just about five inches over one of the barrels. She jerked the bolt back, then slammed it home.

"Give yourself a sec, then take another." Again, the rifle cracked before I finished. Another little burst of gravel, this time off to the right of the barrel. "One more time." The bullet whizzed above the barrel once again.

"Okay, hang on." Still kneeling, I bent over the scope, and gently inserted a dime into one of the two adjustable knobs. I counted four clicks as I twisted the dime counterclockwise. "Try it again."

The first round was off to the right, but the second shot nailed the can, crumpling the top half and sending it flying. "Nice shot," I said, reaching for the box of shells just as Misty pulled the trigger once more. A dry snap; the gun was empty.

I inserted the dime into the second knob, twisting it clockwise for two clicks. Then I loaded the rifle, handed it back to Misty.

She hadn't moved; her eyes were still focused on the cans at the far end of the quarry. As she concentrated, I couldn't help but steal a quick glance at her behind. I ripped my eyes away and handed the rifle back to her. She fired off the five rounds in rapid succession and missed every time, throwing the bullets all around the can.

They weren't landing in one area, so I couldn't tell if the scope was sighted in. "Let me try it real quick," I said, and added quickly, "if you don't mind."

"No, that's okay. I'd like to watch you shoot," Misty said, and scooted over on the blanket.

I eased myself down next to her, grateful that I was lying on my stomach and could hide the growing bulge in my crotch. I loaded the rifle, then pulled it up tight into my shoulder.

"You're putting the crosshairs right in middle of the can, right?" I asked.

"Of course."

Through the crystal clear Zeiss scope, the red and white can looked enormous. I settled the crosshairs right into the center of the huge "B," let my breath out slowly, and squeezed. The gentle snap of the trigger was like touching a DaVinci sketch.

The can rocked slowly, but it wasn't hit. I searched through the scope until I found the bullet hole—directly under the can, about a foot down, a small fresh hole in the barrel. I brought the crosshairs back up and fired again. Same thing. The bullet struck the oil drum just to the left of the original hole. A third round. This time, the bullet nicked the edge of the first hole, nearly grazing the second. All three holes could have fit inside a dime. Okay.

The rifle was sighted in. It was shooting low for me simply because the drop was different. In other words, when my cheek was settled on the stock, my eye occupied a different point in space than Misty's, but it should work fine for her.

I found the can in the crosshairs one more time, then raised the barrel until I was pointing somewhere above the can, about the same distance from the can to the holes in the barrel. I squeezed the trigger, and the beer can popped off the oil drum, spinning end over end until it disappeared behind the barrels. I'd hit the bottom edge, and that had knocked it into the air.

"Nice shot," Misty said. She sounded genuinely impressed. "Now let me try."

I loaded the rifle and handed it back to her. "Just breathe nice and easy. Squeeeeeeze that trigger, real gentle like." I propped myself on my elbows, bringing the binoculars up.

Her first shot was low, second shot high, but the third shot sent another can bouncing off into the gravel. "There you go." Misty nailed two more cans, whispering, "Fucking A plus, you little cocksuckers," then reloaded.

There was something sweet, almost delicious in hearing her smoky voice wrap around a word like "cocksucker." It was almost more than I could handle. I thanked God again for being able to lie on my stomach, hiding an erection that would not be denied.

A sniggering voice floated out across the Quarry to us. "Well, well, isn't this just cute as a goddamn button."

My erection died faster than if I'd seen Fat Ernst naked. I'd heard that voice all night, in my nightmares. I glanced over my shoulder and saw them. Junior and Bert, standing in front of their truck in the middle of the road at the top ridge of the Quarry, silhouetted against the gray sky. Bert waved.

Oh, shit, I thought. *The goddamn Sawyer brothers found me again.*

"Don't stop on our account," Junior hollered. "Just pretend we ain't here. I gotta say, though, I'm downright impressed here, Archie. We been trying for years to get some of that sweet pussy, and you just slid right on in there. Didn't think you had it in you."

"Yeah, Archie," Bert echoed. "Way to go, man."

Something flared in my chest.

"Go back to fucking chickens, dipshit," Misty called out, still concentrating on the remaining beer can.

Junior ignored her. "Hey, Archie, you mind if we get sloppy seconds?"

I got a bad, scared feeling about all of this, overriding my anger. We were out in the middle of nowhere, hidden even from the highway. If Junior and Bert took it into their heads to really give Misty a hard time, nothing was going to stop them.

"You don't mind, do ya, Archie? You sure as hell ain't gonna satisfy a woman like Miss Misty Johnson. I think me and Bert might just have to help ourselves, show this cunt what a real man can do."

"I think we'd better get out of here," I whispered to Misty, but she was already pushing herself to her feet, handing me the rifle.

She stepped forward, hands on her hips. "If you pencil-dick motherfuckers think you're man enough to try it, then you just come on down." Misty's voice sounded confident, tough. I was close enough to see the apprehension in her eyes. It wasn't fear exactly, but Misty wasn't as clueless as I had thought. She knew exactly what kind of mayhem and cruelty the Sawyer brothers were capable of inflicting. Still, she yelled out, "You couldn't satisfy a fucking flea, cocksucker. Go on home and let your mama suck you off if you're in the mood."

I wished she hadn't mentioned Pearl. The air sparked and crackled with charged electricity and the almost playful nature in Junior's voice sharpened into something far more serious. "So. The cunt's got a smart mouth. Let's see how fucking smart your mouth is with my dick in it." I couldn't see the exact expression on his face—they were too far away—but I could tell that Junior meant it. He turned, heading back to the driver's side of the truck.

I still don't know why I did it. Maybe I wanted to impress Misty. Maybe I wanted to simply scare them off. Maybe I just wasn't thinking. I don't really know. All I know is that calmly, almost like a casual reflex, I pulled the Anschütz to my shoulder and blew the tip of the left horn of the bull skull off into nothingness.

Junior and Bert froze.

I jerked the bolt back, slammed a new round into the chamber. "Get the hell out of here," I shouted, hoping my voice sounded braver than I felt.

"You gotta be fucking kidding me. You didn't . . . You didn't just shoot at me, did you? Did you?" Junior hollered.

I yelled back, "I wasn't shooting *at* you. I hit what I was aiming at. When I'm shooting *at* you, motherfucker . . . uh . . . you won't know nothing; you'll be fucking dead."

Junior's open mouth snapped shut. "Well, well . . . You just fucked up seriously, Archie," he said. "We're gonna be seeing you later." I could almost feel the hatred rush across the quarry and wash over me like the putrid water from the pit.

Misty laughed. "Get the fuck out've here, you pussies." She laughed again, a cruel, heartless sound.

Oh, please don't laugh at them, I thought. *Things are bad enough.*

Junior just nodded. "Be seeing you. Be seeing *both* of you." He jerked his head at the truck, and Bert climbed in. Junior nodded at us again, then walked around the front real slow, taking his time. He fingered the broken tip of the bull horn briefly, then climbed into the driver's seat, gunned the engine, and whipped the truck around in a spray of mud and gravel.

"Oh, my God. That was fucking great!" Misty giggled, and hugged me tight before I had a chance to react. "You were perfect," she whispered, and gave me a quick kiss. Right on the lips. It was the first time I had ever kissed a girl, and I gotta say, it felt so good I wished the Sawyer brothers would come back so I could shoot at their truck some more.

wormfood

Then she kissed me again, longer this time.

It finally started to rain and somehow we ended up on the blanket next to the rifle, giggling, whispering, and panting. I don't remember much, just distinct flashes and sudden sensory impressions. It was the contrasts, I think. The way she tasted sweet and salty at the same time. The hard, unyielding surface of the rocky ground and soft flesh. The way the rain made her skin seem slippery, yet almost sticky.

Her breasts were the smoothest things I had ever touched, smoother than glass, than silk, than oil.

Misty pulled out a condom from somewhere. I remember clothes being pulled off, the rough dampness of the blanket, and the strength of Misty's arms and legs pulling me close, closer than I'd ever been to another human being.

I lasted about three seconds.

As it turned out, Misty kept a box of condoms in the glove box.

The second time, I lasted maybe a minute.

But the third time, boy, that was something. And Misty seemed to agree.

Afterward, I stared up into the clouds and felt like the greatest champion in the universe. But yet, at the same time, I felt like the scum that floats at the edge of dead, brackish water. It didn't make much sense. Despite the nagging, ashamed feeling that I had just jumped naked into a giant mud puddle in front of my grandmother, I felt great. No, better than great. I felt like I could walk into Fat Ernst's bar, piss all over the floor, and laugh in his face.

Misty planted her bare feet flat on the wet blanket, arched her back, and wriggled into her blue panties. As her left knee brushed my cheek I saw that a long, ragged scar curled out from the inside of her knee and down her calf. I caught her knee and held it still as she reached for her blouse. The scar looked like a white, curving zipper of melted flesh on tan skin. I slid my middle finger down the length of it, letting my other fingers whisper along her bare leg while I concentrated on the subtle bumps and ridges, feeling the strange logic of the contours.

Misty shrugged and buttoned her blouse. "Got bucked off a horse," she said without any trace of embarrassment or self-consciousness. "Landed on a barbed wire fence and my leg got caught in it."

The bottom dropped out of my stomach, like falling out of the very top of a tall tree. The thought of her getting hurt hit me like a solid kick in the gut, just below my stomach. I swallowed, found my voice. "If anybody ever hurts you ever again, I'll kill them," I said.

She laughed, looked me in the eye, and trailed her fingers down my temple, my cheek. "You're sweet. I never heard that one before."

"I mean it," I said. Then I closed my eyes and kissed her scar.

CHAPTER 16

Misty didn't drop me off at the restaurant until ten thirty, but I didn't care that I was late. I felt too goddamn good. We'd kept our distance the whole ride back, kind of sizing each other up for real this time. Neither of us had tried touching the other one. We listened to country music instead. I was getting a little worried when she pulled into the parking lot, worried that I'd somehow done something wrong. After she stopped her truck out by the sign, she leaned over and gave me another long kiss.

I felt better.

I stopped at the top step and gave a little wave as she pulled out of the muddy parking lot. I saw her wave back through the rear window as the Dodge bounced up onto the highway and tore off, back toward the foothills. I realized too late that Grandpa's 30.06 was still in the gun rack, but that was okay. It just meant that I'd get to see her again. I turned to the front door and realized I still had to face Fat Ernst.

I eased the door open as quietly as I could, feeling a flash of panic at being late. But it passed. I peered around the door and found the bar was empty except for Heck. He swiveled around on the bar stool, staring at me through red, sunken eyes, and greeted me with a tremendous belch that crumbled into wet coughing.

"Morning yourself there, Heck," I said cheerfully, shutting the door behind me. "You need a napkin or anything?"

He shook his head and gave me the thumbs-up sign. I gave him the thumbs-up right back and moved through the tables. I counted three empty glasses on the bar, each coated in some sort of red, grainy liquid. Bloody Marys. Heck was getting started early. One of the glasses had a little purple umbrella sticking out of it. That was different. Fat Ernst must have been in a good mood as well. "Where's the boss?" I asked, heading for the kitchen.

Heck jerked his head toward the restrooms. *Perfect*, I thought. *All I have to do is collect up these dirty glasses and retreat into the kitchen before Fat Ernst gets out of the bathroom.* That way, I could claim I'd been here for at least fifteen, twenty minutes. "Be right back," I told Heck and ducked through the swinging doors. Once inside the kitchen, I stood next to the refrigerator and stretched, reaching up to the ceiling, standing on my tiptoes. Grandpa's boots felt a little stiff, but comfortable. My body felt loose, relaxed, damn near strong. I grabbed the gray plastic bin under the sink and headed back out to the bar.

Heck hadn't moved. He sat, leaning back against the bar, staring out the front windows. I followed his gaze and watched a shadow appear at the front windows. Darkness gathered at the top of the window and grew as a soft blanket of white noise enveloped the building. Rain spattered against the back wall and marched north across the roof. The wall of black clouds rolled out across the highway, slid over the foothills, and melted into utter blackness above the eastern mountains. Raindrops started landing in the flooded parking lot, creating thousands, millions of muddy explosions.

Heck swiveled back around, shaking his head. "Goddamn rain. There goes any business for the day." He sighed, then said, "What the hell. Might as well just have a couple more."

wormfood

I was reaching for Heck's empty glasses when a deep, booming crack of thunder shook the air. That's when I saw Heck's plate. It was sitting directly in front of him and the glasses surrounded it like bloodied cops guarding a horrible crime scene. There was a lot of yellow wiped around the plate, and I remembered that Heck liked his eggs over easy, just barely cooked. Mixed into the bright, primary-color yellow were a few bits of crust and what looked like the chewed ends of a couple of hamburger patties.

Where had that food come from?

Fat Ernst appeared in the restroom doorway, patting his huge belt buckle affectionately. I jerked my hand away from Heck's plate as if I'd been stung. Not wanting to draw attention to myself, I started grabbing glasses and stacked them in the plastic bin. Fat Ernst stomped through the dining area, hitching up his jeans as he barreled along like a freighter in heavy seas. "Mornin'. How'd it go last night?"

The question caught me off guard. What the hell did he mean? I shrugged. "Uh, okay, I guess." It came out more as a question than an answer, but Fat Ernst didn't seem to notice. At least he didn't seem pissed that I was late.

"Good, good." He stopped next to me and Heck and fished around in the front pocket of his jeans for a second, then reached out and grabbed my left hand. I tried not to flinch, but if I did, he didn't notice. Or at least, he pretended not to notice. He just slapped something dry and crinkled into my left palm. Then he waddled around the end of the bar and came toward us on the other side.

I risked a glance down at my palm. A fifty dollar bill was wedged into the crease of skin between my thumb and forefinger. I almost dropped it in surprise. "Yeah, last night was fine," I said.

"Glad to hear it." Fat Ernst met my eyes for a moment and I thought I caught a flash of a smirk on his fat face, but it was gone before I had a chance to register anything clearly. He winked at Heck. "How you doin' there, old man? Looks like you might need another one."

Heck nodded, as if this were the solution to a complex mathematical problem. "Yeah, you know, I think you might be right." He glanced over at the jukebox. "Now, if you could just manage to put a couple of songs from the Sons of the Pioneers on that goddamn jukebox of yours, hell, I'd die a happy man. You know, something like 'Water.'" Heck started singing in a high, warbling tone as I grabbed his plate. "All day I face the barren waste, without the taste of . . . water . . ." He placed both hands flat on the bar and drew himself up, as if his head were attached to a fishing line that was being reeled up to the surface. Heck echoed himself in a high, falsetto voice, ". . . water . . . water . . ."

Fat Ernst grinned, eyes bright. "We'll have to see about that one, Heck."

I decided to take advantage of Fat Ernst's good mood and satisfy my curiosity. It just seemed like the right time to ask. Without really thinking, I opened my mouth and the words tumbled out. "Hey, have you guys ever seen Ma Sawyer? I mean, do you know anything about her?"

Heck crunched his dentures together like a startled snapping turtle. Fat Ernst stood back for a moment, then sagged, leaning on the bar, staring at me. He didn't say anything for a several seconds. "Why?"

"I, uh, saw her last night," I stammered.

"You saw her last night?" Heck scrunched his eyebrows together. "Huh." Then, as if he'd forgotten his question, said suddenly, "I saw her once, man. Way back, before the accident." He stared at the bottles behind the bar. "It was over at Smith's Butcher Block, that place on Third Street." He took a sip of his drink before continuing. "Now this, this was damn near thirty years ago. Them boys, they were just little kids." I had a hard time picturing Bert and Junior Sawyer as little kids. "Pearl had gotten into an argument with the butcher over some damn thing." Heck looked up at Fat Ernst. "You remember old Guy Smith, right? Well, man, she backed him up against the counter and was chewing into him like you wouldn't believe." *Oh, I can believe it*, I thought. "At the time, what took my attention the most was those boys, man. They were grabbing handfuls of ground beef and just flinging them at each other like goddamn monkeys throwing their shit at each other. I couldn't believe it. It was just, well . . ." Heck searched for the word. ". . . uncivilized."

Fat Ernst nodded, settling into his stool, while I stood there, plastic bin on my hip, next to Heck. I thought about climbing onto a barstool, but it was kind of an unwritten rule that employees weren't allowed on the stools. Heck stared at his plate. "But now . . . hell, man, I remember that woman. She couldn't have cared less about what her boys were up to. She was too busy staring old Guy down. I guess she was wanting to know why he wasn't buying any meat from her. Man. Poor old Guy. He kept saying that it wasn't up to him. But she wasn't listening." Heck pounded the bar in sudden recognition. "I remember 'cause it was around Thanksgiving. I was there getting some pork sausage for the stuffing. That's right." He stopped, deep in his memories. "Finally, Guy tried to get away, to get around the meat counter. But Pearl, man, she just struck, like a goddamn snake, just grabbed poor Guy by the balls. She looked strong, I tell you that much. She grabbed old Guy's nuts, I mean hard, man, and hung on, demanding to know why her meat wasn't being bought. She'd shake him now and again and Guy'd turn about the color of this plate here. The last thing I heard was that rusty voice screaming, 'You listen to me 'less you want me take a hammer to your balls again.' I don't know what finally happened, man, but what I remember—clear as daylight—is that you don't mess with that woman."

Fat Ernst nodded. "You got that right. That Pearl, she isn't a woman you mess with. No, sir." I nodded too. I knew exactly how Heck and Fat Ernst felt. I'd seen Pearl, and I didn't want to have anything to do with her. She scared the hell out of me. "Nobody fucks with Pearl. 'Specially now, after the accident," Fat Ernst muttered.

"Why not?" I whispered back, afraid to speak louder.

"Well, let's just say we've all heard the stories," Fat Ernst said, rolling back on his stool. "As far as I can tell, people started talking when she was forced to retire from the DMV. It was the supervisor, remember? John Halkin, I think. Poor goddamn stupid bastard. He shoulda known," Fat Ernst said. "He's the one that fired her. Well, the story goes that he didn't *fire* her, he had to . . . let her . . . go. She hit retirement age, you know? Not too long after that little talk, the supervisor's house gets all *infested* with flies. I mean to tell you, flies were coming out of the fucking woodwork. They were flying out of the goddamn refrigerator, the air conditioning vents, the bathtub drain, the kitchen sink, closets, dresser drawers, electric sockets, cracks in the floor, you know, between the wall and the floor, everywhere."

A creeping, itching feeling crawled up my back and into my hair. It was all I could do not to twist my arm around and furiously scratch at my back. Fat Ernst stared out the front window, watching the rain. "And no matter what the hell this poor bastard tries, nothing works, you know? Nothing. Poisons, chemical bombs, flypaper, a fucking flyswatter—you name it, nothing worked. The flies just kept coming. Finally, he tries to sell the damn property. But every time somebody comes to check out the house, the damn flies drive 'em off." Fat Ernst took a heavy breath, slapping his hands and clasping his fingers together between his knees.

He shook his head. "Finally, this dumb sonofabitch tries to burn his own house down and collect on the insurance. Well, he got caught, convicted, and got sent off to the Monroe County Jail. Had to give up his life, his family, all because of this one woman. Far as I know, he's still there."

"So . . . it was just that one guy, right?" I asked.

"Hell, no. After that, Pearl found an old lawnmower somewhere and started mowing lawns in the summer. At first, I think folks hired her out of pity, this old woman scrabbling for a little change, trying to raise them two wild boys. And for a few years, from what I heard, she did a halfway decent job, mowing lawns with this old, I mean old, rattling lawnmower, driving from job to job in that shitty El Camino. Even when Pearl couldn't manage to pull the starter cord on the mower anymore, somebody'd start it for her, and she'd push it around the streets, going from one lawn to the next without turning it off. I'm telling you flat out, this bit—" Fat Ernst stopped suddenly, then said quickly, "this—ah—*she* refused to even kill the engine while she was pouring gas in the damn thing."

Heck nodded to both of us. "I saw her pushing that lawnmower down the street while it was still running. I just remember praying that nobody got too close."

I thought about the five or six rusted lawnmowers in the Sawyer Brothers' backyard.

Fat Ernst kept talking, more to Heck than me, but I didn't care. "And then her eyes started going. Or maybe she just stopped giving a damn. People got different opinions, but the fact is, people started finding their flower beds, gardens, bushes, everything mowed down to something like three inches. I saw a couple of them yards. You should've seen it. Then I heard that garden hoses were getting all sliced and chopped by that fucking machine. Sometimes, freshly cut grass got . . . *accidentally* dumped into swimming pools. And once in a while, the family cat or some small dog would disappear. Oh, yeah. I heard all about it."

Fat Ernst took a long look around his restaurant. "But it wasn't just the lawnmower." His gaze settled on Heck. "Remember what happened to Harry Knight?"

Heck shrugged. "Just that he died a few years back. Some kind of disease, wasted away in the hospital or something."

Fat Ernst flicked his glance at me for a second, saying, "Harry used to be the vet around here. Ed took over the business after he died. Anyways"—he looked back to Heck—"I'm driving to work one day and I see Harry's truck and the Sawyer truck stopped, side by side, middle of the road. So I figure they're just talking, right? I pull up behind the Sawyers' truck, figuring they'd pull out of the way. But nobody moves. I can't see into the Sawyers' truck, but I can see Harry through his windshield. He's madder'nhell, shouting at 'em. Then he stops, all of a sudden."

Fat Ernst drew back and looked at us, serious as brain cancer. "Then this . . . this arm, I guess, kind of reaches out of the Sawyers' window. Can't explain it exactly. It was just there—one second it's not, and the next it's just fucking *there*. And it ain't Junior or Bert's arm. No way. It looked like one of them arms you might see on an Ethiopian or some poor starving bastard like that. It was that skinny. But see, the weird part is, I just thought it looked too long at first. That arm was so skinny, it took me a minute to figure out that it was holding a stick."

"A stick?" Heck asked.

"Yeah, you know, a fucking stick." Fat Ernst shrugged. "Now, I know that it's Pearl's arm, and I don't wanna know why she's pointing this at Harry. See, I was ready to start pounding on the damn horn, get 'em moving out of the way so I can get to work, but lemme tell you, I saw that goddamn bony arm and I froze. Harry, he sees this stick being jabbed at him, he changes his tune real quick. He takes off, doesn't look at me, doesn't wave, nothing. I don't know what the hell happened there, and like I said, I don't wanna know. All I know is that a couple of days later, Harry is in the hospital."

Fat Ernst lowered his voice. "I heard from Ray later that Harry couldn't keep anything in him. Nothing. He'd eat and eat and eat, but it would just run right through him. I mean, didn't take but ten, fifteen minutes. You could even see that he liked his steak rare. Like shit through a goddamn goose. Spent two days in the john before his wife called the ambulance. Doctors never did figure it out. He died four or five days later. Anything they put in him, any food, any liquids, any injections or anything, just kept leaking out of his ass." He nodded, staring at us. "Like I said, that Pearl isn't a woman you fuck with. No, sir. She's got . . . she can do *things*, and that's a good enough excuse for me to stay the hell away from her."

CHAPTER 17

Slim came in around noon, shaking rainwater off his hat and stomping mud all over the place. I silently ground my teeth and had a nightmarish flash that I would be working at Fat Ernst's until I was an old man, still mopping that goddamn floor while a steady stream of guys in muddy boots kept wandering in and out. Before the door had even closed, I threw the dirty rag in my gray bin and was heading for the kitchen to grab the mop.

"Afternoon, Slim." Fat Ernst said, tearing his gaze away from the television. "How you doing?"

Slim nodded at Fat Ernst and stiffly eased himself down at the bar, setting his hat on the stool between him and Heck. Heck sat slumped over on his stool and stared at his drink. Slim rubbed his eyes tiredly. "Wife's off taking care of the sister-in-law, so I'll take one of those cheeseburgers if you got any left."

"That's something we always got plenty of. Just picked up some this morning, as a matter of fact," Fat Ernst rumbled enthusiastically. "Hey," he said sharply as I reached the kitchen doors. "Fix Slim up a cheeseburger. You know how he likes it."

"Make sure those fries are extra crispy," Slim said, still massaging his forehead. He stopped for a second to point at me and said, "And plenty of onions."

I nodded, surprised that Fat Ernst didn't want me to mop the floor immediately. I ducked into the kitchen, set the bin on the counter next to the sink, and washed my hands. Cooking wasn't much of an art at Fat Ernst's, despite what he liked to tell people. Food was either fried on the griddle or boiled in oil. That was it. I opened the fridge and surveyed the contents as I dried my hands. Two Popov Vodka cardboard boxes were sitting on the top shelf. They were new, so I peered inside. In the first box, I could see the meat that Fat Ernst had just bought, wrapped in butcher paper. Words like "Flank" and "Sirloin" and "Rump Roast" were scrawled across the white paper in black grease pencil. The second box held the hamburgers.

Fat Ernst took a lot of pride in his burgers. He made them about once a week, placing the raw patties in a box lined with aluminum foil so all he had to do was slap those suckers on the grill. He'd dump the ground beef in a large mixing bowl, adding ingredients like bread crumbs, garlic, a couple of eggs, some finely chopped onions, a little barbecue sauce, and maybe a few spices if he had any. All that would get churned together, and then he'd form the patties.

I made sure the stove was on and dropped a burger on the long, flat griddle, where it started sizzling immediately. Then I grabbed a bag of frozen french fries from the freezer and dumped them in a pot of oil on the top of the stove. And that was it.

Slim came in only about every two or three weeks, but he ordered the same thing every time. Cheeseburger. American cheese. With bacon. We didn't have any bacon this time, so I didn't worry about it. Plenty of ketchup. Mayonnaise on the buns, not on the meat itself. Just a touch of mustard. Tomatoes. Four sweet pickles. Lettuce. Relish. Onions—lots and lots of onions. You couldn't put too many onions on Slim's cheeseburger. Once, when he told me, "and I mean *a ton* of onions" and shook his finger at me for about the hundredth time, I piled damn near an entire red onion on that cheeseburger. There was more onion than meat on it. I leaned up against the door, listening. I heard Slim tell Fat Ernst, "Kid finally got it right with the onions. You give him this," and I heard something dry slide across the bar.

I never saw a tip the whole time I worked for Fat Ernst.

I flipped the burger over and grabbed the bag of hamburger buns and Grandma's vegetables from the fridge. Fat Ernst had refused to pay for them because they were all smashed up, but he still wanted to use them. I cut up the onion and crushed tomato as best I could and prepped the buns. By then, the hamburger patty was nearly done so I dropped a slice of American cheese on it and collected the fries. They were crispy enough, I decided. I scraped the burger off the griddle and dropped it on the bun, piled everything up on top of it, dumped the fries on the plate and carried it out to Slim.

"'Bout time," Fat Ernst said, not taking his eyes off the television. As I set the plate down in front of Slim, Heck exploded in a fit of liquid coughing. He grabbed the edge of the bar to brace himself as his body shook and trembled.

"Goddamnit, Heck!" Fat Ernst barked, scowling as he wiped off his arm with a rag. Slim moved his plate over a little and took a bite out of his cheeseburger.

Heck shakily reached into his shirt pocket and pulled out a pack of Marlboros. His eyes had narrowed into slits, his mouth hung open, and deep, guttural sounds bubbled underneath his rasping breath. He fumbled with the lighter and dropped it on the bar.

Slim snapped, "Do you mind? I'm trying to eat here and you gotta light up a cigarette. You want me to come over to your place and spit in your food when you're trying to eat? It's the same goddamn thing." Slim shook his head and took another bite.

If Heck heard Slim, it didn't look like it registered. It didn't look like he was hearing much of anything, actually. He left the lighter on the bar and put the cigarette next to it. His fingers trembled.

I glanced up at the television. A guy in a garish sweater was standing in front of a satellite-fed weather map. A large swirl of white static loomed off the coast while the guy grinned like an idiot and swept his arm across northern California, demonstrating the path of the storm.

Heck grabbed his beer and tilted his head back.

"I'm goddamn sick of this fucking rain," Fat Ernst told the television.

Slim nodded in agreement and crunched his onions.

Heck dropped his head back down, holding his beer out to the side. A thin rope of spit trailed out of his mouth to the bottle. As I watched, the rope broke and drool ran down Heck's chin. It was clear at first, but as more drool slowly oozed out of the corner of Heck's mouth, it got thicker and yellow. Then it got red.

"You feeling okay, Heck?" I asked.

Heck dropped the beer bottle and I heard it clunk and roll away on the wood floor.

"What the hell is wrong with you?" Fat Ernst shouted at Heck. Fat Ernst turned to me, "Clean it up. Now."

Heck started to shiver. He slipped off the back of his stool, swayed for a moment holding his potbelly, then lurched off toward the restroom. Fat Ernst shouted after him, "You better not make a mess this time, you old fart."

Heck fell into the restroom, and a second later, the toe-curling sounds of wet, violent retching filled the restaurant.

"Oh, that's fucking great!" Fat Ernst shouted and threw the rag at the television.

"Good God," Slim said and put his burger back on the plate, eyeing it with disgust.

Fat Ernst swiveled around on his stool and pointed a pudgy finger at me. "You. You go clean it up. Right fucking now. When I get in there later I swear to God I better be able to eat off that toilet and it better smell like a fucking mountain meadow or I will rip your tongue out and use it to wipe my ass. Am I making myself clear here?"

I nodded and darted into the kitchen to get my trusty mop. I didn't look at either Fat Ernst or Slim as I scurried back around the bar to the restroom. When I got there, the door had swung shut. I stopped, bucket in one hand, mop in the other, suddenly unsure of what to do. I set the bucket on the floor and knocked timidly. "Heck? Heck? You okay? I'm gonna come in, okay?"

The door swung open easily with a slight groan from the hinges. The sink was off to my immediate left, the chipped and stained urinal hanging off the wall next to it, and the metal sheet of the stall closed off the back wall, hiding the toilet from the rest of the small bathroom. I could see Heck's boots in the gap under the metal wall.

I stepped inside, saying, "Hey, Heck? You okay?" I left the mop and the bucket near the sink and reluctantly stuck my head around the stall. The first thing I noticed was the blood. It was all over the place. It was splattered across the toilet, across the water tank, across the walls. Across Heck.

He looked dead. He was on his knees, stuck between the toilet bowl and the wall, hunched over and twisted sideways. One hand rested palm up on his thighs, while the other was draped across the bowl. Wet, clinging red streamers of toilet paper were hanging from Heck's chin. It looked like he had tried to wipe his mouth off but had given up somewhere along the line. His eyes were closed and his mouth was open. I watched a thin sliver of crimson drool roll out of the corner of his mouth and drop down toward his chest like a tiny red spider un-spooling her web.

"Heck," I whispered again, crouching down.

No answer. He didn't move, didn't breathe, nothing. I wanted to shout at him, anything to wake him. But instead I reached out slowly, very slowly, and prodded his shoulder with the first two knuckles of my right hand. It didn't feel right to touch him with the bare tips of my fingers.

Still nothing.

I pushed again, harder this time. Nothing.

I didn't know what to do. There wasn't anything I could do except break the news. It was time to tell Fat Ernst. He'd have to call the ambulance, get Heck some help. I pulled my hand away from his shoulder.

Heck's eyes popped open. His left hand, the one curled in his lap, shot out and grabbed the front of my shirt even before I had a chance to scream. His arm shivered slightly, shaking me, and wouldn't let go. I grabbed his wrist and he flung his head back; his skull hit the wall and it sounded like a hard-boiled egg hitting the floor. Boot heels squeaked in the blood as his legs twitched, and one foot flopped back and forth. Something gurgled, deep in the back of his throat.

Heck's head dropped forward, his mouth opened impossibly wide, and his entire body shuddered as if connected to a sputtering electrical current. A torrent of thick blood exploded out of his mouth and nose, splattering against the stall wall two feet away.

I screamed and ripped away from Heck's grasp, my fingers scrabbling on the cold tile. Luckily, not much of the blood landed on me. Heck sank back against the wall and moaned something that only came out in frothy bubbles. I kept scrambling back until I hit the door. I managed to push myself to my feet, fumbling for the door handle. Heck's eyes met mine for a brief second, and all I could see in them was a total, animal kind of pain.

"Uh, just . . . oh, God. Just take it easy, okay, Heck? You're gonna be okay. I'll get you some help. Just hang on." Heck started to gag. I yanked open the door and screamed out toward the bar, "Call 911! Heck's really sick! Call 911!" I turned back to Heck. He had slumped forward, facedown in the toilet. Every couple of seconds his back would shiver spastically and I heard more blood hitting the inside of the bowl.

Fat Ernst's wheezing voice filled the doorway behind me, demanding "What the hell is going on?"

I whipped around, staring up into Fat Ernst's wide face. I could see right up into his black nostrils, and for some reason this reminded me of Heck and my heart broke. "Call 911!" I shrieked, and was about to push out into the hall to make the damn call myself when Fat Ernst shoved me roughly against the sink as he took a step into the small restroom.

"What the fuck is wrong with him?" Fat Ernst asked, hands on his hips.

Heck feebly lifted his head out of the toilet bowl and worked his jaw up and down several times, like he was trying to say something but couldn't get it out. Fat Ernst bent over slightly at the waist, like he was addressing a child. "What's wrong? Are you sick?" he said, carefully enunciating each word.

Slim appeared in the doorway and was just about to step inside when he saw the blood, froze, and said simply, "Sonofabitch."

Heck started flopping around then like a fish that's just been hauled out of the river and onto the rocks. His hands clawed at the air and he kept making those liquid moaning noises deep in his chest.

"We gotta call the ambulance," I said in a high, taut voice. It was getting hard to breathe.

"Well, Ernst, looks like you got your hands full here," Slim said. "I'll settle up with you later." He disappeared into the restaurant.

"Oh, that's fucking great. Fucking perfect," Fat Ernst said, watching the doorway. "Now it's gonna be all over the goddamn county. Bastard'll probably stiff me on the goddamn burger, too." He swiveled his round head back around to stare down at Heck. "Thanks. Thanks a lot, Heck."

Heck just sat there, eyes closed, with a sheet of dark, almost black blood seeping out of his mouth and down his chin.

"Well, goddamnit. We can't just leave him in here. It'll upset folks." Fat Ernst flipped his hand at Heck. "Grab his arms, drag him out here. We'll put him in the back."

"But . . . but you gotta call the ambulance," I stammered.

"I ain't calling nobody, so shut your hole." Fat Ernst suddenly grabbed a fistful of my hair and nearly lifted me off my feet. I got a quick flash that my head was on fire as he dragged me away from the sink and flung me toward Heck. I stumbled into the wall and accidentally stepped on Heck's left hand with Grandpa's boot. Heck didn't move.

"Drag him over here," Fat Ernst snarled.

I grasped Heck's wrist, trying to ignore the warm, sticky blood that coated his arm. I lifted it and tugged gently, pulling his body away from the toilet. Heck's limp form slumped against my leg as I bent over and grabbed his other hand. He still didn't move, and this time I was afraid he really was dead.

I dragged him out of the stall and Fat Ernst took a deep breath and bent over, reaching for Heck's legs. He seized an ankle in each hand as if he were grabbing the handles of a wheelbarrow filled with firewood. He jiggled all three chins toward the door. "Move, dumbshit. Let's go."

I caught the edge of the door with my toe and swung it open. Heck's head rolled over and hung limply between his outstretched arms. I shuffled backward, and we half carried, half dragged him out of the restroom and into the restaurant. We left a shining trail of blood behind us nearly two feet wide on the rough wood floor. I know I should have been worrying about Heck, but all I could think about at that second was that it was going to be a bitch mopping all that blood up if I didn't get to it before it dried.

"Hurry it up, goddamnit," Fat Ernst hissed from between clenched teeth. "This ain't exactly healthy for business."

We were halfway down the bar when Heck starting shrieking again. His body twitched and convulsed; as he jerked, I lost my grip on his right hand and his head and shoulder slammed to the floor. "Oh shit, I'm sorry, I'm sorry," I whimpered, reaching down to pick him up again.

Ray walked in the front door.

CHAPTER 18

We all froze, except for Heck, who was shaking his head violently from side to side, spattering more blood all over the floor like a weak sprinkler on a dead lawn.

Ray swallowed, eyes wide. It was obvious he didn't know what to say. A toneless "Howdy, Ernst," tumbled out of his mouth. As if he were almost ashamed of not being sociable or something, he quickly added, "How's business?"

Fat Ernst dropped Heck's legs. They hit the floor and stayed there. Didn't bounce, nothing. He stared at Ray. "Business? Business couldn't be fucking better."

Ray nodded as if that made perfect sense. He looked down at Heck. "Heck been drinking paint thinner again?"

"Shit. What do you think? Looks like it, don't it?" Fat Ernst said quickly, words stumbling over each other.

"I don't think—," I started to say before I could stop myself.

"Shut. Your. Hole," Fat Ernst said. "I ain't paying you to think."

Ray adjusted his hat and ambled over to Heck's body. "Looks serious. Maybe I better take a look." He knelt down and nudged Heck.

"What's wrong?"

Heck gasped once, and bubbles of blood erupted around his mouth and nose. Each muscle began to slacken, releasing its tension as one by one, the bubbles popped. Then he lay still.

"Is he dead?" I whispered.

Ray watched Heck's face for a moment, then nodded soberly. "Yep. I declare this man officially dead."

"Can't you do something?" I asked.

Ray looked up at me and shrugged. "You want to give him CPR? Go right ahead."

I looked at Heck's open mouth, filled with blood, and didn't say anything.

"Wonder what killed him," Ray said.

"Hell, he's been dying for years." Fat Ernst proclaimed. "If his liver didn't explode 'cause of the booze, then it was the cancer that got him. Or the paint thinner."

"Heck had cancer?" Ray asked.

"What the hell else do you think happened?"

"Maybe it was something he ate," I suggested and immediately knew it was the wrong thing to say.

"Maybe you oughta shut your fucking hole and get to cleaning that goddamn bathroom." Fat Ernst glanced down at Ray. "Grab his arms there. We'll drag him out the back door. Lay him out the loading dock for now. There's a tarp under the sink in the kitchen, roll him up in that."

"Just . . . just hold on a minute here," Ray said, standing and holding up his hand as if he was directing traffic. "As an official of the law, I can't just leave Heck here. I'm gonna have to write up some kinda report on this, you know."

Fat Ernst spoke in a low, firm voice. "There ain't nothing we can do. He's dead and that's tough, but I ain't gonna call anybody just yet. We're going to take care of this quiet. The last fucking thing I need is for this to get out. Business is shitty enough as it is. I don't need some stupid goddamn thing like a dead body to keep customers away." He hitched up his jeans and narrowed his eyes. "You got that, Ray?"

Ray pulled in his chin until it was nearly touching his swollen Adam's apple. "I dunno, Ernst. I mean, this ain't the kind of thing I can just ignore . . ."

Fat Ernst glared at Ray for a moment, then stepped over Heck and shoved me into the restroom. "Be right back, Ray," he said over his shoulder. He slammed the restroom door behind him.

I tried not to step in any more of the blood, but it was too late. Fat Ernst stood with his back to the door, hands on his hips. He looked at the floor and didn't say anything. Finally, he pursed his lips and said, "I need that fifty bucks." My first instinct was to reach into my pocket and grab the money. But I didn't. I held back and crossed my arms in front of my chest in a gesture of defiance instead. Fat Ernst still didn't look at me. "I know it ain't right. You earned it."

You're goddamn right I earned it, I thought.

Fat Ernst said, "I got nothing right now. Nothing, you understand?" He raised his eyes, found mine. "And unless I pay off that asshole," he said, jerking his head in Ray's direction, "he's gonna screw this place. If he calls this little incident in, then that's it. They'll shut me down. So I need help. I need that fifty bucks to help him look the other way. He's got me over a barrel here and he knows it. Now." Fat Ernst folded his arms. "You can either hand over the cash and keep your job, or I can just take it and you can get the hell out of here. Either way, I'm walking out of this bathroom with the money."

I didn't think about it long. I reached into my pocket, handed over the money. Fat Ernst accepted it almost delicately with one of his swollen, sausagelike fists. He said quietly, "Stick with me, boy. I got a plan. You'll double your money." With that, he opened the door and stepped out into the narrow hallway. "You still work here, so get busy." He waddled off, saying, "Ray, let's talk. But first, let's get this stinking sonofabitch out back before he leaks any more blood on the floor."

I grabbed my trusty mop and surveyed the scene. The bathroom was a mess. The smell attacked my eyes and lungs. I didn't know where to start. I slapped the mop against the walls of the stall to let the water wash down. I had to scrape the mop back and forth to get the blood to flake off. As I worked, my mind started wandering. I figured I'd never see that fifty bucks again. Fat Ernst had a plan. Plan, my ass.

I flushed the toilet with the toe of my boot and watched as the blood swirled away. At the last second, I saw something white at the bottom of the bowl. I tensed, holding the mop above the toilet like a spear. Then it was gone, swallowed by the surging water. More worms? If it was another worm, then . . .

I shook my head. I didn't want to think about what that meant. But I couldn't help myself. If there were more worms in the toilet . . . that meant that all that meat, the meat from the steer that I had pulled out of the pit, the steer that was *stuffed with those goddamn worms* . . . that meant that Fat Ernst hadn't sold the meat for dog food at all. He'd just used it for the restaurant. And I had helped him.

Fresh water began dribbling slowly into the bowl, washing some of the blood away. I caught sight of the pale shape again as the bowl filled with clear water. Little blocks of white, arranged in a half circle. Then I figured it out. It was Heck's dentures. They must have landed in the toilet when he was puking. I took a deep breath and held it, thanking God it wasn't the worms.

Still, as much as I hated to think about it, I had to admit that it made a certain kind of sense. It explained Heck getting sick, for one thing. And when had Fat Ernst found the time to take the meat to God knows where for dog food, gotten paid, and then gone and bought more meat from God knows where, all before eight o'clock in the morning? The more I thought about it, the more uneasy I felt. And as I kept thinking about the whole thing, a creeping sense of guilt filled my chest. It felt heavy and hot, like boiling lead. So in the end, I just didn't think about it, and concentrated on cleaning up the blood instead. It was easier that way. But I made a promise to myself to check out the rest of the meat in the refrigerator as soon as I got the chance.

I wouldn't want to eat off the toilet like Fat Ernst had instructed, but it wasn't too bad. I managed to mop up just about all of the blood in the bathroom, except for a few reddish brown stains on the grouting between the tiles in a few places. I dumped the water in my bucket into the toilet and filled it back up with some hot water in the sink.

I carried it out into the restaurant, hoping that the blood hadn't had a chance to dry yet. The place was empty except for the trail of blood that led from the bathroom, widened into a smeared pool near the middle of the bar, and kept going until disappearing under the kitchen doors. I checked the windows; Ray's squad car was gone. I wondered if the bribe had worked. I thrust the mop into the bucket of hot water and then slapped it on the floor. I didn't bother squeezing the excess water out of the mop because I was going to need all the help I could getting that blood off the floor. The stuff was like glue, sticky and congealed. But eventually, with enough hot water and scraping, I managed to wipe the trail clean all through the restaurant and into the kitchen.

It was time for more water. I dumped the bucket in the sink and was about to twist the hot water handle when I heard something outside. A hissed, guttural exclamation, then a hollow thud. I left the bucket in the sink and crept over to the back door. Another exclamation; I could make out the words this time. "Piss brained bag of dogshit." The last word came out as a forced pop of air, and then another dull thud. I recognized Fat Ernst's voice.

I slowly twisted the door handle, trying to think of excuses for opening the door. Nothing came to me, but I pulled it slightly open, just a crack, anyway.

Fat Ernst stood in the rain on the loading dock, chest heaving, fists clenched. Heck's body lay at his feet, just at the edge of the dock. The dock was a square wooden deck, nearly ten feet across, empty except for a stack of rotting pallets next to the door. Beyond the dock was nothing but oceans of cornfields. Fat Ernst kept swearing through clenched teeth. "You sonofabitch. I should've. . ." He trailed off for a second, then came back with a basic "Fuck!" and gave Heck a good solid kick, right in the rib cage. Heck's body jerked and trembled from the blow, but other than that, he didn't move. Fat Ernst stomped on Heck's right hand for good measure. "Cocksucking son of a whore." Another kick, to Heck's head this time, shattering Heck's nose, a dry, snapping sound that reminded me of stepping on a dead, brittle leaf.

Fat Ernst had his back to me, and as he was drawing his leg back for another kick, he suddenly pivoted in place and stared at me. I felt my insides shrinking up and I knew I was going to be the one who got kicked next. But Fat Ernst didn't move, didn't say anything. He just stared at me, thick lips pulled back in a snarl, breathing through clenched teeth. I swallowed, fighting the urge to flee. He twisted back around, spat out "FUCKER!" and kicked Heck in the stomach one more time. Blood erupted out of Heck's mouth in a wet little cloud.

Then Fat Ernst stepped back, still breathing heavily. He stared down at the sprawled corpse and spoke without looking at me. "You get all that shit cleaned up?"

"Yeah, except for the little bit in the kitchen and out here," I answered.

Fat Ernst looked at the sky. The clouds, black and pregnant with rain, filled the sky from horizon to horizon. "What time is it?" he asked finally.

"Uh, around three or four, I think," I said.

"Give me a hand here." Fat Ernst went down to one knee at the edge of the loading dock and flipped open the lid to the Dumpster. It crashed against the metal side with an abrupt, clanging sound that made me wince. Fat Ernst straightened with some effort and took two steps sideways. He bent over and pulled a key ring out of Heck's front pocket, then rolled him on his side and plucked a wallet out of one of Heck's back pockets. Fat Ernst slid the wallet into his own pocket like it belonged to him, then sidled down to Heck's feet. "Grab his arms there, and help me dump him."

I knew it was wrong. Knew I should have called somebody. Knew I should have left. But it didn't matter. I grabbed Heck's bloody arms anyway. I couldn't look at his ruined face. We both lifted, and Heck simply folded in half. Fat Ernst shuffled sideways to the edge, and dropped Heck's legs into the empty Dumpster. It was already starting to fill with rainwater. The rest of Heck's torso slid in, and his arms slipped easily out of my grasp. He hit the bottom of the Dumpster with all the grace of a canvas sack of rotten potatoes falling off a table.

I wasn't sure if Fat Ernst was going to leave Heck in there until the garbage guys came next Wednesday, or if he was going to haul the body out later that night, and I sure as hell wasn't going to ask. Fat Ernst turned his face up to the falling rain for a moment, then wiped his forehead and muttered, "I just can't understand why it is so goddamn hard for a man to make a decent living on his own these days."

I wasn't sure what to say, so I kept my mouth shut.

After a few seconds, Fat Ernst turned and forced his bulk through the back door. He hollered over his shoulder, "Hurry and finish cleaning up. Then you and me are gonna go for a ride. I'm gonna close up early today. We got a lot of work to do before morning rolls around."

CHAPTER 19

Fat Ernst had a huge old Cadillac, with fins and everything, a fat white whale wallowing in a sea of mud. The inside was the color of pomegranates that have been left in the sun too long. Everything was this deep dark red, and I mean everything. The carpet, the seats, the dashboard—even the steering wheel. Only the slivery glints of the metal knobs broke the monotony. I sat down on the edge of the impossibly long bench seat, feeling like a frightened toddler placed upon a pew in some musty old church for the first time. And just like I was in church, I prayed. I prayed there wasn't too much mud on Grandpa's boots to soil the pomegranate carpet. I prayed Grandma was okay. I prayed we weren't going back to Slim's pit.

And I prayed that someday I would forget how Heck's ruined face looked as he landed in the bottom of the Dumpster.

Fat Ernst dropped into the driver's seat like a bomb going off in slow motion. Waves of flesh rolled down, then rippled back up his arms and under his shirt. The car's suspension gave a short shriek of pain, then gave up. Fat Ernst twisted the key and we were off. He didn't say anything and neither did I.

wormfood

The Cadillac followed the highway up into the foothills by the lake. I thanked God that we were headed in the opposite direction from Slim's ranch, but I still got a bad feeling when Fat Ernst stopped the car in front of Heck's store. A rusted gas pump stood outside the store like a stubborn sentry who refused to leave his post. A wooden sandwich board had been propped up near the door and loudly proclaimed LIVE BAIT—FRESH WORMS.

Fat Ernst ignored the "Gone Fishin', Be Back Later" sign hanging behind the glass front door and opened the door using Heck's keys. I decided to stay outside, by the gas pump. Heck was dead, and I didn't need to be inside his store, going through his stuff, looking for God knows what. Behind the store, off to the west, the clouds were churning across the sky, hanging low and fat. It wouldn't be long before the rain started again, flat-out serious this time.

Fat Ernst reappeared, carrying a chunk of cast iron about the size of a basketball. It was bulbous and heavy, with three stubby legs protruding out of what I thought was the bottom. A thick plastic hose grew out of the top and looped over Fat Ernst's shoulder. He carried it to the car, breath coming in short, quick bursts.

"What's that?" I asked.

"Sump pump," Fat Ernst replied, as if that explained everything. He opened the trunk and dropped the thing inside. "See boy, that's how you make it in this world. You gotta always be thinking ahead."

I didn't know what the hell he was talking about but figured it wasn't the time to ask, because Fat Ernst was settling in behind the wheel. I hopped back into the car and Fat Ernst pulled out in a wide U-turn, heading back down into the valley. Before long, I realized that we were headed down Road E, down the narrow road to the gravel track and out to the Sawyers' ranch.

The road didn't improve much in the faint daylight that was still left. It just illuminated the dead trees, broken fences, and scattered litter of tossed beer cans, cigarette packs, fast-food wrappers, and junk that didn't have any logical explanation. A La-Z-Boy recliner, lying on its side. A shopping cart. Broken sawhorses. A pile of microwaves. An old dishwasher, still swathed in fiberglass insulation. Much later, I found out all this was actually dumped by people from town who couldn't be bothered to take their junk to the dump and pay the fee. Instead, they drove out here when they knew the brothers were gone and unloaded their trash.

The Cadillac crested the small hill and rolled down into the hollow filled with deep shadows. As we got closer to the house I could hear the incessant, skin-crawling buzz of the wasps, even through the thick windows. I kept checking and rechecking the passenger window to make sure it was rolled all the way up.

Fat Ernst killed the headlights as he got close to the edge of the house. "Don't want to spook 'em," he said. "Heard they started shooting at a UPS truck that got lost once." After a moment of consideration, he shut the engine off too. We sat quietly in the Cadillac, parked about fifteen yards from the house. Two of the downstairs windows had light spilling out of them onto the tangled grass. But the front door stayed shut. Then Fat Ernst looked over at me. "Why don't you go say hello." Then he told me what to say.

I knew it was coming. Knew it was useless to argue. Fat Ernst would probably just break my nose, then make me go up to the house by myself anyway. So I took a quick glance out at the fig trees, now just splintered, twisted silhouettes against a purple sky, and climbed out of the car. I thought about leaving the door open, thinking it would serve Fat Ernst right if I let a swarm of wasps loose inside the car. But I shut the door and started toward the house.

It still reminded me of a spider; a squat, sick arachnid with broken legs, still waiting patiently in its web of fig trees. A thin strip of cracked concrete took me to the front door. I couldn't feel my legs; they seemed to be moving on their own, and I floated along through the weeds growing in the ragged crevices in the concrete as if I were standing on some crumbling conveyer belt. I just eased on up to the front door and before I could stop myself, I reached out and pressed the doorbell. Nothing happened.

I swore under my breath and raised my fist to knock.

The door opened and Junior grinned out of the shadows at me. "Well, well. If it isn't the sharpshooter. Hiya, Archie."

He stood there wearing nothing but a pair of jeans. A chicken drumstick was clamped in one hand. He glanced over my shoulder at Fat Ernst's Cadillac and took a chomp out of the chicken leg. He pulled his head away, like a dog, and I heard the gristle snap. He said, "Come back for some more shooting practice?"

"Uh, no. Look, I'm sorry about that—I, uh, didn't mean to do it," I finished in a small voice. Uncomfortable silence. I had to say something. "Fat Ernst says he's got another job for you."

"Is that right."

A light flickered on somewhere behind him, to the right, illuminating the foyer of the house. A small, antique table stood against the wall behind Junior. A tall mirror hung above the table. It looked old and dark, as if bubbles and smoke had somehow infected the glass, twisting and obscuring the reflection. And I heard the voice, out of the room to the right. *Her* voice. It sounded like rusty iron being slowly pulled apart.

"What's that pig fucker want?" Dry as death, the words sounded a little slurred and mushy. I wasn't sure if she was talking about me or Fat Ernst.

Junior called back over his shoulder, "Says he's got another job for us, Ma."

In the mirror behind Junior, I caught a glimpse of something pale. The mirror must have been tilted somehow, maybe hung crookedly, because I could see into the room to the right. Maybe it was the living room, I wasn't sure. It wasn't until much later that I began to suspect it was hung that way on purpose, so anyone in the living room could see who was at the front door without leaving the room. The pale shape drifted through the smoky glass like a ghost, but I knew it was her. "What kind of job?"

Junior looked down at me and asked, "What kind of job?" He stuck the now-clean drumstick in his mouth and, in one quick jerk, broke it in half.

"I don't know." My voice cracked and trembled. "He didn't say."

"Archie don't know, Ma," Junior called back over his shoulder, imitating my high, cracking voice. "He didn't say."

The pallid figure in the mirror stopped moving. I could definitely tell it had a human shape now, maybe a little thin, with one arm missing or held in real close and tight, but it was a person. It was Pearl. She was watching me through the mirror. For some reason I could see one of her eyes in the reflection, perfectly clear, utterly black and staring. It felt like she was staring right through my head, right down into the nest of squirming fear that was beginning to spill out into the rest of my body. I felt naked. No, more than naked. I felt like I couldn't hide anything, that all of my secrets were laid bare on a flat rock in the sun and poked at with a stick.

Junior stuck one of the broken ends of the bone in his mouth and started sucking on it, smacking his tongue against the top of his mouth as he sucked out the marrow.

"I know you," Pearl said. "I know you. Saw you last night." The reflection tilted its head slightly. "You're Janine Stanton's grandson, ain't you?" It didn't come out as a question. "Yes, I know you. Knew your grandfather. You look like him. Same scared eyes. I happen to know a few things 'bout your grandma too." I wasn't sure, but it looked like the pale shape in the darkness and smoke of the mirror smiled, a horrible, crooked smile with only one side of her face. "How them boots fit, boy?"

My breath caught and I froze. How did she know about Grandpa's boots? The figure in the mirror drifted back into the smoky shadows and disappeared. Junior flicked one half of the drumstick into the

wormfood

weeds and said, "What the hell does Fat Ernst want now? Tonight?"

I shrugged. "I don't know." Pause. "He just said to bring your shovels."

The blast of a car horn shattered the evening stillness and I flinched. Fat Ernst must have been getting impatient. Junior scowled and said, "Ma don't like a lot of unnecessary noise."

I didn't know what to say. I felt like crawling into a hole and hiding there. Fat Ernst hit the horn again.

Junior picked at his teeth with a long fingernail. "Shovels, huh?"

I shrugged again, helpless. "That's what he said. Said we could all make a lot of money. Just one night's work."

"How much money?"

"I don't know. You'll have to talk to him." I was trying to get Junior to go out to the car and get me away from the house, but Junior didn't move. He just leaned against the doorframe.

"Well, then. You tell Fat Ernst not to get his panties in a bunch and to lay off that fucking horn, and we'll be ready here lickety-split."

I turned to go, saying, "Okay. I'll tell him." Pearl spoke up suddenly, sounding just inches from my ear. "My boys best get their fair share," she whispered. "Otherwise . . . there's a-going to be hell to pay, and I do mean *hell*."

I nodded, and stumbled away. I didn't want to look up, didn't want to see how close she was. "I'll tell him, I'll tell him," I said, moving down the front walk, still nodding like a doll with a broken spring for a neck. I did my best not to run shrieking through the dying light and the circling wasps back to the Cadillac.

I jumped in and slammed the door.

"So? What'd they say?" Fat Ernst asked.

"Junior said not to get your panties in a bunch and they'll be ready lickety-split."

"Okay, then." Fat Ernst lit a cigar. "Took you long enough."

137

CHAPTER 20

I figured it out as soon as we pulled into the little parking lot covered in a thin layer of pea gravel and surrounded by a sagging wrought-iron fence. During the long ride back down the highway out of the hills, the Sawyers following us the whole way, I kept wondering why Fat Ernst had told Junior and Bert to bring their shovels. I was a little worried we might be heading back to the pit, but that didn't make sense. Fat Ernst had enough meat now, but after watching him kick Heck's corpse and drop him in the Dumpster like that, I knew he was capable of anything. Grandma had been right about him.

We were here to dig up Earl's coffin. And steal that buckle.

The sun had disappeared over an hour ago, leaving the valley shrouded in almost total darkness. Fat Ernst killed the Cadillac, sat back on the pomegranate seat, and flicked his cigar stub out onto the wet gravel. He instantly lit another.

Earl had been buried in the Lutheran, Methodist, and Baptist cemetery. The Catholic cemetery was on the other side of the creek, closer to town. And the Mormons had their own exclusive plot of land up north, near their church or temple or whatever the hell they wanted to call it. I guess people who didn't like to associate much while they were alive sure as hell didn't want to lie next to each other when they were dead. They might end up in the wrong heaven or something. This graveyard waited patiently at the end of Route 11, surrounded by walnut orchards, huge trees with vast expanses of branches, silently hulking out in the darkness.

Fat Ernst kept the headlights on and I realized he *had* been thinking ahead when he took Heck's submersible pump. The cemetery wasn't too far from the creek. When they had originally started burying folks out here, the creek was still a ways off, but over the years, especially since they had built the reservoir, the creek had gradually changed its course, carrying away the dark, heavy soil bit by bit, creeping closer and closer to the graveyard.

And now the whole place was under about six inches of water.

The Sawyers' truck pulled in next to my side of the Cadillac and the engine rumbled angrily in the wet darkness. "Leave your lights on," Fat Ernst called out as Junior killed the engine. I looked out over the acre of headstones, rising from the black water, illuminated by the headlights. It looked as though someone had started building a bridge, pouring somewhat orderly rows of various concrete supports and foundations across a swamp, then had given up after a while. I opened the door and stepped into the muddy water, feeling the liquid instantly trickle over the tops of Grandpa's boots and soak into my socks.

Junior and Bert climbed out of the truck and joined Fat Ernst and me in front of the Cadillac, bathed in the harsh glare of the headlights. "If I would've known we were coming out here, I would've brought some flowers for Pop," Junior said, leaning against the Cadillac's hood.

"We're gonna visit Pop?" Bert asked.

Fat Ernst ignored him and asked, "You got your shovels?"

"Yep."

"Well, go get 'em and let's get to work. We're not here for a goddamn picnic."

"Hold on," Junior said, crossing his arms. "We ain't moving until we know why we're here."

"Yeah," Bert said, nodding. He tried to cross his arms as well, but with his right arm still in a cast, it didn't work so well.

Fat Ernst smiled. "You ever seen Earl Johnson's belt buckle? The one made of gold? With a shitload of diamonds all over it?"

"No," Junior said. A moment of silence. Then he smiled back. "But I heard about it."

"Well, I just happen to know that Earl had it put in his will that he should be wearing it when they put him in the ground."

Junior looked astonished and betrayed at the same time. "You mean to tell me . . . that they . . . they *buried* it with Earl?"

"That's what I'm telling you."

"Holy shit."

"Holy shit," Bert echoed. I still didn't think he knew quite what was happening. His eyes were wandering around of their own accord again, and I wondered if he'd been taking his horse tranquilizers on a regular schedule.

"So it's out there, just stuck in the ground with Earl?" Junior gestured at the headstones.

"You got it."

"I'll be damned. Wait a minute—suppose we go get it. How are we gonna split it up? Doesn't make much sense to break it in half."

"No, that don't make much sense at all, does it? You gotta think ahead, like me. See, I'm gonna take it down to Sacramento first thing in the morning, take it in to a pawn shop, trade it in for some hard cash. You'll have your share by noon tomorrow, no later."

"Well, hell's bells, if Earl was that goddamn dumb to wear that buckle into the grave, then let's go get it."

"Now you're talking." Fat Ernst glanced at me. "Go grab a shovel, boy. Time for you to earn those wages."

It started to rain, softly at first. I heard raindrops hitting the leaves of the walnut trees and tiny splashes as the drops began to hit the water all around us. Then it began to come down hard, a wall of fat drops and a deluge of white noise. Within seconds, all of us were soaked to the skin. The rain put out Fat Ernst's cigar. He tried lighting it several times, but no luck. Undaunted, he simply twisted the ashes off and chewed on the end. He spit, still smiling, and said, "Told you I had a plan."

"One more thing," Junior said as if he were just remembering something, and I suddenly found myself face down in the water, a heavy ringing in my ears. It took me a minute to realize that Junior had clocked me in the back of the head with his shovel. When I put it together and tried to sit up, he kicked me in the stomach. A great orange bomb exploded somewhere inside and liquid pain ricocheted through my body.

"That's for shooting at the skull," he said. "How'm I supposed to fix the horn if there's nothing left to fix?" He kicked me again.

"Knock it off!" Fat Ernst hollered. "We're gonna need his help, and he ain't gonna shovel much if you keep kicking him like that."

Junior bent down, whispering, "We're just getting started, you and I." He made a point of stepping on my hand with his cowboy boot, driving it into the soft mud as he turned back to the truck.

Bert started out into the cemetery first, carrying a Coleman lantern that Fat Ernst had also thoughtfully brought along. It gave me a beacon to follow as I stumbled along behind him carrying two shovels, the sledgehammer, and a crowbar, holding my stomach as best I could. Junior was next, carrying the sump pump, plastic tube looped around his shoulders, and trailing a long, heavy-duty extension cord plugged into the generator in the back of the truck. Fat Ernst brought up the rear, wheezing and panting as we splashed through the graveyard. Immediately, I felt the mud grab hold of Grandpa's boots as if it were alive and had a mind of its own. With each step, I sank a little farther and farther into the soft soil, until the water was almost up to my knees.

I wondered how we would find Earl's grave, seeing that they hadn't had time to engrave a headstone or erect one of those giant monoliths that the rich folks seemed to like so much. Everything was completely covered with water, so we couldn't even spot the freshly dug dirt. But as it turned out, it wasn't hard to spot the grave at all. The canopy, used to cover the grave and the mourners during the services when it rained, was still up, waiting down in the far corner of the graveyard, in the Johnson family plot.

As the four of us struggled across the cemetery, shuffling through the mud and floodwater, I realized that Grandpa was buried in here somewhere. Mom and Dad were with Mom's parents on the other side of the river, in the Catholic cemetery. I stopped a moment, looking around. I used to know where Grandpa's grave was located; I used to come out here at least once or twice a month with Grandma, but now, in the darkness and rain and mud, I couldn't find my bearings. All the headstones looked alike, just erratic rows of stone slabs rising out of a black swamp. Our shadows, cast by the headlights, danced and flitted over the stones and mud, looking as if giant ravens flew about, jumping and swirling from one headstone to the next.

I stopped looking for Grandpa's grave and concentrated on the job at hand. Get the job done and get out, this had become my new mantra. Just get it over with and get home.

The Johnson family had its own corner of the cemetery, even had a wicked little spiked fence to keep out the undesirables. We carefully straddled the fence and climbed onto a wide concrete slab that had been poured over the top of Earl and Slim's parents. Once on top of the slab, we rested for a moment, staring into the dark water under the canopy. Oddly enough, while Junior and Bert and me fought to catch our breath, panting and bent over, bracing our hands on our knees, Fat Ernst seemed the least tired. I had never seen him with that much energy. He paced the length of the slab, maybe seven, eight feet at the most, chewing on his wet cigar and slapping his hands together. "All right then, gentlemen. Let's get to it. There's at least fifteen, maybe twenty, twenty-five thousand bucks down there waiting for us. All we gotta do is dig down six goddamn feet and grab it. That's it. Easiest goddamn money you ever made. Come on, let's move it."

"You start digging then," Junior said, still catching his breath.

"You know I got a heart condition. So quit your bitching and get to work."

Junior picked up both shovels and violently tossed one to me, and we got to work. The beginning was the hardest. We stabbed the shovels blindly into the water, wrenching great, dripping piles of sludge out of the mud and slopping it over to the side. Eventually, Junior and I built up a sort of wide, low wall around the area where we guessed the grave was. The pain in my side receded into a dull ache that I knew would hurt like hell tomorrow. Fat Ernst carefully lowered the submersible pump into the water and plugged it into the extension cord. Junior adjusted the plastic hose so the water was pumped out over the little dike we had built. I was hoping for a break while the grave was being drained, but Fat Ernst wasn't in a break kind of mood.

We pried more sludge out of the hole. I dug until my back and arms were screaming for relief; blisters rose up on my palms almost instantly, breaking and oozing from the rough wooden handle and the silt. We kept at it, settling into a ragged rhythm of digging and lifting. Bert hummed the theme to some other TV show for a few minutes. I think it was *The Munsters*, but Bert wasn't very good. Fat Ernst finally slapped him on the back of the head and that shut him up. Fat Ernst didn't say much either, just kept pacing back and forth, mincing along in the rain as if he were being forced into some formal dance and had to take a leak really bad.

We kept digging, excavating a square hole roughly six feet wide and six feet long. The pump died when we were about four feet down. The motor started in with this hiccupping whine for a while, then simply stopped. There was only thick mud coming out of the end of the plastic hose at that point anyway. Junior unplugged the pump and threw it out of the grave. Fat Ernst ignored it. We kept going, lifting out shovelfuls of mud that had the consistency of wet concrete and slapping it over the dam around the hole, until I couldn't feel my arms anymore, couldn't feel my hands, and the only thing I could hear was the sucking, squelching sounds as each bite was taken out of the earth and splashed over the wall.

It wasn't too long after mud strangled and killed the pump that Junior's shovel hit something solid. He pulled it out, tried again. The blade sank into the muck nearly up to the handle, and this time there was no mistaking the sound, like a baseball bat cracking a rock under water. I stabbed my own shovel into the mud and, sure enough, felt the tingling jolt up my dead arms when it connected with something solid.

"That's it," Fat Ernst whispered in a tight voice. "That. Is. Mother. Fucking. It."

CHAPTER 21

Without a word, Junior and I kept digging, holding the shovels sideways as we scraped mud out of the hole, flinging it away in looping, uneven arcs out into the rain and darkness.

It didn't take long to figure out we had hit the concrete shell that held the coffin. I stood back while Junior went to work with the sledgehammer, pulverizing the cement lid. Within minutes, the rough slab collapsed around the coffin. I started throwing chunks of concrete out of the grave.

About three feet of the casket extended into the hole; the rest was buried under the south wall. We had been close, but we hadn't dug down directly on top of the whole thing. It looked like we had found the top end, because I could see the seam where the lid was cut in half, in case you felt like lifting it up and saying goodbye during the funeral.

Fat Ernst had to wake Bert up by slapping him on the back of the head again. But once he was awake, even Bert could see that we were getting close, and he took his job seriously, kneeling at the top of the dike and holding the lantern out over the hole.

"All right, then." Junior said, and stuck his shovel into the mud and left it there. "Gimme that crowbar."

Fat Ernst thrust the three-foot bar into the hole, nearly crunching my skull in the process. "Do it. Pop that bitch open."

"Oh that's what I'm gonna do all right," Junior said in a velvet, seductive voice as he felt along the edges of the coffin. "Gonna pop your sweet little cherry like a virgin on prom night. That's right, baby."

I backed into the far corner, giving Junior some space as he got romantic with the coffin. He found a spot he liked, along the side and near the grooved seam along the top. He took the crowbar and jammed it up under the overhanging lip on the side, then wrenched it down in a rushed, savage motion. The wedged tip snapped clean out of the groove and flipped up and popped Junior in the nose. He went back against the side of the pit, landing hard, and before he had even burbled out "Mudderfugger," blood started gushing out of his flattened nostrils as if somebody had cranked open a faucet.

"Shake it off," Fat Ernst commanded.

Junior didn't do much except make fists, little grabbing motions in the air in front of his face, and blink rapidly.

"That must hurt like hell," I said.

"Popped *your* cherry," Bert said, and I guess that struck him as particularly funny, because he started giggling uncontrollably, and the lantern started to shake, throwing our huge shadows around the hole like lurching giants.

"Come on, come on," Fat Ernst said. "We're almost there. Quit fucking around."

Junior blinked a few more times and shook his head, spraying blood all over the place. With a tremendous, "You fucking fuck!" he raised the crowbar above his head and brought it down on the coffin with all his strength. The impact left a slight dent and made a hollow boom, but that was all. This pissed Junior off even more, and he attacked the coffin in ferocious spasms, flailing away at it like an old blind woman trying to kill a rattlesnake with her cane.

Finally, he gave up, exhausted and spent. Blood was still running freely from his nose, but Junior ignored it and stared at the coffin like he was trying to scare it into opening. "Gimme that sledgehammer."

Fat Ernst dropped it into the hole. Junior bent over the coffin, inspecting the dents and grooves that he had inflicted on the lid. Sliding his finger along the seam where the lid was cut in half, he found a small notch, a chip broken out of the surface. "There we go," he whispered.

He caressed the notch, then gently worked the blade of the crowbar into the narrow space. "Hold this," Junior said to me, indicating the bar. He held it upright, directly in the center of the lid, as if he was about to stake a vampire.

I did what I was told, firmly grabbing the cold steel with both hands, holding it snug into the little chipped space. If I had realized what Junior was planning, I probably wouldn't have been so quick to grab the damn thing, because he stepped back, swinging the sledgehammer up and over his head. He said, "Watch it," and smashed the hammer flat down on top of the crowbar in a tiny burst of sparks and stinging chips of metal. The jolt vibrated up my arms into my chest and it felt as though I had grabbed hold of an electric fence. I'm lucky I didn't let go, and managed to keep the crowbar in an upright position, because the second blow came just as fast. I stepped as far away from the coffin as I could, holding the crowbar with one straight arm. Junior kept whipping the sledgehammer over his head and swinging it down, like he was working on a railroad, driving iron spikes into solid rock.

After about five or six blows, my hand went numb. It took a few seconds to realize that I wasn't even holding onto the crowbar anymore, yet it was staying upright. Junior had managed to pound it almost an inch into the seam in the coffin lid. He kept at it, bringing the hammer down and grunting every time it smashed into the crowbar.

"All right, open wide for daddy," Junior said as he straddled the coffin, crowbar between his legs, and grabbed the tool with both hands. "You like it, don't you?" He screamed this last part out as he wrenched the crowbar forward, then back. It gave a little, but not much.

"You know you want it!" Junior kept screaming and spitting blood, but I guess the coffin wasn't in the mood for sweet talk. That crowbar didn't budge. After a moment, Junior said, "Bert, get your ass down here." He looked at me, disgusted. "Unlike like the Amazing Human Noodle over here, I need somebody with a little weight, a little fucking strength."

"You got it," Bert said, and slid into the grave. Junior hopped off the coffin and told me to get on it. "Sit down, put your back against the wall, and push at it with your feet. Me and Bert'll pull." He positioned Bert at the head of the coffin and stood next to him. I braced my boots against the crowbar, spread my arms, put my hands flat against the dripping mud wall behind me, and got ready to push. On the other side of the bar, Bert wrapped his left hand over my boots. Then Junior encircled Bert's hand with both of his fists, interlocking his fingers. "Now, when I give the signal, we're gonna pop this old girl open." He winked. "And that's a goddamn promise."

Maybe it was Bert. Maybe it was my legs. Maybe the coffin finally just succumbed to Junior's romance. I don't know. Whatever it was, when Junior shrieked, "NOW!" I kicked out as hard as I could and they jerked backward on that crowbar. I heard a deep, satisfying crack. The crowbar suddenly flopped over toward the Sawyer brothers, and they tumbled into the mire at the bottom of the grave. I looked down to see a long, ragged crack running between my legs, up toward my ass. This made me vaguely uncomfortable and I scooted off the top of the coffin right quick.

"Yes!" Fat Ernst shouted, clenching both fists.

And suddenly, only one thing became real. The buckle was close now, close enough to smell, close enough to taste, close enough to touch. All of our aches and pains and blisters, the rain, the mud, all of it faded into the background, became unimportant. Junior worked the crowbar around in the crack, slamming it back and forth like a man desperately trying to churn smooth butter out of cheese. The opening got wider and he worked the crowbar down the coffin, trying to crack the lid in half lengthwise.

The whole lid split right in half. The bottom half wouldn't open much because at least three feet of the coffin was still buried under the mud wall, but Junior pried open the top half enough that he could force his fingers inside and pull. It swung open with a groan from the mud-caked hinges, but it was open, by God, a quarter of the lid pried up and waiting.

Nobody said anything. Fat Ernst lowered the lantern down into the hole and Junior grabbed it, held it over the open part of the coffin. Bert stood at the head and I stepped closer, joining Junior along the side of the casket. Junior tilted the lantern sideways to get light into the ruptured coffin. "Huh," he said. "I guess these things leak."

The coffin was full of black water.

"Who gives a fuck," Fat Ernst hissed down at us, on his knees at the edge of the dike. His hands kept fluttering around, as if he were a puppeteer and could control us by manipulating the strings. It didn't work though; nobody in the grave moved. "Holy fuck, just reach in there and grab it!"

"I ain't sticking my hand in there." I thought this was one of the most intelligent things Junior had ever said.

Fat Ernst nearly had a fit. "If I woulda known that I hired a bunch of pussies . . ." He gritted his teeth. "Just reach in there and grab it!" he shouted, high and shrill, with one pudgy finger stabbing violently toward the coffin. "Hey, boy!" The stabbing finger found me. "You. You reach in there and grab it. Do it, and . . . and I'll double your share."

Well, there was no way I was going to stick my hand in there, not for any amount. Before I could say anything, Bert shrugged, said, "No big deal," and reached into the black water, holding his cast away from the coffin. His eyes rolled back and crossed as he felt around inside the flooded coffin.

"Good job there, Bert. Glad at least one of you has a set of balls," Fat Ernst shouted happily. "Keep going, boy, you'll know it when you find it."

Bert pulled his hand out of the coffin and we all tensed. But he merely inspected a glob of fatty tissue curled in his palm. He rolled it between his thumb and forefinger, sniffed it, decided it wasn't important, and flung it away. Then, without hesitation, he plunged his arm back in there, concentration etched into his face.

"Find anything?" Junior asked.

Bert shook his head. "Old Earl didn't make it in here in one piece, did he?" he called up at Fat Ernst.

"No, no, he didn't," Fat Ernst said. "Thanks to you knuckleheads, he ended up in the ditch." He chuckled. "He wasn't exactly in the best of shape when they fished him out."

I couldn't help myself and asked, "What's it feel like, Bert?"

He thought hard for a moment, the tip of his tongue sticking out of the corner of his mouth, like a pink, blind animal that's cautiously testing the wind before venturing out of its burrow. "Gooshy," he said finally. He pulled his arm out one more time, but this time he was clutching a black cowboy boot full of water. He tipped the boot up, pouring the water into the mud around our feet. "He's . . . he's all mixed up."

"You just keep going there, Bert. It's in there. I know it," Fat Ernst said.

Bert jammed his arm back into the water, felt around for a minute, then reached in deeper, until he was practically bent over double, water up to his shoulder. He grunted, trying to push his arm farther. His eyes narrowed. "I think I got it!" Bert dragged a dripping pair of jeans and a thick leather belt out of the coffin. Sure enough, that gold and diamond belt buckle was clutched in his left hand.

But it was the worms that caught my attention.

Two of them, both as plump as Fat Ernst's cigars, hung off of his left forearm, twisting and undulating, slowly chewing into the soft flesh up near the elbow. I don't think Bert actually felt the worms on his skin until he saw them, but when he finally did see them, he freaked. He shrieked and scrambled backward, kicking away from the coffin, and dropped the jeans and the buckle into the mud. Junior went after him, trying to help.

"Get the fucking buckle!" Fat Ernst screamed.

While Junior was busy pinning Bert's left arm in the mud and grabbing at the worms, I scuttled over and managed to grab the buckle, a heavy goddamn thing, before Bert's kicking legs drove it even deeper into the muck.

"Oh, thank Christ!" Fat Ernst breathed. "Give it to me." He reached out toward me, leaning closer.

"Little fuckers!" Junior hissed through clenched teeth, a squirming worm between his fingers. He flicked it into the mud and stomped on it. Bert yanked the undulating second worm out of his left arm and wiped it on his cast.

"Give it to me!" Fat Ernst was really reaching now, still on his knees but leaning way over the edge, stretching his arm out to me. I turned to him, an automatic response, and lifted the buckle toward his hand.

A sound caught my attention, a sort of deep, groaning sound that seemed to come from far away.

Bert suddenly screamed, slapping at his cast. I turned and saw that the worm had squirmed its way between the flesh and the plaster, at the inside of his elbow. He whipped his arm out, catching Junior right in the nose. Junior went to his knees, fresh blood pouring from his nostrils. Bert clawed at his cast, whimpering at first, then flat-out screaming when the groaning, sucking sound got louder and louder. I turned, got a quick flash of the bulging mud wall, and suddenly understood.

I whirled around and scrambled onto the coffin as the whole west side of the grave collapsed, snuffing the light out, Fat Ernst riding the crumbling wall of mud on his knees all the way down. Junior yanked Bert out of the way as a tidal wave of water exploded into the grave and I found myself clawing and kicking at the mud attacking me, fighting my way to the east wall. The water swirled and surged up underneath me, lifting me toward the canopy. I kicked out even harder, thrashing and fighting the quicksand muck. Somehow, I managed to find the edge and pull myself out of the rushing, boiling water.

I rolled down the other side of the dike and got twisted around. In the darkness, I wasn't sure where I was at first, whether the grave was behind me or in front of me. I'd been too close to that lantern for too long and, as a result, couldn't see much of anything for a few minutes. The lantern had been at the bottom of the grave and was long gone. There was just rain, mud, and water. I felt something, looked down, and could just make out a few tired glints from the buckle still clutched in my right hand.

By then my eyes were starting to get used to the darkness, and I could see the canopy and the surging, swirling water where the open grave had been. I heard someone coughing on the other side of the canopy. "Holy Jesus," Fat Ernst coughed weakly. He gagged again, spitting into the water. I saw his shadow wearily climb onto a faint gray shape in the night—the slab.

Everything was getting clearer; my night vision was kicking back in. I saw Junior's back as he crawled out of the water and onto the slab. He rolled around on his stomach and peered back into the water. "Bert!" he called out.

I heard vomiting off to my right. Junior scrambled over to that end of the slab and reached out, grabbing Bert by his hair. Fat Ernst suddenly sat up and shouted, "Who's got the buckle? Oh, sweet Jesus, one of you fucks please tell me you've got it." Junior pulled Bert onto the slab, pounding on his brother's back. Bert kept vomiting and I wondered how he'd managed to swallow that much mud.

"Oh fuck, oh fuckohfuck." Fat Ernst started weeping. "Please, please tell me somebody got it."

Bert suddenly twitched, kicking his long legs out in the mud. "I . . . I think that thing just crawled up under my cast," he said in a quiet voice.

wormfood

I looked down at the buckle clenched in my right fist. The diamonds managed to catch whatever light had filtered through the thick clouds and rain and glittered seductively in my hand. I suddenly realized that I could just run. Keep the buckle for myself. Just turn and run like hell and disappear into the darkness.

But then what? Where would I take it? I couldn't get to Sacramento to a pawn shop. I couldn't exactly march into the town bank either, drop the buckle on the counter and demand to be paid for it. And it wasn't like Fat Ernst wouldn't know who had taken it. He'd hunt me and the buckle down and probably kill me without thinking twice about it. I didn't have much of a choice.

"I've got it," I called out. If I gave it to Fat Ernst, at least I had the possibility of getting a little cash out of it.

"You do? Oh, thank Christ. Give it here. Hurry!"

"It's in my arm . . ." Bert started to cry and snot ran across his lips, leaving clear, glistening tracks in the mud on his face.

"Not yet. I want to make a deal first," I said, trying to keep my voice strong, and unclipped the buckle from the belt and jeans.

"What kind of fucking deal? Just bring it over here and we'll talk."

"I want a bigger share. Five hundred bucks. That's fair. If this thing's worth fifteen, twenty grand, then you can pay me five hundred easy. If you don't think that's fair, then I'll just toss it back into the grave, and you can fight those fucking worms for it," I said, tossing the wet jeans back into the mud. I realized that might have been the longest speech I had ever made to Fat Ernst.

"Don't you fucking dare. You stinking goddamn . . . All right. Fuck. All right. You got it. Five hundred. You got it. I swear. Just bring the buckle here."

I edged around the grave, staying on the outside of the canopy. The last thing I needed to do was to fall back into that quicksand nightmare. As I reached the stone slab, Bert started shrieking, clawing madly at the white plaster, "It's in my fucking arm! It's inside!"

Junior grabbed Bert's cast.

Fat Ernst sidled past Junior and Bert, hand out. "Okay, boy, you made your point. Five hundred. I won't forget, I promise. Just give it to me."

I handed it over. Fat Ernst smiled, jerking the buckle out of my hand and slipping it inside his shirt.

Junior said, "I can't see shit, Bert. You sure it went in there?"

Fat Ernst drew himself up, saying, "Gentlemen, I'm going to clean up and then I'll head to Sacramento first thing in the morning." He nodded and added, "You fellas did a good job here."

Junior gently wiped Bert's face with the tail of his shirt. "Come on, Bert, let's go home. Get you some more tranquilizers." Then he wiped some of the blood away from his own mouth.

We splashed back through the long shadows thrown by the head-lights, abandoning the pump, the sledgehammer, the shovels, and the lantern. The rain was still coming down hard, but it felt good as the water slowly washed away the mud and grit on my skin. Fat Ernst didn't say anything else, just plopped into his Cadillac and took off im-mediately, roaring away through the walnut orchards. Junior helped Bert into the truck and paused long enough to reel the extension cord back in. Then they too were gone, leaving me alone in the darkness and rain.

But I didn't mind walking home. Like I said, the rain felt good on my skin. Clean, somehow. And as I walked, I had plenty of time to think about Misty.

And those goddamn worms.

CHAPTER 22

When I got home, Grandma was asleep in her chair, her snoring softly echoing the white noise and static on-screen. I was glad. I didn't want to have to explain all the mud and blood again. I'd been spending too much time with dead things lately. So I stripped out of my filthy clothes in the backyard and just sat on the steps for a while, letting the falling rain wash the rest of the mud away. After a while, I quietly crept inside and took another long, hot shower. Grandma was going to wonder why the gas bill was so high this month.

After the shower, I grabbed the W and X volume of the Encyclopedia Britannica that Grandpa had bought years ago. One winter he decided to work his way through all of the volumes. I carried the encyclopedia back to my room and turned to the section on WORMS.

It wasn't much help. There wasn't a lot of information that fit what I knew about the worms I'd seen. But what did I know about them, really? They ate meat, both alive and dead . . . So, let's see, call 'em carnivores. And from what I could tell, they lived in water, both salt water and freshwater. It seemed like they burrowed into the body, eating it from the inside. But other than that, I wasn't really sure. Whatever they were, they sure as hell weren't night crawlers. The only halfway useful thing I did find was something called a "Pompeii worm." Those things lived in scalding water at the mouths of hydrothermal vents on the ocean floor and could withstand temperatures up to 176 degrees Fahrenheit. That would explain how the eggs or pieces or anything else could survive being cooked inside the hamburgers, if that's what killed Heck.

Other than that, there wasn't much. There weren't any pictures of worms that came even close to the things in the meat that I'd seen. Most of the worms in the encyclopedia were segmented, while the worms I was looking for were quite smooth. The section on parasitic worms looked hopeful at first, but then I realized they were all too small. You couldn't even see most of them with the naked eye. Then it struck me—these things lived underwater. In the pit, they squirted around in the water as if propelled by rockets.

So I replaced the W and X volume and grabbed the F volume. The FISH section was huge, so I skimmed through most of it. It wasn't a simple trout or goddamn goldfish swimming around in Slim's pit. It wasn't sharks either. But then I started reading about primitive fishes and knew I was getting closer. Especially when I saw a picture of a lamprey. Lampreys are like eels, almost snakelike in their appearance. Their mouths are round, and they seem more like a leech than anything else.

The lampreys in the picture didn't have the tendrils around the mouth. Close, but not quite. Something else was mentioned in that section, something called a hagfish, or "slime eel," but there weren't any pictures.

Hagfish, I thought. Something about the name sounded right.

I grabbed the H volume, flipped through a few pages, and there it was, staring at me, in full color and ugly as anything I'd even seen. Even Fat Ernst on the toilet couldn't compare. A goddamn hagfish. The picture wasn't exact; the worms I had seen had black spots running the length of their bodies, and it seemed like the tail was a little different, but it was awful close. Then I started reading, and wished I hadn't.

wormfood

Hagfish lived in the cold mud on the bottom of the ocean, in dense groups, up to *fifteen thousand* in one area. My scalp started itching, and it was all I could do not to scratch, because then I'd be scratching wildly at my whole body, chasing phantom worms all night. They would burrow into dead or dying fish and eat them from the inside. They had a large, circular mouth with a muscular tongue and two rows of strong, sharp teeth. I rubbed the circular wound on my hand. The scab was healing nicely, but it still hurt like hell.

The hagfish could reach lengths of up to three feet.

I swallowed, trying to not to picture one of those worms that big. Hagfish mostly fed off of dead whales, crawling in through the mouth, the eyes, or the anus. Ray's voice popped up in my head, talking about Earl, ". . . and I ain't talking about his goddamn mouth, neither."

Everything fell into place, into perfect clarity, as if I had suddenly managed to focus my binoculars. Earl falls off the boat, dies, and sinks to the bottom, right there at the mouth of the Klamath River. Then these things, these hagfish, or something close, some kind of mutant aberration maybe, don't ask me, slide into his body, chowing down on his insides, and lay their eggs, or simply go to sleep in there or whatever. A week later, his body gets pulled out of the water and shipped home. He's in his coffin, being taken to the cemetery, when I manage to hit the hearse with the Sawyer brothers' truck and knock the coffin into the ditch. And the baby worms get set loose in the ditch water. I figured the difference between freshwater and salt water didn't bother them much. Look at salmon; they're born in freshwater, swim downstream into the ocean, into the salt water, then swim back upstream into freshwater to spawn. So the worms, they headed upstream, up the ditch, maybe smelling meat from Slim's body pit, I don't know, but they end up in the pit and God knows where else. But they're in the pit, that's for goddamn sure, feasting on all those dead carcasses . . .

And then we had to go and pull one of the steers out for meat.

I shut the book with a snap. I'd read enough. I'd read more than

I wanted to. I shook my head to clear out some of the images of those things, of hundreds, even thousands of hagfish inside of a dead whale; those things eating Earl's guts; the colony of worms in the pit; the worms in the middle of the steer intestines; and the burning pain in Heck's eyes as he died. I crawled into bed but I didn't sleep much. And when I did finally drift off, I wished I hadn't.

I blinked once, twice. I shook my head and looked around. I was sitting in the middle of a small rowboat as it floated out across endless ocean swells that melted into a dull sky. I couldn't find any oars, so I just hung onto the bench tightly. The wood felt soft and wet, like an old sponge, and I was scared the seat would crumble into wet splinters under my fingers. Fishhooks and old fishing lines lay in a tangled heap at the bottom of the boat.

I sensed a pale sun somewhere behind me, floating just beyond the low clouds, giving the water and sky a flat, gray color. I risked turning my head to look behind me for any sign of land and the little boat tilted to one side with a sickening feeling. For one gut-wrenching moment, I felt the tiny craft lurch over and I thought I was going to fall in. So I whipped my head back, desperately trying to find the balance that had kept me safe this long. Naturally, the boat rolled over unsteadily the other way. I clutched the wooden sides and shifted slightly, and the boat's rocking slowly subsided.

The wind died.

I felt something on my head and looked up, felt soft wetness splash my face. It was raining. The drops felt unnaturally warm, like a shower. I spread my arms, momentarily forgetting where I was, and let the rain gently wash my fear away. The water ran down my naked chest and back, cleansing and refreshing. It felt . . . wonderful. I opened my mouth, drinking in as much of the rain as I could. It tasted sweet, and I swallowed. But as it trickled down my throat, it left a foul aftertaste, like something had died long ago and had been soaking in the water ever since.

I closed my mouth suddenly and opened my eyes.

wormfood

The raindrops were now a dark, unsettling color. I pulled my arms back in and tried to wipe off my face, my shoulders, my chest, but it was no use. I was covered in slimy, brackish water. It gave off a sick odor as well, like fish that had washed up on a cold, desolate beach and had taken a long time to decompose. The rowboat was rapidly filling up with rainwater.

And it was beginning to sink.

I spit off to the side, trying to clear my mouth of the ugly aftertaste, and breathed through clenched teeth. The gob of spit floated slowly away on water that was now flat as glass. I looked down; the discolored water was now up to my ankles. The hooks and lines floated around in it like a confused spiderweb. I pulled my bare feet quickly out and propped them in the bow of the boat.

A splash.

The floating ball of spit was gone, leaving nothing but expanding circles of ripples.

Despite the color of the rain, the ocean seemed clearer somehow, as if the lack of swells made the depths more visible. I could see speckled, constantly shifting bands of weak sunlight stabbing down into the gloom. Something dark was moving down there. It glided slowly, almost lazily, into the shafts of light, moving upward.

My heart began to beat a little faster and I felt a sudden sense of vertigo, as if I were floating above an immense sky, so I cautiously centered myself in the boat. The gut-churning vertigo made my hands shake. It felt as if I was about to fall from an immense cliff.

The rain continued, and the water in the bottom of the boat got deeper. I brought my hands together and cupped them, trying not to upset the balance while flinging water out of the boat. A crack appeared in the floorboards, growing silently until it disappeared beneath me. A tiny group of bubbles grew from within the narrow space of the crack and floated gently to the surface. They broke and fizzed quietly.

I tried to bail faster.

The dark shape got closer. It was big. Several other shapes joined the first. They swam in wide, slow circles, always creeping upward. I kept trying to hurl water from the sinking craft. One of the thing's backs finally broke the surface, right under my hands. The skin was rotting. I could see the remains of scales, but these were peeling away, revealing spongy, infected flesh.

Another shape rolled through the water nearby. It rose up and sluggishly slid along the surface long enough for me to catch a quick glimpse of a huge, puckered mouth with many, many small teeth, then dove into the depths and vanished.

The rain came down even harder, driving the small boat deeper into the warm ocean. The horizon tilted drunkenly to the left, and I desperately tried to climb up onto the right side. For a second, this helped to balance the craft, until the entire rowboat cracked in half.

And just as I pitched headfirst into the dark, silent water, the alarm went off.

CHAPTER 23

I was up and moving quickly despite my lack of sleep and the bruises that left me stiff and sore, slogging through wet fields in a straight path to Fat Ernst's restaurant. I sure as hell didn't want to be late, not on a morning when I was supposed to get my paycheck. But I had another reason for getting to work earlier, one that had nothing to do with getting paid. I didn't want Fat Ernst around for what I had to do.

The wind screamed up out of the valley, driving rain into the foothills and whipping the drops past my face almost horizontally. One field to go. I just had to climb a fence, hike across a flooded pasture, then scoot down the highway a few hundred yards. I had put Grandpa's boot on the bottom strand of barbed wire and slung my other leg over the top of the fence when I heard the sound of screeching, sliding tires behind me.

My first thought was that the Sawyer brothers had found me again, right in this precarious position with my balls suspended a few inches over angry barbed wire. I saw who really was behind me and almost wished it had been Junior and Bert.

A pickup slid to a stop next to me in a flurry of splattered mud.

Slim stared out of the window with sunken eyes. His face was pale, drawn. He stared at me for a few quiet seconds, and from the expression on his face I wasn't sure if he was going to drive away or shoot me on the spot.

Finally he spoke. "That's private property, boy." He sounded like he'd swallowed a fistful of dry fertilizer.

I didn't know if I should climb off the fence or not, so I kind of froze there. "Um, just heading to work," I said.

"Work." He coughed and brought his ever-present handkerchief up to his mouth. He automatically checked the contents, stowed it safely back in the pocket of jeans. He swallowed, grimacing as he did so, and turned back to me. "What's going on in that goddamn kitchen?"

"What? I don't know . . ."

"I haven't felt right since eating that cheeseburger yesterday. My guts are burnin' up. Feel like I gotta shit, but nothin's comin' out." With a quivering arm, he slid the gearshift into PARK. "So I want to know what the hell is going on. Where'd Ernst get that meat?"

I damn near slipped off the barbed wire fence but managed to grab the steel post just in time. "I, uh, don't exactly know where he got it. Costco, maybe?"

Slim coughed again. "Bullshit." He sniffed. "I know my meat, boy. Hell, I eat a steak, I can tell you how old the steer was, just how long ago it was killed, whether it had been frozen, what the animal had been eating, whether it was corn, or grain . . . Didn't realize it at the time, not with Heck gettin' sick and everything, but that cheeseburger wasn't any"—he broke down in a fit of hacking coughs, gasping for breath between each cough that made his whole body shudder—"goddamn good."

"Maybe you ought to see a doctor about that," I said in as much of a helpful tone as I could manage.

Slim finally got his coughing under control and hawked a large brown ball of phlegm into the mud. He pulled the handkerchief back out and blew his nose forcefully. It seemed like he'd forgotten I was there. He wiped his nose and again automatically checked what he'd deposited on the stiff blue cloth.

Slim flung the handkerchief out the window and wiped his hand frantically on the front of his shirt, biting off quick gasps of air. He fumbled with the gearshift, finally pulled it down into drive, and stomped on the gas pedal. The pickup lurched forward, fishtailing out of the weeds and onto the asphalt. I ducked down as globs of sticky mud flew all around me like shrapnel. A few drops stuck in my hair, my shirt, but at least I didn't get any in my eyes. Slim's pickup headed into the foothills.

Then I saw the handkerchief at the edge of the weeds.

I should have left it. I should have just climbed off the damn fence and walked off into the wet pasture. But curiosity got the better of me and I climbed down and pushed through the weeds to the side of the road. The handkerchief looked harmless enough as I crouched down on my haunches next to it. Still, I didn't want to touch it, so I found a small twig in the weeds and stuck one end under the closest corner of the handkerchief and lifted the flap.

Three tiny gray worms squirmed over each other in a slimy smear of snot and blood.

I jumped back and flung the twig away. I wanted to climb the fence and run though the flooded pasture and leave this behind. Instead, I froze. What if these goddamn worms wriggled their way into the mud here in the weeds? God knows what might happen if they made it to the pasture; it was covered in at least three, four inches of water. They could go anywhere. I gritted my teeth and brought the heel of Grandpa's boot down on the handkerchief, grinding the worms and the snot and blood into the asphalt. When I pulled my foot back, I could see there wasn't much left of the worms. That made me feel a little better. But then I realized Slim was still out there, still infested with more of the worms. I jumped the fence and took off on a run across the pasture, splashing my way to work. I'd be goddamned if anybody else ate that meat.

I got lucky. The place was empty. Fat Ernst was in the bathroom once again when I slipped through the front door. I crossed the floor hastily, not worrying about the mud from my boots, and went into the kitchen. Fat Ernst had already started the stove. I yanked the fridge open and there they were, waiting on the top shelf in the sickly yellow light like two malignant tumors, the white Smirnoff boxes. A crinkled sheet of aluminum foil rested within each box, covering the contents.

I didn't want to touch the boxes with my bare hands, but I didn't have much choice. I had to do this quick and quiet. I slipped my fingers underneath the box on the right and slid it out toward me. There was no way I was going to stick my hand in there. For all I knew, those worms could be waiting underneath the thin sheet of aluminum foil, having eaten all of the hamburger meat, and were hungry for some more. Some more *fresh* meat. So I didn't hook my fingers over the side, nothing. I lifted it gently out of the fridge, set it on the stove, and grabbed the second box. I carefully put the second box on top of the first and picked them up, carrying them out in front of me like a bomb that might explode if I made any sudden movements.

To open the back door I had to prop the boxes against my chest, because there was no other way to do it in a hurry. I gritted my teeth, let the boxes slump against my T-shirt, and scrabbled at the door handle with my left hand. It opened easily and I glided outside onto the loading dock. The Dumpster lid was still wide open, and for a second I couldn't remember if I was the one who had left it that way. Then I got to the edge of the dock and dropped the boxes inside the Dumpster as fast as I could.

Too late, I realized that Heck was still inside, slumped in about a foot of rainwater, staring up at the falling rain. His mouth was open, and his face had taken on the pale color of mushrooms that have never seen the sun. The boxes landed right on his chest, spilling raw hamburger meat into the rainwater, and for a split second I caught a quick glint of something shiny in the hamburgers, probably the aluminum foil.

I sucked in a breath. I wanted desperately to back away and run like hell. I couldn't believe I had forgotten where Fat Ernst had left Heck. No, scratch that. It wasn't only Fat Ernst. It had been me as well. I had helped. I had helped Fat Ernst drag Heck into the Dumpster. I had helped Fat Ernst in lots of ways.

To hell with it then. I didn't care if Fat Ernst did own the land and the trailer. Things had finally gone too far, gotten too out of hand. Grandma and I would figure something out. We'd find somewhere to live. I'd sleep under a goddamn bridge for the rest of my life before I worked for Fat Ernst one more minute.

CHAPTER 24

I knew I couldn't march in there and demand my share of the buckle. I couldn't let on that I intended to quit. If Fat Ernst suspected that, then he would naturally assume I would be calling the cops, letting them know exactly what he'd been feeding the customers. Of course, that's what I intended to do, but I wanted my fair share of the money first. Maybe it was hypocritical of me, waiting until I got paid before I split and called the cops, but I figured that if me and Grandma were going to have to find a new place to live, then we were gonna need all the money we could get our hands on.

As I filled the plastic bucket with hot water for the last time, I felt a sense of peace settle through my body, knowing that after this, I wouldn't have to mop the goddamn floor again. I dragged the bucket and mop out front and started splashing water near the front door. I had about got all the mud that I had tracked in cleaned up when Ray shouldered the front door open. He stood in the doorway like he was afraid of stepping inside and let his right hand settle around the handle of the .480.

He nodded at me, saying, "Fat Ernst around?"

I was about to point toward the restrooms when we both heard the sound of a flushing toilet. Fat Ernst appeared, hitching up his jeans. He ignored me and glared at Ray. "What do you want?"

"Thought I'd stop in for a quick bite. See how things were going."

I wondered if Ray knew about Earl's belt buckle.

Fat Ernst sighed. "Okay, but it'll have to be fast. I gotta run down to Sacramento, take care of some business."

I thought Fat Ernst was supposed to have gone last night, coming back this morning. I almost said something, but Ray stopped me.

"What's going on in Sac?" Ray readjusted his gun belt and holster as he bent his sticklike figure slightly to sit on a barstool.

Fat Ernst stopped for a moment as he rounded the bar, fixing Ray with heavy-lidded eyes. "Business," he said flatly.

So Ray didn't know about the buckle. Good. That meant more money for the rest of us. Fat Ernst scratched the boulder of his stomach. "What do you want?"

"How about some of that chopped steak, couple of eggs?"

Fat Ernst swiveled his blunt head around to stare at me, still trying to clean the new mud around the front door. "You heard the man. Steak and eggs. Hop to it."

I straightened, holding the mop in front of me. "Uh, I don't think you've got any more meat."

"Got some more in yesterday, 'member?"

"You're out now. There's nothing in that refrigerator."

Fat Ernst folded his massive arms and leaned back. "What?"

The rhythm of my words was steady, but my voice was a little strained. A little squeaky. "I didn't see any meat in there."

Fat Ernst stood, started back around the bar, moving slow, but he didn't look tired. He moved languidly, like a bored shark going after a drowning seagull.

"Well, hell, if you don't have any meat, that's okay. How about some pancakes, then?" Ray asked.

"Oh, no, we've got some meat. We've got plenty of meat," Fat Ernst answered, glancing at Ray. "Seems to me there's been a . . . mistake." With the last word, his eyes nailed me to the wall. But then his eyes slid up and over me, staring out the window to my left. "Christ, what's she want?"

I turned to look. Through the rain-streaked window, I could see a red Dodge pickup bouncing through the deep mud of the parking lot. It stopped next to Ray's police car and Misty Johnson climbed out.

CHAPTER 25

Ray pulled his shoulders back and did his best to straighten up his hunched posture. He licked his fingers and smoothed out his pencil mustache, then his eyebrows. "Probably wants to talk to me."

Fat Ernst slowly backed up to the bar. I knew he was worried that she'd been out to the cemetery. Hell, I was worried too, worried that she'd been out to the cemetery, worried that she'd been talking to her uncle Slim. But I had to admit, it was nice to see her. She jumped out and dashed through the rain to the front door. I opened it for her and she stepped inside, shaking water droplets out of that perfect blond hair. She was dressed almost exactly like yesterday, with a white blouse and jeans that looked like blue skin.

"Hey there," Misty said to me.

"Hi," I said, trying not to smile too much.

"Howdy," Fat Ernst nodded. "Get you anything?"

"No, thanks. I was just stopping by, wondering if you guys had seen my uncle anywhere this morning."

I knew enough to keep my mouth shut.

Fat Ernst shook his head. "Nope. Haven't seen him since, let's see . . . yesterday. Came in, had a burger around lunchtime."

"He got real sick early this morning, took off a couple of hours ago. Aunt Gertie is having a nervous breakdown."

"I'm sure he'll be fine," Ray said, hitching his belt and reaching down desperately for a deep voice. "If you want, I can drive you around, and we can look for him."

"He's sick?" I asked.

"Yeah, he's been throwing up, and—"

"Stomach flu's been going around," Fat Ernst cut in. "Hell, I ain't been feeling so good either."

Ray stood and puffed his chest out, pulling his chin in so that his Adam's apple protruded out damn near equal to his nose, still talking like Darth Vader. "So, uh, like I said, why don't we go look for him?" He pushed his cowboy hat back. "Ever been for a ride in a real police car?"

"Oh, motherfucking Christ. Not now," Fat Ernst said in a low growl, staring out the window again. I whipped my head around, and saw the Sawyer brothers had just plowed through the parking lot. This place was turning into Grand Central Station. Junior stopped behind Fat Ernst's Cadillac, shut off the engine, and jumped out. He had several strips of gray tape across his nose, probably from last night's mishap with the crowbar. Bert followed, wobbling around the front of the truck.

Misty casually moved sideways a few paces, putting me between her and the front door.

Junior kicked the door open. "Mornin'."

"Mornin' yourself." Fat Ernst said, lips drawn tight against his teeth, and folded his arms once again over his stomach. "What are you doing here?"

Junior grinned. "Thought you might need some help today. In Sacramento."

Fat Ernst shook his head. "Nope. Now, we talked about this last night. You go on home, and we'll . . ."

Junior suddenly noticed Misty. His grin got even bigger. "Well, hey-hey-hey there. Wondered if that was your truck outside." He sidled over to Misty. Bert leaned against the doorframe and stared blankly at the bar through bloodshot eyes.

Ray stepped forward, hand on his gun. "Why don't you fellas do like Fat Ernst said and go on home now."

Junior took a whirling step and snarled up at Ray's Adam's apple, "Why don't you lick my ass?"

Ray flinched. "Wouldn't take much to put a bullet in that thick head of yours. The only thing that's stopping me is all the goddamn paperwork I'd have to fill out."

They reminded me of a couple of dogs, sizing each other up to fight over a scrap of meat. But Ray was the one bluffing; he kept swallowing, and you couldn't miss that Adam's apple bobbing up and down like a buoy in a storm.

Junior laughed in Ray's face. "You think you got the balls, you try it."

"Jesus tap-dancing Christ. You stupid fucks knock it off," Fat Ernst barked. "Junior. Get out've here. We'll talk later."

Junior turned away from Ray and faced Fat Ernst. "No. You ain't going nowhere with—"

Fat Ernst slammed his hand flat on the bar and it sounded like a gunshot, echoing around the wooden walls and floor. "This is *private* business—watch your mouth." His eyes flickered over to Ray and Misty and settled back on Junior. He waited a moment, letting his meaning sink in, then spoke quietly. "We can discuss this later."

Junior shook his head. "We're discussing this right fucking now."

Fat Ernst started to say, "I mean it," but Junior jumped in and stopped Fat Ernst cold.

"That ain't what Ma wants."

The restaurant got quiet. Fat Ernst finally said, "I don't give a flying fuck," but the weight of his words sounded false. "This ain't got nothing to do with your ma. This is between us."

"That ain't what Ma said. She said, 'You boys either come home with the money or the buckle.' And I'm not arguing with her."

"What buckle?" Misty asked in a low voice.

"Never mind," Fat Ernst snapped. "This ain't any of your concern."

"Hold on a minute here," Ray spoke up. "Buckle?"

Fat Ernst sucked in a long, long breath, ignoring Ray's question. He never took his eyes off of Junior. "Now you listen. You listen but good. We had a business arrangement. You agreed to it. Now you want to change the arrangement. You wanna break our contract. Fine." Fat Ernst drew himself up and eyeballed Junior. "The way I see it, we got two ways we can do this here. We can do it the easy way, the way we agreed, or we can do it the hard way. It's your choice. But I gotta tell you, you ain't gonna like the hard way. You ain't gonna like it *at all*."

"Shit," Junior spat. "You think you're dealing with some fresh pussy here?" He snorted. "Hard way. Don't make me laugh. Ma'll show you the hard way. She'll fuck you up the ass with a chainsaw."

"You wanna push it? You wanna find out?" Fat Ernst stepped forward, curling his hands into fists the size of footballs.

Junior only came up to about Fat Ernst's sternum, but he didn't back down, I'll give him that. He just nodded slowly, saying, "If that's the way you want it, then—"

Junior never did get to finish the sentence because Fat Ernst's right fist lashed out and smashed into his taped nose. Junior's head snapped back, and before he could either fall or take a step backward, Fat Ernst's left fist swung up and popped his nose again. This time, Junior landed on the floor in front of Bert.

Bert looked down. "Hey, Junior, your nose is bleedin' again."

Fat Ernst stepped forward, clenching and unclenching his fists. "Yeah, you're one tough customer all right. Told ya you weren't gonna like it the hard way."

Junior coughed wetly, made a gagging noise at the back of his throat, then spit blood onto the floor. He rolled over, trying to find his feet. Fat Ernst planted the sole of his boot on Junior's butt and pushed him back to the floor. "Stay down, asshole. I want you to think about this for a while."

Misty's hand found mine and I squeezed it hard.

Ray chuckled and knelt next to Junior. "See what happens when you fuck with real men? Go home to your mommy, you little pansy."

Junior swallowed. "Suck my dick," he said in a thick voice.

Ray thumped the top of Junior's head with his thumb and forefinger. "Don't you got enough sense to know when you're beat?"

Junior just grinned at Ray, and suddenly shot his head forward like a cobra, sinking his teeth into the meat of Ray's calf. Ray screamed like a little girl, falling and kicking wildly. Junior hung on, shaking his head like a pit bull, refusing to unclamp those jaws. Ray kept screaming, "Mother . . . motherfucker . . ." in a high-pitched shriek.

Fat Ernst sighed and kicked Junior in the head. Junior's body went slack, and he finally let go, a bloody scrap of Ray's pants between his teeth. As Junior slumped against the floor on his back, I could see his eyes had rolled up white.

Ray scrabbled away from Junior, still shrieking, "Motherfucking motherfucker . . ." He clutched at his bleeding leg for a few seconds, then grabbed a table and pulled himself to his feet. He flailed at his holster. It took both hands to pull out that gigantic Redhawk.

"I'll kill you!" Ray shrieked, forgetting all about his deep voice. He managed to shakily point his pistol at Junior, still lying on the floor. "Kill you fucking dead!"

"Do it," Fat Ernst hissed in a low, urgent voice. "Shoot the motherfucker! Teach him a lesson." I realized what Fat Ernst was doing. He was trying to get Ray to eliminate the competition. Ray would take the blame for killing Junior, and Fat Ernst would get the buckle all to himself. "Shoot him!" Fat Ernst commanded again.

Ray clicked the hammer back. I held my breath, wondering if Ray would really go through with it, would actually shoot Junior in the head at point-blank range. That close, the bullet would simply dissolve Junior's head. I couldn't decide if I was scared or happy. But just then, out of the corner of my eye, through the window, I happened to catch Slim's pickup swerving wildly down the highway toward the intersection.

At the last second, Slim roared off the asphalt and smashed right into Fat Ernst's neon sign, going at least thirty miles an hour. The pickup bounced over the cement foundation in an explosion of sparks as the sign and the pole toppled over and hit the mud with a resounding crash.

CHAPTER 26

Ray froze, pistol twitching.

Nobody else moved either, except Bert, who leaned over and looked out the other window. "Hey, I think Slim just hit your sign."

Out in the parking lot, Slim's tires were spinning in the mud, but the pickup must have been stuck on the jagged stump of the sign.

The phone rang, a heavy, black, blocky thing behind the bar.

Fat Ernst ignored it and yanked the front door open. "You fucking fuck! What the fuck do you think you're doing?" he roared, stomping out to the wooden stairs.

Slim swung the driver's door open and fell face first into the mud. The phone rang again.

Ray finally let the pistol drop, ever so gently squeezing the trigger and easing the hammer down with his thumb. I didn't think he had it in him to shoot someone in cold blood. "We'll be picking this up later, I guarantee." He slid the Redhawk into the holster and spit in Junior's face. Junior didn't react. Ray joined Fat Ernst out on the front steps.

The phone rang one more time, an insistent, authoritative sound. I couldn't take it anymore and reached over the bar. I jerked the heavy receiver up to my ear and said, "Fat Ernst's Bar and Grill." I turned back to the window. Slim had pulled himself out of the mud and was leaning back into his pickup.

Silence on the other end of the phone. I hoped it wasn't Slim's wife.

Then, "Arch, is that you?" Grandma's voice shouted out at me as Slim turned away from his cab and I could see he was now holding a rifle.

"Get down!" I shouted at Misty and crouched between the bar stools, still holding the phone up to my ear.

Through the open door, I could see Slim brace his rifle in the window frame of the driver's door. He flicked his wrist, chambered a round with the bolt action. I heard Fat Ernst yell, "What do you think you're doing?"

Slim didn't answer. Instead, he fired, sending a bullet through the front window. A cloud of glass burst into the restaurant next to Bert like a swarm of wasps as the television above the bar exploded. Misty dropped to the floor, crawling under a table. Bert stepped back, blinking furiously. He turned to Junior, brow knit in confusion. Tiny shards of glass stuck to his face. Dots of blood appeared, welling up as if by magic, then rolled down his cheeks, his chin, as if he were crying blood.

I felt kind of sorry for him.

Grandma hollered from the phone, "Arch? Arch?" She sounded out of breath.

"Dirty motherfucker," Fat Ernst said as he scrambled back inside, followed closely by Ray. They hit the floor next to Junior, and Ray kicked the front door shut.

Grandma kept shouting, coughing to get the words out. I caught something that sounded like, "Watch yourself—the damn—," but Slim fired again, and the receiver was yanked out of my hand. The phone popped off the bar above my head and bounced into the bottles behind the bar as the echoes of Slim's shot slammed into the restaurant.

For a second, I thought Slim had hit the phone on purpose, to stop anybody from calling for help, but as I scuttled across the floor toward

Misty and peered over the window ledge, I realized that Slim didn't have much control over the rifle. He wasn't aiming at all, just swaying back and forth on his feet, hanging onto the door frame for support. Blood ran freely out of his nose and mouth. He coughed, sending a fresh wave of blood down the front of his chest.

"Sonofabitch!" I heard him yell weakly. "Come on out . . . here . . ."

Misty curled up tight next to me, hanging onto my arm, and suddenly things didn't seem quite so bad. Slim fired again, and as the window crashed down around us like a deadly waterfall, I changed my mind quick. Things were bad.

"Where'd you get it?" Slim hollered. He fired another round, and the mirror above the bar shattered. I brushed the broken glass from Misty's back as best I could.

Fat Ernst grabbed Ray's collar, shouting into his ear, "Shoot back!"

"But—I don't know—," Ray croaked, swallowing furiously. It was obvious he'd never fired a gun at anyone in his career as a deputy and had no idea what to do.

Fat Ernst slapped him. "Shoot him, you fucking moron! Shoot! Back!"

Junior raised himself to his knees, peering groggily at his bleeding brother.

Fat Ernst spoke slowly. "Ray. You pansy-assed fuck. Get that fucking pistol out and shoot that cocksucker or I'm gonna jam it so far up your ass you'll blow your head off every time you brush your fucking teeth."

Slim fired again.

Ray scooted over to the open window by the Sawyer brothers, yanked the revolver out of his holster, stuck it blindly out the shattered window frame, kept his head down, and pulled the trigger.

The report from the Redhawk sounded like a goddamn cannon had been fired inside the restaurant. Ray's hand popped up from the recoil like he'd waved suddenly to a friend, then fired again. His eyes were shut tight. I knew he hadn't hit anything and had just wasted four bucks on those two rounds, but I cautiously raised my head and looked anyway.

wormfood

Sure enough, Slim was still standing, loading more shells into his rifle.

Since Slim was busy reloading, I stuck my head up a little more, searching the highway. It was empty. No help there. I took another quick glance around the parking lot and found that Ray had, in fact, managed to hit something. A splintered hole about the size of an apple was now in the middle of the windshield of Fat Ernst's Cadillac. I got pissed. "Nice shooting, Ray."

Fat Ernst crawled over to Ray's window. He stuck his head up and said, "You're gonna pay for that, you stupid fuck." He grabbed Ray's pistol and lifted himself heavily to his feet, facing the window. Squeezing the pistol tightly in both fists, he raised it with straight arms and yelled at Slim, "Stand still, dammit!"

He fired and put a fist-sized hole in the pickup's front fender, almost three feet from Slim, who was bringing his rifle back up and didn't seem to know or care where Fat Ernst's bullet had gone.

Before Slim got the rifle barrel back through the pickup's door, Fat Ernst fired again. The bullet punched through the driver's door and hit Slim in the stomach, slamming him back against the cab as if a horse had just kicked him in the balls. The rifle landed in the mud next to him.

Ray stuck his head up, saw Slim go down, and whispered, "Shit-fire. Damn!"

"That's how it's fucking done." Fat Ernst dropped the pistol in Ray's lap, yanked the door open, and stomped down the stairs.

Ray twisted the pistol around his lap until the barrel pointed at his chest and fiddled with the cylinder. He finally popped it out, dumped all of the shells, both empty casings and loaded cartridges, and started reloading from scratch. I thought about mentioning that he was loading a gun aimed at his head but said to hell with it. The dumbshit would have to figure it out for himself.

"Oh, shit," Misty whispered. Her face looked drained, eyes wide and unblinking. She pushed herself away from me, found her feet, and was out the door before I could stop her. I followed her out into the rain.

Fat Ernst waddled furiously through the mud over to his fallen sign and Slim's pickup. Misty was right behind him, splashing straight through the puddles. Behind me, Ray came slowly down the wooden steps. "Is he dead?" he called out to Fat Ernst.

Fat Ernst stopped at Slim's feet and put his hands on his hips. "Close enough," he called back over his shoulder. Misty and I stopped behind Fat Ernst, neither of us saying anything. Ray stood nervously off to our right. He kept checking to make sure his pistol was back in the holster.

Slim, sitting with his back to the pickup, coughed weakly and blood splattered into the mud. There was a small hole in his stomach, a few inches above the waistband of his jeans. Blood had bloomed across his white shirt, encircled the pearl buttons, seeped down across his leather belt, and run down his jeans. It hurt just looking at him. He stared at his lap, apparently unable to lift his head. "I should . . ." Slim mumbled under his John Deere cap. "You sonofabitch . . ."

"Me? Fuck you. *You're* the stupid sonofabitch who tried to shoot *me.* You can't just go around shooting at people."

". . . Gonna put a bullet . . . right in your goddamn head . . ." Slim's right arm fumbled for the rifle at his side, but he couldn't move very well and his hand just slapped at the muddy stock.

"Don't move, you fucking moron. You've been gut shot."

"Please don't move," Misty begged. "Please. Just hold on. I'll go get help."

"No." Slim coughed. "No. Don't. There ain't no point . . ."

A jackrabbit shot across the muddy expanse of the parking lot as if its tail were on fire and disappeared into the cornfield along the parking lot, the same one Slim had driven his own Cadillac into the day of the funeral.

Slim tried to push himself up using his rifle as a crutch, but his hands kept slipping in the mud. He coughed again. "Where'd . . . where'd you get that meat?"

wormfood

Oh, shit, I thought.

"I went . . . went up to the pit and counted . . ." Slim spat.

I heard something out in the east cornfield, a vast, rushing sound, almost like a wave. I turned to the field and saw another jackrabbit come bounding out from the tall green stalks and race past the restaurant.

Misty said, "Don't try to talk, okay? Save your strength. We'll get you some help." She looked at Fat Ernst and said, "We have to get him to a hospital."

Fat Ernst ignored her. He stared back at Slim. "I don't know what the fuck you're talking about," he declared.

The rushing sound got closer and as I looked out across the field, toward the northeastern foothills; it looked like wind or something was tearing into the corn, making the stalks shudder and shake.

The front door slammed and Junior and Bert worked their way down the steps. Junior looked a little more awake now. He shouted over to us in a thick voice, "You fucked up! You fucked up real bad this time! We're gonna go home and tell Ma! Then you just wait and see what happens."

Ordinarily, the idea of a grown man threatening to go home and tell his mommy that someone had hurt him would have been funny, but since this was Junior, and he was talking about his mother, Pearl, it didn't seem funny at all.

Nobody else was paying much attention, not with Slim lying in the mud bleeding to death. He kept talking, forcing the words out through mouthfuls of blood. "I counted 'em . . . there's one missing. Goddamn you . . ." Misty bent down, tried to get close, to help him somehow, but Slim waved her away. "Get out of here . . . leave . . . can't you see—I've got 'em inside . . ."

"What?"

"I can feel 'em moving . . . moving inside of me . . ." Tiny bubbles of blood appeared at the corners of Slim's mouth. It reminded me of Heck.

A sheet of brown water surged out of the east cornfield and washed over the parking lot. It foamed and splashed around Slim's legs and the truck's tires. Within seconds, the cold water was four or five inches deep.

"What the hell is this?" Ray asked. "Do you . . . ? Shit. You think the reservoir flooded?"

Junior started his truck with a roar. He gunned the engine a few times, popped the clutch, and rammed the back of Fat Ernst's Cadillac. The bug-spattered, rusty grille smashed into the white car almost as if it wanted to eat the smaller vehicle. The truck's engine groaned and the tires slipped in the mud as it shoved the Cadillac forward, crumpling the front end of the car under the restaurant.

"I'm gonna kill that prick," Fat Ernst said.

Slim slapped at the water and started to gag, deep in his throat. A terrible, wet retching sound, it twisted my stomach into knots. He kept slapping at the water, his chest hitching and shivering.

Junior reversed the truck, leaving the Cadillac dead under the window, and pulled around so he faced the highway. He popped the clutch again, flinging buckets of mud at the restaurant, splattering the walls and shattered windows. The truck bounced past us, leaving two large wakes in the muddy water as it surged onto the road and tore off down the flooded highway, heading for the mountains.

"Misty," Slim croaked. "You go on . . . get the hell of out here."

"But—," Misty said.

Slim kept talking. "I can feel 'em . . . I can feel 'em moving inside . . ."

"Feel what?" Fat Ernst shouted over the sound of the flood.

"These—," Slim said, and pulled the rifle across his chest so the end of the barrel was under his chin.

He closed his eyes.

And pulled the trigger.

CHAPTER 27

I didn't even hear the report as the top of Slim's head erupted in a chunky mist of blood, bone, and brains. Most of the blood and flesh hit the ceiling of his truck, sticking there for a second, then dripping down onto the seat and the dashboard. As the rest of his head bloomed into the air like a red mushroom cloud, bits and pieces started falling back into the water around us. Misty screamed and kept screaming, her shriek rising higher and higher into the falling rain.

Something landed in my hair, but I couldn't move. Fat Ernst turned to us and mumbled, "Fuck me." His face and chest were dripping with blood and flecks of flesh. He blinked rapidly several times, as if some of the blood had gotten into his eyes.

Misty stopped screaming suddenly, just clapped a hand over her open mouth, eyes huge, and froze like that. Tiny droplets of blood were scattered across her white face as if someone had playfully flicked a paintbrush in her direction.

My eyes snapped back to Slim's corpse. The top half of his head, from the eyes up, was pretty much gone; his skull resembled the top half of a chipped coffee mug, jagged around the edges. The rifle slid out of Slim's hands and I found myself focusing on it, afraid to look at his head. A Winchester, Model 70. Slim's shoulders slumped forward onto his knees, his chin flopped forward, and what was left of his brain, looking like the ground meat inside of a charred bratwurst, came sliding slowly out of the ruined skull, dribbling slowly onto his jeans.

Five or six thin, short, gray worms squirmed out of his head, wriggled into the cold, muddy water washing around his legs, and disappeared.

I don't know if anyone else saw them because Ray suddenly started slapping at his face. "Ow! Oh, fuck! Fuck!" He kept slapping at his head and face. It took a second, but I could see that parts of the blood and meat on his face were squirming around.

The thing in my hair started to move. I plucked at it, and my fingers found something soft and slimy in the midst of all of the sticky blood. A worm squirmed slowly between my thumb and forefinger. I dropped it with a cry of disgust, realizing too late I had just dropped it into the rising floodwater, setting it free.

Fat Ernst started grabbing at his face and chest as well and as I kept looking around, I could see the bloody worms all over the place. Falling from the ceiling of Slim's truck. Probing around in Slim's brain pan. Wriggling across the front of Fat Ernst's shirt. Hanging off of Ray's bottom lip. And curled up on Misty's shoulder.

I jumped toward her, brushing the worm off her white blouse. Her eyes darted from my face to her shoulder and back up to my eyes. I realized we had to get out of the water, so I grabbed her hand and started pulling her back to the restaurant. Already I could see worms, some up to six, seven inches long, skimming along the surface of the water. And the water was getting higher.

Ray squealed at Fat Ernst, "Get 'em offa me! Get 'em off!" He yanked at the worm trying to chew into his bottom lip, pulling it away from his teeth. "Get it osh! Get it osh!" The worm popped free and he flung it into the water.

Fat Ernst ignored him and started backing away from Slim's pickup, slapping at his arms and chest. His face had this hard, set look, like he had just seen the worst the world could throw at him and he'd lived through it. "Fuck this," he said, turning and splashing back to the restaurant.

Ray kept standing in one place, turning in circles, trying to get a glimpse of his back, spinning like a dog chasing its tail. He finally moved away from the pickup when a worm appeared in the water and started crawling up the outside of his boot, following the bloodstains, heading toward the wound where Junior had taken a bite out of his leg. Ray uttered a short shriek and punched at his leg, smashing the worm.

I held on tight to Misty and helped her as we made our way to the wooden stairs. The water was surging around our knees now, and combined with the sucking mud of the parking lot, it was getting harder and harder to keep my balance. Fat Ernst charged past us like an enraged bull and stormed up the stairs. He paused at the top to glance at his Cadillac, crumpled underneath the west window as if it had tried to crawl underneath the building. He shook his head and kicked the door open, then stomped inside.

I put Misty's hand on the railing and gently pushed her up the steps. She didn't say anything, and I got worried that shock might be settling in, creeping in around her brain like a comfortable, hazy fog. I hoped she was okay, because I wasn't sure how I could get her to a hospital. Now that I was out of the floodwater, I wasn't in any hurry to jump back into it.

At the top of the stairs, I turned back and surveyed the frothy brown ocean that used to be the parking lot. The landscape had suddenly become flat, unreal. The telephone poles and the couple of vehicles rising above the surface of the water were the only things that gave any proof there was solid ground under all that water. Ray stumbled to the bottom of the steps, fighting the floating cornstalks that were propelled by the current like ragged spears.

He looked up at me, eyes frantic. "I got any on me?" he asked hoarsely, jerking his legs out of the water. I gave him the once-over and shook my head. He didn't seem to believe me and kept slapping at his shoulders, twitching his head. "You see that?" he asked. "I mean, did you fucking see that? Fucking worms, Jesus, man, they came right out of his fucking head." Fresh blood trickled down Ray's chin from the hole right under his lip. "I mean, they were fucking *inside* of him. Jesus."

I nodded and stepped into the restaurant. The lights had gone out, and the gray light that spilled in through the open windows gave the whole room a dark, dead look. Fat Ernst leaned back against the bar, staring at the floor. Misty was standing by herself near the tables, looking out at her uncle's pickup through the shattered window. Ray pushed past me and staggered over to the bar, still slapping at himself. "I got any on me?" he pleaded to Fat Ernst.

"Shut the fuck up, Ray. I gotta think here."

"But . . . but . . . do I got any on me?"

Fat Ernst sucked at his teeth, finally looking up at Ray. "Turn around."

Ray was more than happy to oblige. He spun around, pivoting on his boot heels, arms straight out as if he had been crucified.

Fat Ernst nodded. "Yep. There's one by your ear there."

Ray went nuts, clawing at both ears, crying, "Jesus, oh Jesus . . ."

I had watched when he turned around and knew there weren't any worms by his ears. There might have been one somewhere else, but I could see there weren't any on his head. At least you knew it when these things bit you; it hurt like hell, not like some mosquito or leech you didn't notice at first. Still, it made me nervous enough that I forced myself to run a shaking hand over my own head and around the back of my neck. My hand came away smeared with bloody mud, but that was all.

I checked Misty, looking her over, but she was okay. She just stood there, face white, unblinking. I led her over to one of the booths and helped her into the seat. She clasped her shaking hands together on the table in front of her like she was praying. I sank into the seat across the table and put my head in my hands. Despite everything, I just hoped Grandma was okay. I hoped the dry creek bed hadn't flooded and she had been calling about something else.

Ray finally calmed down, realizing that Fat Ernst was only fucking with him, and asked something we were all wondering. "What the fuck are we gonna do now?"

Fat Ernst waddled around the bar and sank onto his stool with a grunt. He took a deep breath, let it out slowly through his nose. "You got any ideas, I'd be glad to hear 'em," he said, reaching under the bar and grabbing a bottle of tequila. He unscrewed the cap, tilted it to his lips and took one long gulp. "Sit down, Ray. Relax."

Ray didn't want to relax; he kept pacing up and down in front of the bar stools but eventually gave up after a few minutes. It was as if all the fight, all the energy, all of the adrenaline, had left him at the same time, like air escaping a balloon. He dropped onto a barstool in front of Fat Ernst and didn't say anything.

In a rare gesture of generosity, Fat Ernst pushed the bottle of tequila across the bar to Ray. He took it without looking up and gulped from the bottle. I watched from the booth and hoped this was a sign that things might have changed. I should have known better.

Fat Ernst took another drink, sat up straight on his stool, and said, "Ray, go on out to your car and radio for help."

Ray lifted his head, then slowly swiveled around on the barstool, looking at his squad car through the open window. He slowly shook his head, once, twice. "I . . . I can't get there."

I looked out the window. The squad car was at least thirty feet beyond the trunk of Fat Ernst's Cadillac. Ray would have to wade through all that floodwater to get to his car. It looked like the water was at least two feet deep now. Too damn deep, too damn far, too many goddamn worms in the water. Ray swiveled back around to Fat Ernst and shook his head again, more decisive this time. "Nope. No fucking way. You go out there."

Fat Ernst pulled the bottle off the bar and shook his head. "What a goddamn pussy."

I glanced back out the window. Misty's pickup, nearly halfway to Slim's pickup, was too far as well. We were stuck.

Ray jumped off the bar stool, shouting, "I'm a pussy? I'm a pussy?" He gestured wildly toward the front door, his voice a taut, vibrating wire. "You're so goddamn tough, you go on out there. Go ahead. Be my guest."

"Settle down, Ray." Fat Ernst looked over at me. "What about you, boy? You wanna be a man? Go get us some help?"

I shook my head. "No, thanks."

Misty suddenly shoved the table toward me, got up, and stalked over to the bar. For a second, I thought she was going to ask Ray for the keys to the squad car. I don't know what I would have done then. Instead, she snatched the tequila bottle out of Fat Ernst's surprised hand and came back over to the table.

"You're gonna pay for that," Fat Ernst said.

"Put it on my tab." Misty spit on the floor and slammed the bottle in front of me. "You. Drink."

"I don't really drink much."

"I don't care. Drink. Now."

What else could I do? I gingerly grabbed the neck of the bottle, put the rim to my lips, and tilted it up. The tequila tasted like somebody pissed in a kettle full of bathwater, heated it up, and bottled it. If anything, I think I preferred the taste of Junior and Bert's whiskey. I managed to swallow, fought the expected rising gorge. I didn't think Misty would be too impressed if I puked all over the table.

"Take another one."

I forced down another gulp. The second time tasted even worse. Then I noticed the worm, cold and dead at the bottom of the bottle like a carefully preserved little cat turd.

"Now. You're going to tell me what the hell is going on around here."

I shrugged, still holding onto the bottle. "I guess the reservoir flooded. I mean, we were just up there yesterday, so you saw how high the water was."

∫ wormfood

Misty just looked at me. "You know what I mean. What happened to my uncle?"

I sensed Fat Ernst tensing up behind the bar, but he didn't seem as important as he used to. "I, uh, I don't know."

"Take another drink."

I didn't know if I could handle another drink. But I took another sip, a small one. Misty grabbed the bottle, took a few swallows herself. Over at the bar, I could hear Fat Ernst mumble something as he produced another tequila bottle. He unscrewed it, took a long drink, and pushed it over to Ray.

Echoing Fat Ernst, Misty slid the bottle back to me. I took it and drank a solid gulp without being asked. It seared the inside of my throat as it went down, all desert heat and piss, exploding like a soft bomb when it hit my stomach, sending drops of liquid shrapnel into my blood. The room got warm all of a sudden.

"Now," Misty said in a low voice, so Fat Ernst and Ray couldn't hear her, "you tell me what happened."

I started to say, "Well, Slim got these worms in him," but realized that wouldn't explain much of anything. I took another drink, and the room got hotter. But I felt okay. In fact, I felt better than okay. Not great, but certainly not as bad as I had been. I thought about it for a moment, then decided the best place to start was at the beginning. I pushed the bottle back to Misty. She drank, then pushed it right back to me. I took another deep swallow and started talking.

"Okay. I don't know about all of this, but it's the best I can figure. I think it started with your dad." I kept going, telling Misty about the worms that ate into her dad when he was in the ocean, and since he hadn't been embalmed, nobody'd seen the worms, and it would have never mattered, but he ended up in the ditch on the way to the funeral and the worms had gotten into the irrigation system and had swam off to God knows where, including Slim's property, and I just kept going, drinking and talking, up to when me and the Sawyer brothers had pulled a dead steer out of the body pit.

"Wait a minute," Misty said. "You guys stole a fucking dead cow out of my uncle's pile of dead animals?"

"Well, it was a steer. And it wasn't so much a pile exactly. More like a big hole in a ravine, all filled with water."

Misty only nodded, eyes sharp.

I told her about taking it back to the Sawyers' barn, and all the worms that came out of it, and after that I didn't know what happened to the meat. Just that the next day Fat Ernst all of a sudden had two boxes of fresh meat.

Misty closed her eyes.

I kept going, words escaping out of my mouth. "Then Heck got sick. I mean, he got *real* sick. And then, uh, he died." I didn't tell her he was still out there in the Dumpster. "Slim saw it, watched Heck die, and I think he might have been eating a cheeseburger or something maybe, I don't really remember. He took off and that's all I know."

"And you let him eat it."

"What?"

"The cheeseburger."

I didn't want to mention that I had cooked the goddamn thing and served it up to him as well. "I didn't know . . . I really didn't." I took another swig from the bottle. "Look, as soon as I figured it out, I came in here this morning and dumped all that meat out. Just grabbed it and dumped it in the Dumpster. It's gone, gone, *gone*." I whisked my hands together like I was brushing off some dirt.

Fat Ernst choked on his tequila and coughed hoarsely.

Misty ignored him. "Gone, huh? All I know is that because of you, I'm stuck in here with you three assholes. My father's body is all fucked up and my uncle is dead now too. Because of you."

I didn't know what to say. In a way she was right. No, scratch that. She was right, period. I was reaching out to take another drink of tequila when she punched me, hard. I never even saw it coming. One second, I'm reaching for the bottle; the next, her fist was nothing but a blur as it slammed into my chin. I got a quick flash of the ceiling and then my head smacked into the wall behind me.

She started to cry then, rubbing her knuckles. I guess I deserved to get punched. I hoped it made her feel a little better. Then she kicked me under the table, heel sinking into my balls. I don't think I deserved *that*.

My world collapsed into tiny folds and misshapen shards until a tidal wave of pain took over completely. White-hot seething agony rocketed up out of my balls into my stomach, my chest, my face, into my skull, then bounced back down and said howdy to everywhere else it hadn't touched. I couldn't breathe. Every muscle, every fiber, every nerve suddenly shrieked as if I'd fallen into a boiling cauldron of hurt. I tipped over sideways in the booth, alternately clutching at my groin and drawing my hands back, afraid to touch anything.

I don't know when Misty got up. I somehow heard our bottle of tequila explode into more bottles somewhere over Fat Ernst's head. I didn't care. Everything hurt too goddamn much. I think they started yelling at each other around then, but the only thing I remember clearly at all was the floor rising in a wave as Fat Ernst's Cadillac suddenly exploded through the floor and wall.

I slid out of the booth involuntarily and hit the floor, still curled up in a fetal position, clutching at my balls, wondering how the white Cadillac had managed to drive itself up into the restaurant. Part of the ceiling crashed down, covering the jukebox, which blurted, "Lord, I'm coming home to you—," before falling silent. Underneath the building, the wooden six-by-six supports groaned.

I rolled over and gasped for air just in time to see Junior appear in the crack in the front wall, running up the inclined hood of Fat Ernst's Cadillac. He ducked under the sagging roof, slid down the chrome grille, and landed heavily on the pitched floor. Clutching a lumpy gunnysack to his stomach, he slammed sideways into the bar, sending stools flying.

Ray pushed himself away from the canted bar and went for the Redhawk. He hadn't quite managed to pull the nine-and-a-half inch barrel clear of the holster when Junior thrust the gunnysack at Ray's head. It seemed to pop open in the air, falling away from a short length of thin, twisting rope. Junior hit the floor and rolled onto his left shoulder, still moving fluidly, still one continuous explosion of movement since he jumped off of the Cadillac's hood. The broken nose didn't seem to slow him down at all.

The patchy brown rope landed in Ray's face, curling around his head for a brief second, then fell away. Ray cried out once, dragging his pistol away from the holster. I realized the brown rope was a goddamn baby rattlesnake about the same time Ray shot himself in the foot. I felt, more than heard, the powerful report, and saw the front half of Ray's right foot instantly burst into a thick cloud of red meat.

By this point, Junior had leapt onto the bar and was kicking Fat Ernst in the head. I could only watch all of this through a fog of agony from my spot on the floor. Misty was somewhere behind me, crouching under one of the tables. Fat Ernst slipped off his stool and fell out of sight behind the bar. Junior didn't quit; he jumped off the bar and landed on Fat Ernst, savagely kicking and punching him the whole time. Ray pitched forward, still clutching his pistol. He hit the floor hard and didn't move. I wasn't sure where the snake had slithered off to.

Junior finally decided Fat Ernst had had enough and came around the end of the bar. He winked and blew Misty a kiss, stopped long enough to deliver a solid kick to my stomach. To be honest, I barely felt it. All I know is that I slid back into the wall, the floor got soft and warm, and darkness closed around my head like a wet blanket.

CHAPTER 28

When I opened my eyes, I was lying on the floor in front of the bar. Pain ricocheted through every inch of my body. I tried to sit up, but something yanked me back down. I looked over and discovered that my right wrist had been handcuffed to the brass railing that ran along the bottom of the bar. It must have been Ray's handcuff. I kept blinking, trying to make sense of my surroundings. The walls and floor had taken on warped, surrealistic angles, like I had fallen into a bad dream. On the floor next to me, I watched some kind of liquid, water or tequila, trickle steadily toward the front door. I realized that the warped angles weren't my imagination; the walls and the floor were buckled, twisted, and mangled from the impact of the Cadillac.

That didn't make much sense either, so I tried to move my head slowly to the left. The smashed front end of Fat Ernst's Cadillac had been forced into the western half of the restaurant. The only thing I could figure was that Junior had hit the back of the Cadillac with his truck, driving it into the building.

I kept blinking and the blurry, dark spots in my vision started to slip away. A large, fuzzy blob directly in front of me swam into focus.

It was Fat Ernst. He was tied to one of the dining chairs with barbed wire. His wrists had been bound together behind him at the small of his back. More wire was wrapped around his ankles and the front chair legs. The strands stretched tight against his chest, barbs sunk deep; the two ends must have been twisted together with a pair of pliers. It looked like Fat Ernst was unconscious; his head lolled around on his chest, eyes shut. Actually, I wasn't quite sure if his eyes were closed or not; it was hard to tell through all the blood on his face. Junior had really gone to town on him.

I kept blinking spots out of my eyes and saw Misty. She was sitting in the booth, back to the window, with the burlap gunnysack covering her head. I hoped the snake wasn't in it. I couldn't see her face because of the sack, but I knew she was awake; I could hear soft, strangled sobs and see her chest hitch once in a while. Her hands were tied in front of her with what looked like an extension cord. A flat strip of leather, like some kind of dog leash, trailed down her chest and wrapped around the table column.

Ray lay facedown on the floor near the restrooms, twitching a little once in a while. His face was turning black and puffy

The hood of the Cadillac creaked, and that was when it finally hit me.

We were all in very big trouble.

Junior appeared, carrying a dark bundle of rags on his back. He eased down the chrome grille, gently lowering the tangle of clothes to the tilted floor. The rags produced a cane, and the misshapen bundle lurched up the tilted floor toward Ray. The cane, a knotted and twisted piece of dark, shiny hardwood, thunked into the floor every now and then.

Pearl was here.

And my blood turned to ice water.

Pearl jabbed at Ray with her cane and got a low moan in response. She clucked something, turned toward the bar, and I think she smiled, but it was hard to tell. She wasn't much fun to look at. If I had to guess, I'd bet that she looked more like Bert than Junior, and I suspected they had two different fathers.

It was downright impossible to know for sure what she had looked like before the accident with the lawnmower. She kept her left arm curled in close to her chest; the limb looked ravaged and useless. It reminded me of the short, tiny arms of a Tyrannosaurus rex. Her head was cocked to the side, like a bird watching a bug, and her greasy, clotted hair started somewhere around the top of the crown of her head, hanging down to the back of her neck in gnarled clumps. I'd seen her before, that night when we brought the dead steer back to the Sawyers', and I knew she was thin, but I wasn't prepared for just how little flesh covered her bones. I wondered how she had the strength to even move.

I'd seen her from a distance, even heard her voice up close, but nothing scared me as bad as watching her limp up the inclined floor to me and Fat Ernst.

"See, Ma?" Junior said proudly. "Got everybody tied down just like you told me." He still had duct tape on his nose, but his eyes were bright and excited.

"Yesssssss," Pearl said, sounding too much like another goddamn rattlesnake as she got closer. "You done good, Junior." Her body was scary enough, but her face was worse. Like her sons, she didn't have many teeth left. The left side looked like the doctors had just gathered up all the loose skin—pulling it sideways across the top of her head, keeping it unnaturally tight on the right side of her face, and then stapling and stapling all that extra flesh to her skull in wild, irregular folds. Her jagged right eyebrow was up near the top of her forehead, giving that eye an arched, perpetually surprised look, while the hair of the left eyebrow was gone completely. The flesh around the brow sagged down to the left cheek, leaving nothing but a curving, hollow slit, and the skin on the left side of her face rippled and dribbled down to a chin so sharp I could have sliced tomatoes on it.

The Cadillac creaked again, and Bert appeared in the splintered hole, ducking under the low roof. He looked around, wobbling a little, taking everything in without expression. He'd lost the old tie he had been using as a sling, and now his cast dangled limply down around his hip. He slid down the grille and sat on the bumper. His face, normally a kind of bleached gray color, had lightened even more, taking on the color of the belly of a dead fish. He reminded me of Slim when I was on the fence watching the rancher blow his nose that one last time into the blue handkerchief.

Pearl stopped near Fat Ernst, leaning on her cane. She fixed that staring, round right eye on me, and again I got the skin-crawling feeling that she was somehow looking directly into me, deep into my thoughts, seeing right into my darkest fears. Which, at that point, were probably painfully obvious. I tried to pull my legs in, anything to try and get as far away from her as I could. She smiled again, the left side of her face curling inward, creating all kinds of fun new folds and wrinkles in the ruined flesh.

Junior was happy. "Can I have her now, Ma?"

Something went cold inside of me, something almost worse than Pearl looking at me. I flashed over to Misty. She hadn't moved.

"First thing's first, Junior." Pearl lifted her cane and jabbed it into the back of Fat Ernst's fleshy skull. "Wake him up."

Junior edged around the chair until he was directly in front of Fat Ernst, bent down, and spit in Fat Ernst's face. "Rise and shine, you fat fuck."

Fat Ernst didn't move.

Junior clamped Fat Ernst's nose between his thumb and forefinger, shaking the bigger man's head. Finally, Fat Ernst opened his mouth, sucking in a halting breath. I could see his eyes open, but just barely, just thin slits that cracked the dried blood. He coughed, deep in his chest.

"That's right, wakee wakee, little snakee," Junior said. "Take a good look around, Mr. Tough Guy. Hard way?" Junior laughed, a prickly sound that bounced around the slanted walls and sunken floor. "Hard way my ass, you fat fuck. I'll show you the fucking hard way." He slid his fingers into Fat Ernst's nostrils and yanked. Fat Ernst's chins jiggled up and out; his fingers popped open, then clenched back into massive fists. The muscles in his forearms tightened, and I could see the skin around the barbed wire get white, straining around the wires, anchoring the barbs even deeper in his flesh.

"That's right. Smell the bacon, you puddle of puke. You're the one who wanted it the hard way." Junior put his hands on Fat Ernst's knees and froze, whispering. "We just want the buckle. That's all. Just give it up, and we're gone with the wind."

Fat Ernst didn't say anything for a moment. When he did, it sounded like wet concrete coated his throat. "This is my place. You best get the fuck out of here before I get pissed."

Junior just nodded. "I'm gonna ask you one more time. Just once more—that's it. You answer me, and, hey, we're outta your hair. You wanna be a tough guy, then it's gonna have to be the hard way. It's gonna hurt. It's gonna hurt bad." He leaned in even closer, kissed Fat Ernst on the forehead. "Where's the buckle?"

"Get fucked," Fat Ernst replied.

Junior patted Fat Ernst's flattop. He smiled, and it seemed genuine. "I warned you," he said simply, then stepped back, shrugging at his mother. Pearl limped forward, clomping around Fat Ernst's chair, slamming the cane into the floor with a disquieting rhythm. Fat Ernst managed to raise his head. I could tell that he flinched when he saw her face, even though he tried to hide it.

Pearl shook her head slightly, looking like a god-awful ugly vulture tearing a piece of gristle out of a dead squirrel. Even though he was wired to a chair, her knifelike chin only came up to his flattop. Fat Ernst had his head down, breathing heavily through his mouth. Pearl jammed the bottom of her cane into the soft folds of his throat, forcing his chins up. She regarded him for several quiet seconds with her right eye, then said to Junior, "Me and him got some talking to get done. You go play. Have fun."

Junior started shaking like a puppy that didn't want to piss on the floor. "You sure you don't want some help, Ma? I can help. I can get him talking."

The left side of Pearl's face curled into itself again, and she shook her head. "No, it's okay. This here calls for a woman's touch," she said, watching Fat Ernst the whole time.

Fat Ernst didn't like the sound of that. I saw his fist clenching again, but he did a good job of keeping his face still. But I didn't care about him. Pearl could feed him to the worms for all I gave a damn.

Misty was the one that I was worried about.

Junior sauntered over to the booth, saying, "Got me a *date*." He pulled the sack off Misty's head and said, "Wanna dance?"

A piece of me snapped, deep inside my chest. "Leave her alone, you fucking—"

The cane came out of nowhere and cracked into the left side of my skull, knocking me sideways, smashing my head into the floor. Pearl whispered in my ear, "Now you watch your tongue around my boys. I don't put up with none of that filthy talk. Especially from a Stanton like you." The cane settled softly on my left temple, increasing slowly but steadily in pressure, until it felt like someone was standing on top of a railroad spike, driving it into my head. Pearl's warbled, calm voice came again, "Speak again and I'll have Junior cut out your tongue."

I knew she would do it, so I did my best to keep my mouth shut. I tried to nod though, anything to get that cane out of my skull. I guess that satisfied her, because the cane suddenly withdrew, leaving me gasping on the floor. Hot tears stung the inside of my eyes. It was all my fault. Everything was my fault. And I couldn't change that.

But if I could get out of this handcuff, I could try and make things right. And if that meant killing anyone, everyone, all of them, any so-nofabitch between me and Misty, then so be it. In fact, I'd happily kill all of them.

I kept my head on the floor as Ma shuffled back to Fat Ernst. Misty finally lifted her head. Tears had left clean tracks through the drops of Slim's blood on her face, but she wasn't crying anymore. She had some kind of dog's choke chain wrapped tight around her neck. A large padlock kept it snug enough that she couldn't pull it off. The end of the chain was attached to the leather strip, a leash. Junior untied the leash from the table column, then stood and stared down at Misty.

She stared right back at him and said, in a slow, strong voice, "Well, Slick, I don't dance unless I get some drinking done. Drinking always gets me dancing. Drinking gets me all fired up." She gave him a quick grin and blinked a couple of times. "So . . . you wanna get me a drink?"

Junior nodded back, hard. "My kind of girl." He blew her a kiss, ran across the floor, jumped over me, and landed on the bar. As he grabbed Fat Ernst's bottle of tequila, I twisted my head over and studied the handcuff. It had been ratcheted tight around my right wrist and was secured snugly around the bar. I figured I could slide it back and forth about three feet between the thick fittings that anchored the brass bar to the wood. I yanked my arm, hard, but the effort wasn't worth it; the handcuffs were Ray's, genuine police issue hardened steel.

Junior ambled back across the floor, holding the bottle up triumphantly.

"Bert!" Pearl snapped, still staring into Fat Ernst's face with her wide, unblinking eye. "Make yourself useful."

"Okay, Ma," Bert said, pushing himself away from the front door, swaying as he found his feet. He rubbed his shoulder, saying, "What do you need?"

Pearl thrust her knifelike chin at Ray's body. "Drag him outside. But don't push him all the ways in the water. Not yet, anyway. Dangle his head out there for a while. Use him for bait. See if we can't catch anything. Only damn thing he's good for." She looked for me and I realized that she knew about the worms too, as if she were reading my mind again. "Case somebody don't feel like cooperating."

She glared down at Fat Ernst. He wasn't moving or saying anything, just staring at the floor through half-open eyes. Bert bent over Ray, grabbed the deputy's leg with his left hand, and dragged him over to the front door. Bert's broken right arm dangled from his shoulder as if it were attached with just a piece of rope. It swayed back and forth, bouncing off his hip once in a while. He let Ray's leg drop back to the floor and Ray whimpered once. He wasn't dead yet, but I figured it wouldn't be long. Bert opened the front door and pulled Ray out to the steps.

Junior had dropped into the seat opposite Misty and was taking a long swallow of tequila. He jerked the bottle away from his lips and held it out to Misty. She grabbed hold of it with her bound hands, tilted the bottle back. A sudden flash of hot jealousy washed over me and I almost said something, but I didn't want to piss off Pearl again. Misty had been drinking tequila with me just a half hour ago, dammit. Junior whispered something at her and then Misty had to go and wink at him, taking another swallow of tequila.

That bitch! I thought.

Slow down, slow down. I realized that she was just playing Junior, trying to fake him out. Buying us some time. At least that's what I hoped, that's what I assured myself, but as hard as I tried to believe that, a small sliver of doubt got stuck between the prayers.

Pearl let her cane fall sideways across her body, where she caught it deftly in the crook of her ravaged left arm. Her right hand trailed up Fat Ernst's body, blackened fingernails sliding up his rayon shirt in a flurry of ragged whispers. She extended her index finger, knuckles standing out like knots in a twig, and caressed Fat Ernst's bulging chins. Her fingernail scraped against Fat Ernst's thick gray stubble and it sounded like the tip of a knife being drawn through sandpaper. She slid her finger up his cheek, through the nest of blackheads along the side of his wide nose, pausing at the corner of his right eye. He shut both eyes, squeezing them tight.

"You know," Pearl said, "it don't have to be this way. It ain't nothing to make you wish you was dead." Slowly, damn near gently, she increased the pressure of her index finger, forcing it slowly into the tender gap between Fat Ernst's eye and the bridge of his nose. It made me squirm just to watch, but I couldn't look away. He tried to pull his head back, but there was nowhere to go. Pearl just kept pushing, pushing. Fat Ernst's boot heels lifted off the floor, driving the pointed toes into the wood. But he never made a sound.

Pearl sighed. "You're one tough nut to crack, I'll give you that." She withdrew her finger and I could clearly see the moisture clinging to the fingernail. One single gossamer strand stretched from the tip of the blackened nail to the corner of Fat Ernst's eye, snapping as the finger drifted down his face, stopping long enough to massage his thick bottom lip. "I really don't want to hurt you."

I glanced over at Junior and Misty. They were staring at each other, giggling and whispering. Junior had his right hand under the table, on Misty's knee. The bottle was almost empty.

Pearl started swaying her hips, slowly, almost imperceptibly at first, index finger still lingering on Fat Ernst's lip. Then her shoulders got into the act, dipping and rising and rolling with the rhythm of her hips, knees rocking back and forth. It took me a second, but I finally realized that Pearl was dancing. Not just dancing, but lap dancing, like some long dead, rotting stripper that couldn't give up the job.

I almost wished she'd stop and shove her finger back in Fat Ernst's eye.

Fat Ernst didn't seem to like it much either. His boot heels had settled back on the floor, but he couldn't tear his eyes away from the twitching scarecrow between his knees. His right eye had gotten all puffy and red, and a glistening track of tears rolled down his cheek, collecting at the base of his nose. I think he was testing the strength of the barbed wire around his wrists, because I could see welts of blood gathering under the thin metal cords.

Pearl kept dancing. I could hear her humming something softly under her breath but couldn't place the song. Her knees kept getting farther and farther apart, until the outsides of her sticklike legs were pressed firmly against the insides of Fat Ernst's knees. Then she started thrusting her pelvis around at odd angles like she was trying to imitate some moves she had seen long ago, but her hips just weren't letting the rest of her body perform properly, so it kind of looked like she was having an attack or something.

Between the humming, she started whispering to Fat Ernst. "See?" More humming. "It doesn't have to be bad. I don't want to hurt you." She spread her legs and her pelvis swayed and dropped, like she was doing the limbo. "You've been good to the boys, treated 'em fair. So I don't want this little"—she made some sort of big band, trumpet, *wah-wah* sounds softly with her mouth—"misunderstanding to end our relationship." Her knees hit the floor and her right hand clutched at Fat Ernst's chest, squeezing his nipple.

Bert stuck his head in the front door. He looked even worse, worried too, like he might throw up at any minute. "Hey, Ma? There's these things, these . . . worms, they been eating at Ray's head."

Pearl snapped her head over Fat Ernst's thigh. "I'm busy here, boy. You go on back out there, keep an eye on things. I'll let you know when you need to come back in."

Bert nodded, scratching at his cast, then stepped back outside.

Over at the booth, Junior threw his head back, tilting the bottom of the bottle toward the ceiling. When he dropped his head down, a puckered little tequila worm was caught between his teeth. He grinned proudly at Misty, then leaned across the table, shoving his face at her. I got a quick glimpse of Junior biting the worm in half as his mouth closed over Misty's lips. Her body shuddered slightly, but she didn't pull away. As he dropped back in his seat, Misty chewed once, twice, then swallowed. The worm was gone.

CHAPTER 29

Fat Ernst still wasn't saying anything. Pearl kept swaying her hips around, still on her knees between his legs, face right in his crotch. Her right hand crawled over and squeezed his other nipple, then slid back down the rayon shirt in another round of ragged whispering until it finally stopped at the huge belt buckle. I wondered for a second if he'd been crazy enough to simply hide Slim's gold and diamond buckle in plain sight as it were, just wearing it himself, but when Pearl carefully unbuckled his belt, I could see that it was just his usual buckle.

Then she unzipped his jeans, and in the silent restaurant, the zipper sounded like Junior starting his chainsaw.

Fat Ernst started breathing hard.

Pearl licked her uneven lips with a very long, very pink tongue.

I wanted to look away; I really did. I wanted to look at the floor, the ceiling, the rain outside the shattered windows—anything, anything at all—but I couldn't tear my eyes away from the sight of Pearl kneeling before Fat Ernst, face right in his crotch. It was like watching two trains smash into each other; you couldn't look away.

Pearl peeled the top of Fat Ernst's jeans away from the zipper like she was opening a well-read book. Fat Ernst's eyes were still shut tight; I don't think he wanted to see Pearl's ruined face so close to his dick.

Junior slid out of the booth, gently pulling on Misty's leash. "I want you to watch this. Maybe you can learn something." Drawn by the leather leash, she rose to her feet. Junior gripped Misty's waist, pivoted her so she was facing Fat Ernst and Pearl, then pulled her back against him. He rested his chin on her shoulder, watching with her. His hands crept forward around her hips and slid into her front pockets. "Ma's the best. The *best*."

Junior couldn't see Misty's face. But I could. She glanced at Pearl kneeling on the floor between Fat Ernst's knees, then looked me dead in the eye. Her face was blank, cold. I couldn't tell what she was thinking.

"Such a big, strong man," Pearl breathed, flicking her long tongue out to lick Fat Ernst's white briefs. Fat Ernst didn't look too happy. Like me, I think he wished Pearl would just jam that blackened fingernail back in his eye instead. But she kept licking at his white underwear like she was attacking a large vanilla ice cream cone. She fiercely clutched the top of his left thigh, rolling her head around like a snake rising out of a wicker basket. She darted her head forward, licking at the front of Fat Ernst's underwear, then pulled back for some more head rolling.

Despite himself, I'm sure, a bulge started to grow in the front of Fat Ernst's underwear.

The left side of Pearl's face crinkled up in satisfaction, and she applied more pressure to her licking, dragging her tongue up and down the bulge in slow, gliding movements. Finally, she slid her right hand back up his thigh and worked her fingers into the waistband of his underwear, pulling it down, releasing Fat Ernst's penis.

Fat Ernst had the biggest dick I had ever seen.

Don't get me wrong here. It's not like I've seen a lot of guys' dicks or penises or anything—or even want to—but, Jesus, this thing was huge. It looked like a telephone pole was erupting out of his pants. "Please don't," Fat Ernst said in a strangled voice.

"Don't what?" Pearl said slyly, staring up at him with her good eye. Fat Ernst gritted his teeth.

Junior slowly pulled his hands out of Misty's front pockets and slid his palms up her stomach, inch by inch, until he was cupping her breasts. Misty's expression never changed. Junior stuck his tongue in her ear and wriggled it around like a fat worm. I vowed to cut *his* goddamn tongue out if I ever got the chance.

"You want me, don't you? You want this, don't you? Don't you?" Pearl opened her mouth wide, flicking her pink tongue up and against his dick. "Tell me. Tell me where it is and I'll suck you off until you explode." Then she took Fat Ernst in her mouth and suddenly I found I could close my eyes.

The slurping sounds didn't help.

"Tell me where it is!" I heard Pearl say, panting a little.

No answer.

More slurping.

After a couple more long seconds, I heard "Tell me!" again. "Tell me where the buckle is and I'll finish you off, big boy." Pearl paused for emphasis. "And I'll *swallow*."

I'll admit it, I peeked. Pearl was on her knees, staring up at Fat Ernst, right hand wrapped around his dick, giving him that lopsided smile.

"Fuck you, you ugly old bitch," Fat Ernst said, spitting little flecks of blood into the air as he spoke. "I don't care what the fuck you do, you ain't getting jack shit outta me."

Pearl froze.

Just for a second. Then she nodded. But the lopsided grin never left. She opened her mouth wide, and I suddenly feared that she was just gonna bite Fat Ernst's dick right off. Instead, she said in a low voice, "Junior, get your ass over here."

Junior stopped kneading Misty's breasts. "But, Ma . . ." he whined. "I was just getting started."

"You mind your mother," Pearl snapped. "Less you want to sleep with the hogs again. Besides," she said, not taking her eyes off of Fat Ernst. "We get that buckle, and I'll let you take her home."

"You mean it?"

"Of course. You can keep her as long as you want. This flood here, nobody'll know what happened to her. If you're careful, she'll last weeks, maybe even months, if you're extra damn careful."

Junior licked at Misty's eye and whispered, "You stay right here now. I'll be back right quick." He pushed her down into the booth and left the end of the leash on the table.

Misty gave him a smile I hoped was fake.

"Drag that goddamn deputy back in here. Find out if we caught anything," Pearl said and let go of Fat Ernst's dick. She put her hand on his thigh for support and pushed herself to her feet. "You don't know what you're missing." She didn't zip his pants back up, and that made me nervous.

Junior and Bert yanked on Ray's cowboy boots and slid the body back inside. Once Ray's head cleared the doorframe, Bert dropped the leg and sank into a nearby chair. His face had gone nearly totally white, and he kept scratching at the skin around the top of the cast, where his arm joined his shoulder.

"You got your knife?" Pearl demanded, leaning on her cane, still standing between Fat Ernst's knees.

Bert nodded feebly, working his fingers under the top of the cast.

"Junior. Cut his head off."

That got Fat Ernst's attention. His eyes snapped open, jerking up to Pearl's face. She grinned back down at him. "You had your chance," was all she said. The muscles in Fat Ernst's arms tensed, and fresh droplets of blood started rolling down his wrists, the backs of his hands, collecting in small puddles on the floor.

Misty methodically twisted and rotated her wrists, still bound in the extension cord. I kept staring at her, but she wouldn't look up.

Junior bent over, plucked the huge Rambo knife out of Bert's boot, and sank to his knees by Ray's head. Ray's legs were pointing toward me, and I couldn't see much. Junior cocked his head for a moment, studying Ray's long, crooked neck, readjusted his grip on the knife, then brought it down like he was pounding on a stubborn nail. He sawed the knife back and forth for a moment, and a dark pool of blood began to grow under Ray's shoulders.

After a couple of seconds of sawing, Ray's head rolled lazily away from his body and came to a stop, resting on the left cheek and ear.

"Bring it on over here," Pearl said, waving Junior over.

Junior drove the tip of Bert's knife into the table. Bert looked like he wanted to focus on the quivering handle, but his eyes wouldn't work right. Junior picked up Ray's head by the thinning hair, holding it out as if Ray wanted to keep an eye on the floor, and carried it over to Fat Ernst's chair.

Ray's eyes were closed. His mouth was open, fat tongue hanging limply between his teeth. His eyes had nearly disappeared inside his orbits, as if they had been pushed aside, driven deeper into the skull. The huge Adam's apple had been raggedly severed in half.

"Well, well, well. Let's see what we caught here," Pearl said, taking Ray's head by the hair. She dangled it in front of Fat Ernst's face for a moment. The fingers on her ruined left hand stretched out, forcing Ray's jaws open even farther. The thumb and forefinger slithered inside, pushing the tongue out of the way. She yanked the head away from her chest with her right arm, and there, pinched between the thumb and forefinger of her ruined hand, was a worm. Maybe three inches long, slick with blood and slime, squirming and twisting between Pearl's two fingers.

Pearl flung Ray's head at me. I flinched and jerked out of the way as it hit the bar and bounced into my lap. I bucked, kicked it down the bar, yelling something, and looked frantically down at my T-shirt. No worms, thank God. Nothing had crawled out of his head.

Pearl held the worm up to Fat Ernst's nose. "I think he likes you," she said, and laughed, a high, whistling, joyless sound that seemed to be more of a wheeze than an actual laugh. The worm contracted, drawing its tail up to its head until it was nearly a complete circle. It slapped its flat tail back against Pearl's thumb, sliding sluggishly, urgently around the liver-spotted, leathery skin. "Told you, you had your chance," she said, and without any kind of warning she dropped the worm onto Fat Ernst's naked dick.

Fat Ernst started screaming then, a soul-shredding sound that filled the restaurant, inarticulate strangled gasps and sobs between each shriek of pain. His body bucked and jerked against the barbed wire, taking the chair on a shuddering dance around the dining room. Pearl leaned on her cane and watched. Finally, he tipped over backward and crashed into the wooden floor. I heard something crack.

Oh God, please let that be the chair, I thought. *If I can just distract Pearl and Bert long enough for Fat Ernst to get loose, then we might get out of this alive.* All Fat Ernst would have to do would be to roll over, crawl six or seven feet toward the jukebox and grab Ray's Super Redhawk. I'd like to see the look on Pearl's face *then*.

In the meantime, Bert clawed frantically at the skin around his shoulder. His motions were getting so frantic he was starting to draw blood.

Fat Ernst kept rolling and twitching, sliding the back of the chair around on the floor, his head whipping back and forth, and I got a blurred impression of his white face, mouth open in silent horror.

Hang in there, I thought. *Just keep going. Don't quit yet. I need you to snag that fucking revolver.* The black and white slivers of his eyes found mine and glared at me accusingly.

Pearl clomped around to Fat Ernst's head and gazed down at him. "We could have had something," she said, almost sadly, and gently placed the sharp tip of her cane in the hollow of Fat Ernst's right eye. He stopped shaking and started making sounds then, just gurgling moans really, but it was enough to let Pearl know that he felt the pressure on his eye. She leaned forward, putting all her weight on the top of the cane. I saw the tip of the cane slide into Fat Ernst's eye about an inch and hold for a moment. Fat Ernst flopped and jerked against the wires, but they held firm.

"Fuck . . . all of you . . . Ahhhhhhhhh—*shit* . . ." Fat Ernst gasped.

Pearl put more weight on the cane, and something popped. The cane suddenly sank another four or five inches into Fat Ernst's head. His body jerked and he farted, a deep, ripping noise that filled the restaurant with the pungent aroma of ripe shit. The smell made even Pearl wince.

Fat Ernst twitched once, twice, and that was it.

CHAPTER 30

Fat Ernst was dead and so were my escape plans.

Pearl yanked her cane out of his right eye, and forced it down deep into his left eye as well, just for the hell of it, I guess. She paused for a moment, working the cane back and forth, really scrambling Fat Ernst's brains, back curved, leaning over Fat Ernst like some kind of thin buzzard hunched over a dead squirrel on the highway. She rested and took a moment to catch her breath. The cane in Fat Ernst's eye socket stood up all by itself.

Pearl took another deep breath, let it out slowly, and jerked the cane out of Fat Ernst's head. She slammed the cane on the floor, shaking off tiny spatters of blood and bits of meat and shouted, "All right then, boys. Boys! Bert! Get over here, stop screwing around. What the hell's wrong with you?"

Bert didn't look up. "I . . . I can feel it moving . . . in my arm. It hurts . . ."

"Quit whining or I'll give you something to whine about. Now," Pearl leaned on her cane, swiveling her head around. "You boys peel this place open like an orange. This goddamn cocksucker hid that buckle in here somewheres. I can smell it."

"What about him?" Junior pointed at me. Everything got tight and frozen inside, down deep under my stomach.

Pearl fixed her staring eye on me. She chuckled. "If Ernst wasn't gonna tell us, what makes you think he'd tell this little pip-squeak?" She leaned over me, slamming the cane into the floor between my thighs, too damn close to my crotch. "Eh? You know where it is?"

I shook my head enthusiastically. "Fat Ernst never told me anything." I was hoping that would be enough, and because I couldn't help them, they'd have to let me go.

Pearl nodded, leaned back. "That's what I thought. Junior, drag his hide out back, dump him in the water. Let them worms chew on him for a while."

Blind terror scrabbled up my chest and filled my throat. I opened my mouth, but nothing came out.

"Hey," Misty said. "Stop picking on him. He's just the fucking dishwasher. He wouldn't know anything."

Pearl whipped her head around and said, "Shut your hole, bitch. This don't concern you none. You keep quiet or I'll take care of you myself. And let me tell you, there's far worse things that can happen to you than just letting my boys loose on you. Things worse than that pretty, empty little head can ever imagine." She was quiet for a moment, waiting to see if Misty would say anything else.

Please, please, keep quiet, I thought. I'd rather die than see her get hurt. Misty dropped her glare, clasping her hands together. I could see the knuckles grow white.

"Junior," Pearl said sharply. "You do like I asked now."

"You got it, Ma," Junior said, digging around in his jeans for a moment. He pulled out Ray's key ring, squatting down in front of me. "This'll teach you not to go around shooting at our truck, you little bastard," he said and unlocked the handcuff.

"Please," I whispered, as Junior jerked me to my feet. "Please, wait, I—"

A guttural cry from the corner stopped Junior. The cry started low, then rose to a high-pitched, almost childlike scream. Bert was on his feet, back to the front window, broken arm raised high. His scream reached a fever pitch as he brought the cast down against the table. The dirty plaster cracked with a dull crunch. Bert jerked his right arm up, brought it down a second time. Plaster crumbled off. He smashed his arm down against the table again and again, clawed at the disintegrating plaster. Ragged chunks of the thick plaster were peeled away, revealing a swollen, bulbous upper arm, almost black from the congealed blood inside. Bert stopped to catch his breath and jerked his Rambo knife out of the table.

"You put that—," Pearl started to say, but before another word made it past her lips, Bert brought the knife around in a tight arc across his chest and sank half of the thirteen-inch blade into his shoulder, just above the cracked top of the cast. It didn't seem to bother him much, because he yanked it out and jabbed it in again. And again.

"Bert!" Pearl shouted. "You stop that this instant!"

Bert wasn't listening. He stabbed himself a fourth time, sinking it awful damn deep this time, then worked that handle around, twisting it into the thin meat of his shoulder like he was digging for clams at the beach. Blood cascaded down the black skin and yellow cast. He kept at it like a man possessed.

We all watched, transfixed, nobody moving until finally Pearl snapped out of it and yelled to Junior, "Stop him! Now!"

Junior brought his left elbow up in a swift jab and smashed it into my nose. I fell back into the bar and sank to the floor, my butt landing painfully on the brass bar. Then there was some sort of scuffle between Bert and Junior, but the only thing I really remember clearly was that at some point Bert was on the floor, like me. He slowly pulled something long, flexible, and bloody from his wounded shoulder and held it triumphantly out for his mother and brother to see. He flicked his wrist, flinging the thing away from him, and Junior promptly ground it into the floor with his boot.

Several long seconds of heavy breathing. I heard Junior say, "Too goddamn much blood. He ain't gonna make it."

Quiet for a moment. Then Pearl, "Go get my bag."

The next thing I knew, I was lying on my back on the bar, and Pearl was saying, "Now you hold still," as she jabbed something cold into the crook of my right arm, at the soft part at the inside of my arm at the elbow. It was some kind of goddamn needle attached to a long stretch of surgical tubing.

The only thing my fogged brain could think of to say was, "Hey, hey, waitaminute . . . is that thing sterile?"

Pearl gave me her lopsided smile as the yellow tube grew red, starting at my arm and traveling down into Bert's arm. He was down beneath me, lying on a table that had been shoved against the bar. He looked unconscious or dead. His shoulder was wrapped with the rags that Fat Ernst used to mop up spilled beer on the bar.

"Wait . . . wait. We don't even have the same blood type," I croaked. Of course, I was just guessing, but it seemed like the smart thing to say.

Pearl smiled at me again, and it was clear that she could care less. "Blood is blood," she whispered, sliding her finger down my forehead. "It don't matter when life is leaving." Her touch on my nose left something warm and slimy behind. After a moment, I realized she was marking me, painting something on my face. "Everything you think you know, all your science, all your books and facts and bullshit, it means nothing. Nothing. There are forces out there, powers beyond what is known, out beyond your pathetic nightmares, little boy."

She turned to Bert after finishing with me, and dipped her finger into a bowl filled with something black. She left a streak of the liquid straight down his bare chest. On either side of the line, she started drawing weird symbols and shapes, mostly around Bert's heart. "I can read clouds. I can hear what the wind whispers. I can see in the dark." She dug around in her bag for a moment, pulled out some kind of metal shaft. It glinted in the gray light and I realized it was a goddamn scalpel.

Without hesitating, she bent back over Bert and started tracing the lines with the scalpel. Blood seeped out, ran down his chest. "I can talk to snakes. To wasps. To cockroaches. To worms," Pearl said proudly. "And I can control blood. Hell, I brought Junior back three times now." She looked across me to Junior, standing on the other side of the bar. "'Member that truck? Thought you'd never wake up. Good thing that driver was a big pig of a man, held a lot of blood in all that fat."

My blood continued to drain down the tube, into Bert.

Pearl started chanting something in her hissing, garbled voice as she cut into Bert, carving, slicing, permanently etching those strange shapes and symbols into his flesh. It sounded a lot like what she had been singing when I had seen her at the burn barrel in her backyard that night we slaughtered the steer. *I'm not dying like this,* I thought. *Not like this, with my blood slowly being siphoned out of me like some asshole sucking gas out of a car's goddamn gas tank.*

I tried to raise my right hand but couldn't. I rolled my head over to the side and found out why. Junior was holding me down against the bar. I couldn't move, couldn't fight, nothing. My life kept slipping away, my blood being sucked out of me, down into Bert's cold, white body. This wasn't fair. I didn't want to die. Not like this. "Please stop," I whispered.

Pearl stopped chanting long enough to say, "Not yet. Not yet."

"Please don't," I said. Cold lethargy settled through my limbs, anchoring my body to the smooth finished wood of the bar. I wished Misty would say something, anything, now; I didn't care what they did to her. But I couldn't see where she was. The reality of the situation hit me hard. No one was going to save me. I realized with an absolute certainty that I was going to die; I was going to die, my blood stolen, drop by drop. I had to think fast. But my mind was a blank gray slate. Nothing.

Pearl resumed chanting, cutting away at Bert.

My blood kept sliding away, my unforgiving, betraying heart

unknowingly pumping it out of my arm, down the greasy tubing. Something sparked in my mind, fizzled quietly. I blurted out, "I know where the buckle is."

Silence filled the restaurant.

"Bullshit," Junior said.

I sensed Pearl watching me, so I said, "I know where it is. I know where Fat Ernst hid it. I watched him."

"Is that so," Pearl said quietly.

"He hid it in one of the hamburgers," I whispered. "I saw him."

"In the hamburgers?" Pearl asked.

"Yes, I saw it."

"Well," Junior said, "thanks for the tip, Archie. We appreciate it."

I spoke fast, feeling a faint numbness creeping through my body. "Kill me and you'll never find it." That got their attention. "It's not in the fridge. I put the meat somewhere else."

Pearl grabbed my chin, jerking my head over so I was staring into her melted-wax face. "Where is it?"

I stared her dead in the eye and repeated, "Kill me and you'll never find it." Pulling my right arm out of Junior's grip, I reached over and yanked the needle out.

Pearl looked down at Bert. She reached out and touched his neck, feeling for a pulse. After a moment, she said, "He's back with us." She turned her attention back to me and nodded. "He's alive but just barely. You show us where the buckle is, and we'll let you go." She said evenly, "If I find out you're lying, I'm gonna cut off your dick and choke you with it. Then I'll feed you to the worms. Understood?"

I nodded. "And if I give you the buckle, you'll let me and Misty go."

Junior grinned when I mentioned Misty.

Pearl said, "Of course."

"Okay. I'll give it to you. But I'm gonna need gloves, a plank out of the wall over there, your snow shovel, and a shitload of duct tape."

CHAPTER 31

Junior shouldered his way through the dangling insulation and splintered wall back into the restaurant, stomping across the Cadillac's hood, carrying what I needed. He pulled me off the bar and held me up as my legs found the strength to stand. I swayed back and forth, dizzy from the loss of blood, feeling empty somehow. I looked up, found Misty watching me carefully from her place in the booth. We locked eyes for a brief instant, but it was enough. Enough for her to wink, slowly, deliberately. Enough to know that she was worried about me, that she was with me.

"Where is it?" Junior asked, clamping his fist around the back of my neck.

"Out back," I gasped, and felt my feet almost lifted off the floor as Junior marched me along, slamming my face into the swinging kitchen door. He shoved me into the stove, hard enough to drive the air out of my chest in one quick rush. I watched the tiny blue pilot light dance and disappear. Before I had a chance to take another breath, Junior yanked open the back door and threw me out onto the loading dock. I hit the wet wood and rolled to the edge, nearly falling into the open Dumpster.

wormfood

The rain was still falling. I put one hand on the metal edge of the Dumpster. It was almost completely filled with black rainwater. Several dark lumps floated at the scummy surface. I pushed myself to my feet, scanning the horizon frantically for any signs of help. Nothing but water and the distant trees lining the freeway. Another foot and the water would be washing over the loading dock. Everything, as far as I could see, was under at least three or four feet of floodwater, leaving a surging brown landscape of foam, trash, and floating cornstalks.

And somewhere down there, down in the cold water and mud, the worms waited.

Junior smoothed his pompadour back and stepped closer. "Where is it?"

I tilted my head at the Dumpster. "In there."

Junior shook his head, dropped the plank onto the dock, and tossed the gloves and duct tape at me. While I got ready, the water got higher, rising another three, four inches. In about an hour or so it was going to wash over the loading dock and into the restaurant, covering the floor. I stood at the edge of the loading dock, looking down into the Dumpster. My arms were wrapped with several layers of duct tape from my shoulders down to my wrists. Huge leather gloves encased my hands, floppy leather fingers sticking out at least two to three inches from the tips of my fingers.

Junior waited impatiently on the other side of the shovel, arms crossed, ignoring the rain that ran through his hair and left greasy trails down his face. Pearl waited in the doorway, out of the rain. She said she didn't want the rain ruining her makeup. But she kept a tight grip on Misty's leash.

Misty watched silently from near the doorway.

I hoped my guess about the buckle was right. At first, I had thought that Fat Ernst would have hidden it in his Cadillac, but that would have been too obvious. Then, at the last second, I remembered the glint of something shiny peeking through the raw hamburger meat

217

when I dumped the boxes in the Dumpster. It was time to find out.

I dropped the plank across the Dumpster, shook it to make sure it would hold, and eased out over the black water. I'd wrapped duct tape around my boots and legs, up my knees, as well. I was hoping it would be enough to stop the worms from chewing through to my skin but had no way of knowing whether it would work. I inched out to the center of the plank, keeping my butt planted firmly on the splintered wood, legs splayed, feet braced against the top of the Dumpster walls.

Junior handed me the shovel and said, "You got five minutes, zipperhead. After that, no buckle . . . no more nice safe seat." He put his boot on the edge of the plank and gave it a little shove to demonstrate.

I held the shovel on my lap, taking several deep breaths. The stench coming out of the Dumpster reminded me of Slim's pit. Actually, the two places weren't too different. Both were full of rainwater, rotting meat, and the goddamn worms. Except this Dumpster was worse. There wasn't just rotting meat under that water; Heck's body was somewhere down there too. I didn't want to think about what the worms had done to him. So I held my breath, got a good, solid grasp on the handle, and slowly sank the tip of the blade into the thick black water.

Instantly, thousands of tiny worms rose to the surface. It was worse than I had thought. Not only had Heck's body been infested with the worms, the meat from the boxes was also full of them. There had been plenty of food, plenty of water, and plenty of time. And now the Dumpster was literally teeming with thousands, maybe millions of worms. My skin started to crawl, and it was all I could do not to drop the shovel and roll back onto the loading dock.

"Four minutes," Junior said, as if reading my mind. He wasn't wearing a watch, and I knew I was at the mercy of his patience.

I forced the shovel deeper into the muck, trying to remember where exactly that bottom box had landed. The handle kept slipping deeper and deeper into the rancid water, until just six inches remained above the surface. I prayed it wasn't Heck's body when the blade struck something rigid. I pushed the handle forward, bracing it on my knee then pushing down, using my knee as a lever. The resistance split, and the shovel slid into the mass easily.

And while I prayed I hadn't touched Heck's body with the shovel, I prayed harder that the plank was strong enough to handle the extra pressure.

The plank held and the shovel blade broke the surface. The soggy, shredded remains of a white box slipped off the side and landed in the water with a *plop*. A mound of gray, raw hamburger meat rested on top of the blade. Hundreds of tiny worms squirmed and wriggled in and out of the meat, spilling away and falling back into the water. I jiggled the handle a little, slowly shaking chunks of hamburger meat off the shovel. Soon the meat was gone. No buckle.

"Three minutes," Junior reminded me.

I stuck the shovel back in, deeper this time, not worrying about whether I hit Heck's body or not. I tried again, scooping up a giant, soggy mound of squirming meat, but the buckle wasn't there.

"Two fucking minutes," Junior said, and slid the plank sideways a few inches, almost pitching me into the water. I shoved the shovel into the water, again and again, bringing up dripping piles of meat. Once I brought up a ragged piece of Heck's shirt. I forced myself not to worry about it, just to keep going.

Pearl, who had been silently watching from the doorway the whole time, finally spoke up and said, "That's enough. It ain't out here. This little shit has wasted enough of our time."

I kept pulling meat out of the Dumpster. "But it's in here, I know it." I jabbed the shovel back into the water. "Just give me a little more time. It's in here."

Junior leaned harder on the plank. "Time's up, Archie."

I struggled to lift one more shovelful. As usual, the blade was heaped with meat and alive with worms. I started twisting the handle back and forth, same as every other try, dribbling little bits and pieces into the flooded Dumpster. I didn't know what else to do.

Out of the corner of my eye, Junior stood up, putting most of his weight onto his left foot, as his right foot slid across the plank and prepared to kick it into the Dumpster.

And then I saw it at the end of the shovel. The buckle.

Covered in gray hamburger meat, a golden notched edge hung out over the side of the shovel blade. The diamonds captured the somber dark light that filtered down out of the storm clouds and flung that dead light back out into the air in brilliant sparkling patterns. *Here's my chance*, I thought, and got a better grip on the shovel's handle.

"I'll be damned," Junior breathed, still leaning back, right foot resting against the edge of the board.

I jerked the shovel away from the water, twisting my upper body around as fast as I could, flinging the mound of meat up into Junior's face.

Junior jumped, faster than I had guessed, and most of the meat, maybe seven, eight pounds of it, hit Junior in the throat. A little stuck to his face, his eyes, his mouth. It was enough to distract him when he landed heavily at the side of the Dumpster and fought for his balance. The buckle bounced off his ear and went sailing toward the back wall of the restaurant.

Pearl screamed something, a shrill, jagged sound that echoed out across the floodwater. She rushed at her son in a stuttering, crablike movement, but Misty grabbed hold of the leash, right up near her throat, and yanked Pearl back.

Junior lost his fight with gravity and landed on my shoulder and right side hard, slamming me sideways into the plank. The wood groaned and cracked. I swung the empty shovel back around, like I was trying to hit myself in the head and managed to strike Junior's neck, but he barely noticed it. He balled up his fist and hit me in the temple before I even had a chance to let the shovel fall back away and reverse my grip.

My head bounced off the plank and stars burst behind my eyes.

Junior clamped his hands around my throat and sank his knee into my stomach. I couldn't breathe. My left leg fell off the plank. I hoped the duct tape was thick enough to stop the worms.

Arms taut and shivering, Junior stared down at me through slitted eyes, lips pulled back, yellow teeth clenched and bared in a wild and savage grin. "Motherfucking piece of shit."

The pressure around my throat suddenly vanished as Junior released me and grabbed at his own throat. I caught a quick flash of Misty's face over his right shoulder. Her jaw was set, eyes on fire. She had that leash wrapped around Junior's neck and was doing her best to choke the life out of him.

Pearl's cane cracked through the sky into Misty's skull. Misty dropped to the loading dock, but she didn't let go of the leash. Junior arched his back, clawing at the leather. Pearl brought her cane down again, viciously striking Misty in the jaw. Misty let go then, rolling into a ball, covering her head with her arms. Pearl whipped the cane over her shoulder, bringing it down in a whistling arc, smacking into Misty's body. It reminded me of Junior hitting the crowbar in the coffin. She kept hitting Misty, again and again, cracking that cane into Misty's arms and head and hands.

Before I could react, Junior grabbed a fistful of my hair and twisted, almost rolling me off the plank. He pulled me sideways and shoved my head down toward the black water. Worms rose out of the surface, reaching, straining for my skin as if they were steel shavings drawn to a magnet.

"Don't kill him yet. We need his blood," I heard Pearl yell, then saw her lopsided, leering face under Junior's arm, watching me with her bright right eye. She held the cane in her right hand, buckle in her left. "And his liver."

Junior rolled me back onto the plank and squeezed my throat again. The gray sky got darker. I heard Junior's harsh breathing coming down a long, winding tunnel. And then—almost at the other end of the tunnel—I heard Grandma's voice.

"That's enough fun for today. You best let go of my grandson."

CHAPTER 32

Junior jerked his head around. Under his arm, past Pearl's hunched figure, I saw Grandma's short, squat frame filling the back doorway of the
restaurant. She wore her giant straw hat and Grandpa's thick neoprene
fishing waders up to her ample waist. The .10 gauge rested comfortably
on her walker. For a second, I wondered how she'd made it through the
worms, but then I realized the waders had protected her.

Junior squinted down at me and didn't move.

"Maybe you didn't hear me," Grandma said, casually bringing up
the side-by-side barrels of her shotgun. "I swear to the good Lord, I'm
gonna scatter your innards to hell and back." She paused. "I mean it, son."

Pearl started to say something, but Grandma wasn't in the mood
and squeezed the trigger. The blast disintegrated the bottom five inches of Pearl's cane and drove a hole the size of a grapefruit through the
loading dock. Grandma rode the recoil, letting the gun rock and buck
in her hands, and when the gun smoke cleared, the barrels were aimed
at Junior's head.

Pearl stared down at her feet. "You . . . you shot me."

Junior instantly let go of my throat and scooted backward onto the

wormfood

loading dock, asking, "Ma? Ma? You okay, Ma?"

I sucked in a giant breath, coughed like hell, and almost rolled off the plank into the open Dumpster. I remembered that my leg had been dangling in the water and jerked it out with a splash. I couldn't feel whether any worms were eating into my leg; I couldn't seem to focus my eyes. Everything had gone numb except the inside of my throat and lungs. Each breath felt like I was swallowing gulps of lava.

"Arch? How you doing?" Grandma asked.

"I'm here," I said, and my voice sounded hollow and scratchy. "Thanks."

"What's all over your face?" Grandma asked me, but kept her eyes and shotgun on Pearl and Junior.

"I dunno," I said, crawling off the plank. "She marked my face for some kind of something." I watched Pearl's expression closely, feeling guilty, like I'd just crossed a line by admitting that Pearl had tried to kill me. "They wanted my blood."

"You people are goddamn lucky you didn't hurt my grandson or this girl any worse," Grandma said, her tone calm and controlled, but a deaf guy could have heard the hatred seeping through the spaces between each word.

Junior ignored her. He kneeled before Pearl, inspecting her feet. "Jesus, Ma," he nearly sobbed, "You been shot." Pearl stood still, bracing herself with her good arm on Junior's head, staring at Grandma. Junior wiped at Pearl's shoes with trembling fingers. A dozen tiny round bubbles of blood, no bigger than peas, kept rising up at the top of the leather after each sweep of Junior's hand.

"Don't you worry about that none," Pearl said to her son, never taking her eyes off Grandma. "It don't hurt."

I knelt over Misty as thunder growled out across the valley. Her left arm rested across her chest and I flinched when I saw her hand. The fingers stuck out in all directions, mangled, as if she'd stuck her hand in a fan belt. Blood ran down her temple. Her bottom lip had

223

been split, and one eye was nearly black, swollen shut. Her other eye was closed. At least her breathing was slow and steady.

"I been waiting a long time now," Grandma said quietly, watching Pearl carefully. "Kept watching the town, ever since the day you dumped that blood all over the sidewalk in front of the butcher's. That's when I knew. Been praying I'd find you like this one day."

Pearl drew her cracked lips back from her decayed teeth in a defiant, tight smile. "You shoulda prayed that you'd never see me ever again, you shriveled teat. When I get tired of you and your chicken-shit little grandson here, you're gonna pray for death instead." Pearl raised the blasted, splintered end of her cane until it pointed at Grandma's torso, where the waders stopped, just under Grandma's large breasts.

"Pearl," Grandma said with a tired smile, "you couldn't scare a goddamn chipmunk away."

"You'd be surprised at what I could scare away. Got your grandson shaking in them old boots." Pearl fingered her cane, stroking it slowly, obscenely. "I can still smell Bill in 'em."

Grandma exhaled sharply. "I ain't here to talk about my husband. He's gone." She coughed. A tiny trickle of blood ran from her right nostril and collected on her bottom lip.

Pearl's smile got wider and her eye got brighter. The cane quivered. "In some ways, maybe. Maybe not. Dead? Yeah, he's dead. Gone?" She shook her head slightly. "Naw. He ain't gone. Not by a long shot. He still . . . lingers. Like them boots. He's still around, you just gotta know how to listen." Pearl paused a moment, giving all of us a chance to listen as the rain softly hit the surface of the floodwater, the roof, the loading dock. "He talks to *me* now. And sometimes, when the wind is just right, I can still hear his screams. Screaming out there in the dark. Cryin' for you, for anybody, to come and save him. Course, toward the end, he doesn't get many words out, as such. Just starts in with them screams. Sounds like a goddamn helpless old woman. It feels . . . well, it helps me sleep, listening to him out there, out there in that hog pen,

224

wormfood

just screaming, screaming."

"Don't push it," Grandma said, easing the shotgun up to Pearl's head. More blood slipped from Grandma's chin, dripping onto her sundress.

"Go ahead and shoot me then, if you think you can. You don't have the balls, you worthless old bitch. You should have let him go. He would have been happier with me. And he knows that now. I would have satisfied him, showed him what a real woman could do."

Grandma smiled thinly and licked her lips. Her tongue smeared the blood, making it look like she'd applied a serious shade of lipstick. She said, "He wanted a real woman; that's why he chose me. Not some goddamn skinny sideshow freak. He married me, remember?"

"I remember. I don't forget anything. And you oughta know that." Pearl let the cane drop for a moment, holding it with her curled left arm, and reached up to the folds of the rags at her throat, pulling out a string of yellow blocks. It was a necklace of some sort, with dozens of irregular, knotted chunks of what looked like wood or bone, all tied together with a piece of twine around Pearl's scrawny neck.

She grinned. "Forty-four teeth."

Grandma swallowed and I saw her finger tighten around the shotgun's trigger.

"And you know where they came from. You know. That big old boar. That one that stared at you the whole goddamn time them county boys pulled all those pieces of Bill out of the mud."

"I don't give a damn what you've got there. I . . . I sold those hogs at the auction. All of 'em. They're gone." Grandma clenched her teeth and swallowed, and I feared she was swallowing blood.

Pearl shook the necklace, making the pig teeth dance in a dry, crackling, snapping sound, like a hardwood campfire. "Nothin's ever gone. Didn't you pay attention back in high school? Matter never goes away. It just changes. It just gets recycled." Pearl brought the cane back up. "Who do you think bought them hogs, you stupid bitch? We, me and the boys, we ate every last one of them pigs, everything, right on down to the bone marrow. Sweetest, most goddamn tender meat I ever tasted. Like honey."

I'd had enough. Hot fury bubbled up and I snapped, "Shut up! Just shut up!" I shook the haze out of my head. "Evil fucking bitch." I jumped up, away from Misty, and grabbed the shovel. I brought the blade around, feet nearly three feet apart, hips locked, shoulders rolling, arms braced, like I was trying to hit a home run, wanting nothing more than to knock Pearl's head off, send it skipping out across the floodwater like a flat stone.

Pearl raised her right hand, caught hold of the blade, and stopped it cold. I felt like I'd just tried to chop down a steel beam. The tingling jolt rushed up my arms, vibrating deep in my chest.

Pearl ripped her stare away from Grandma, forced the shovel down, pinned me down like a bug. "You ain't nothing but a speck on flyshit, little boy."

While Pearl's gaze was fixed on me, Grandma shot forward, bringing the double barrels of her .10 gauge down in a short, vicious arc, cracking it into Pearl's skull. Grandma grunted, spat, and hit Pearl again.

Pearl dropped to her knees, wincing in pain, grinning the whole time.

Something tickled the back of my mind, something important.

Next to me, I heard Misty whisper, "Kill her . . . just kill her . . ." Her eyes were nothing but slits, but she was conscious. She pushed herself up into a sitting position. ". . . Kill her . . ."

Pearl lifted her right hand to her head and touched the raw spot where the barrel had connected. "You hit like a girl," she said to Grandma.

I jabbed the shovel at Pearl again, just to keep her off balance, on her toes, so to speak. Boiling fury still popped inside of me and I said, "Gimme that fucking buckle. It ain't yours, it belongs to her." I jerked my head at Misty.

Pearl looked at me and the left side of her face folded into a smile. "You think you're man enough, you come and get it." She held up the buckle for a moment, clenching it in her fist while she slid her knees apart on the dock, then lifted her dress and shoved the buckle up between her legs. She spread her arms wide in an invitation. Judging from the look on her face, I'd say she liked hanging onto the buckle.

I didn't know what to do. I sure as hell wasn't going to go after it.

"I've listened to enough of your evil garbage," Grandma said, biting off each word as if it tasted bad. Blood still dripped off her chin. "I may be a tired old woman, but I will kill you and your whole family if you so much as sneeze."

I'd never been prouder of my grandmother.

Pearl hissed, "You just wait, you sad, leaking sack of meat. My boys? They're gonna catch up to you. Someday, somehow, you'll wish you'd never been born."

I finally figured out Junior was gone.

One minute, all five of us had been grouped into a rough circle on the loading dock, and I could remember Junior at his mother's side up until she pulled out the tooth necklace. But when I had lost it, trying to hit Pearl in the head, I realized that Junior hadn't been there. He had vanished like smoke.

I brought the shovel back up, saying, "Grandma, he's—"

Junior screamed, "Eat this!" from inside the kitchen. Thunder cracked across the loading dock, and blood exploded from Grandma's chest and back. She was lifted off her feet and flung forward, shoulders rigid, knocking the walker into Pearl. I jerked my head around just in time to see a short bark of flame leap out of the darkness of the kitchen. That was it; that was what I had forgotten.

Ray's Super Redhawk, lying on the dining room floor.

A wall of fire unfurled out at me. Searing heat washed over the loading dock, and the concussion followed an instant later, slamming into my chest, my head, snapping my bones. It felt like I'd been hit by a burning truck.

It was the gas.

When Junior had shoved me against the stove, the burst of air knocked out of my lungs had blown out the pilot. So the whole time we were out on the loading dock, the colorless natural gas had been silently filling the kitchen, the dining room, until Junior pulled the trigger on Ray's revolver.

The initial wall of flame had blown itself out, and through the haze I caught a quick glimpse of Junior. He was on fire, stumbling toward the front door; the grease in his pompadour seemed to be especially flammable. I hoped it hurt bad enough he wished he was dead. I hoped he thought he had just been flung into hell. He threw himself at the front door, burst through it, and hurled himself into the water in a cloud of smoke and steam.

Grandma fell facedown on the dock, flattened by the impact of the gunshot and the wall of heat. Her right palm slapped the wood, then crumpled under her body as she slid forward. The .10 gauge slipped out of her grip, bounced once, and slid across the wet wood into Pearl's hand.

Pearl landed hard on her bony hip at the edge of the Dumpster. The shotgun slid past my head, right into her good arm. She swung the heavy barrels around toward Grandma. "Shoot me?" she rasped. "I'll eat your heart, you bitch, just chew it up and shit it out."

I rolled onto my side, twisted, and kicked Pearl in the face with my right foot. It wasn't much of a kick, but the impact snapped Pearl's head back and the shotgun went off; her pointed chin popped up as the buckshot exploded into the flames in the kitchen. The force of my kick, combined with the heavy recoil from the .10 gauge, knocked Pearl's upper torso back, and ever so slowly Pearl toppled and fell into the Dumpster headfirst. She held on to the shotgun all the way, refusing to let go even as the Dumpster water swallowed her head, shoulders, hips. Her sticklike legs followed, kicked once, then slid off the loading dock and disappeared into the thick, dark water. A few bubbles popped on the surface. The shotgun was gone.

"Please don't be dead," I whispered, scrambling to Grandma. She was lying on her stomach. A red cloud grew violently on her back, right between the shoulder blades.

"Oh no," I whimpered and gently rolled Grandma over on her back. It was worse than I had feared. The bullet had left a crater the size of a coaster in her chest. I could see three, four inches down, into her chest, into her heart. Both of her eyes were closed. "Grandma," I whispered into her rain-streaked face. "Grandma?"

She opened her eyes.

"Hang on, just hang on, okay?"

"He shot me, didn't he."

"Yeah, he shot you." The air in my chest suddenly caught, and I found I couldn't take a breath.

"The hell did he shoot me with?"

"A .480 caliber," I said.

She exhaled ever so slowly and died.

CHAPTER 33

I rocked back on my knees and howled at the dark sky. A deep, heartrending hurt unfurled from somewhere in my chest and spread throughout my body like cancer. I kept howling, screaming, shrieking at the black, rain-filled clouds. Grandma was dead and I was ready to die too. To lie down, rest my face against the wet, cold wood, and drift off with Grandma, slip away to a quiet, numb place. A sound, like someone gasping for air, stopped me. I stared down at Grandma, hoping, praying that she was alive, fighting to draw air into her lungs. But Grandma hadn't moved. Her eyes were still. The sound came again. I glanced over my shoulder.

Pearl was climbing out of the Dumpster.

Tiny worms hung from nearly every inch of exposed skin, as if she'd suddenly grown thick, squirming hair all over her face and shoulders. She flopped forward on her chest, wriggling her hips and kicking her legs, sliding onto the loading dock. I couldn't move. With a grunt, she pushed herself to her feet, then looked at me. Actually, I wasn't sure if she was looking at me or not because several fat worms hung out of her right eye socket. Still, she must have seen something, because she raised her good arm and pointed at me.

"Ooooooh," she croaked. I realized that she was trying to say "You," but when she opened her mouth, blood washed out over her bottom lip and her knife-edged chin. It looked like a dozen or so worms were eating her tongue. Part of her outstretched arm fell off. The muscle between the elbow and the back of the shoulder just fell free with a wet ripping sound and landed limp on the wood, hundreds of worms squirming through the fibrous meat.

Without a muscle to hold it up, her arm flopped back to her side.

She took a step forward.

More flesh started falling off, hitting the wood with soft plops. A couple of fingers. Part of her scalp. She took another step forward, and the jolt of her foot landing made more parts fall onto the dock. A giant chunk of her thigh. Her nose. Something that might have been part of an intestine slid out from under her dress and down the inside of her leg. The gold and diamond studded buckle fell from between what was left of her thighs. And all of her, everything down to the thin layer of skin covering the cartilage of her nose, was alive with worms, *infested* with them.

She shuffled a few more feet until I couldn't take watching her anymore and simply placed my gloved hand in what was left of the exposed rib cage and pushed. It felt like shoving a stack of empty aluminum beer cans over. Pearl opened her mouth and four or five teeth tumbled out of gums that looked like Swiss cheese. Gurgling something, she fell back into the Dumpster. Her outstretched arm hit the opposite side and simply broke off, falling out into the floodwater, flinging clots of worms and meat into the air. Water filled her open mouth.

The last thing I saw of Pearl was her chin. The jawbone lazily separated from the rest of the skull, floating at the surface for a moment as worms swarmed eagerly over it, then vanished into darkness, swallowed by the black water.

Smoke curled out of the open doorway and rolled across the loading dock. I couldn't see anything but bright, strong flames through the back door. The restaurant was finished; the building was burning out like a doomed ship on the open sea. But at least the sailors on burning ships could try and fight drowning or sharks. Those deaths would take time. They didn't have to worry about the worms, the worms that would squirt through your open, flailing fingers and dig into your soft flesh, chewing, squirming, forcing themselves into your *orifices*.

Misty coughed, fighting the smoke that drifted across her body. Her right hand held the bottom of her shirt to her mouth as a kind of air filter. Shit, with Grandma, I'd forgotten. All it took was one little cough, and I realized that I didn't want to die anymore. Not as long as Misty was still alive. Out at the quarry, on the blanket, I'd vowed to protect her. And I still meant it.

I tried to think of something, some way we could escape. We couldn't go through the back door into the kitchen; the flames were too big, too strong. We couldn't exactly jump in the water, either. We needed time, I decided. Maybe somebody had seen the smoke. Maybe help was on the way.

"Okay, okay. Now, you hang on." I grabbed her shoulders, gave a little shake. "Just stay here, keep your feet. I'm gonna fix it so we can get on the roof, okay?" I said, looking into her battered face. I think she nodded back.

The wood beneath my feet suddenly shifted and dropped. Cold fingers clutched at my stomach and I felt that same kind of nauseating vertigo from my dream. The whole building was starting to collapse. Floodwater seeped across the loading dock, washing parts of Pearl around. Worms were everywhere.

I pulled the plank off of the Dumpster, dropped the bottom on the pile of rotting pallets, then slammed the top edge against the wall, as a kind of ramp. The top was at least two feet under the overhanging plastic gutter. It didn't matter. It would have to work. We'd just have to stretch a little, that's all. Already, four or five worms were clustered around my boots, probing and biting, inching up the leather. "You goddamn little shits," I whispered down at them through gritted teeth and pulled Misty close. She took a good look at the plank, tucked her broken hand in close to her stomach, and started climbing.

The entire building shuddered and shifted. More water splashed across the loading dock, rocking Grandma's body. I didn't want to leave her there, but I knew I didn't have the time to carry her up to the roof. I grabbed hold of the wood, pulled myself out of the water, and blinked the tears out of my eyes.

Above me Misty slowly dragged herself onto the sloping roof with her good hand. I followed as fast as I could, scrambling onto the slippery shingles and up the angled roof to the crest. Misty rested on her knees, coughing a little, trying to clear her throat.

I stood up and saw that the flood had swept through the flat valley, washing over the highway, across the ditch, through the fields, leaving nothing but an ocean of filthy water littered with garbage and cornstalks. I couldn't see anything other than an empty horizon and knew that no help was coming.

Down to my left was the crumpled back end of Fat Ernst's Cadillac, wedged between the front wall and the Sawyer brothers' truck. Ray's cruiser was twenty or thirty feet farther. Slim's truck sat out by the highway, water halfway up its doors. And over to my right was Misty's bright red Dodge, sitting by itself, maybe fifteen, twenty feet from the edge of the roof. The water only came up to the bottom of the frame, so I figured the engine was still dry.

"Do you have your keys?" I asked Misty.

She nodded and dug into her jeans pocket with her right hand, gingerly holding her mangled left hand up and out of the way. She dropped four keys and a dangling bottle opener into my open, gloved palm and asked "How are you gonna get there?"

I shrugged and stuffed the key ring into my pocket. I slid carefully down the front half of the roof and squatted at the edge, trying to estimate the jump from the roof to the pickup. I'd never make it.

I'd end up fighting my way through the water while the worms got a free lunch. Even if I made it to the pickup, I'd bleed out before I could move the pickup closer to the building for Misty.

As if reading my mind, Misty called down to me, "I wouldn't. Those things'll get you before you get five feet." The roof shivered, and the west edge dropped half a foot. I heard something over the rain and the flames, a low, strumming sound.

The telephone wires. A lone, thin wire stretched from the upper corner of the roof off to my right out to a telephone pole at the edge of the cornfield, halfway between the restaurant and the highway. If that wire could hold my weight, then I could swing hand over hand to the pole, where it joined several other heavier telephone wires. Those wires crossed right over Misty's truck. It was a hell of a drop to the pickup.

"There," I said, pointing at the wires.

"Do you think they'll hold?" Misty asked.

"Shit, I hope so," I said, more to myself than anybody else, as I scurried along the top of the smoking roof to the west end and tested the wire. I couldn't see how it was attached to the building; it simply ran in through a little hole under the eave and disappeared. I stuck my foot over the edge and pushed down as hard as I could. The wire held, so I grabbed hold with both hands and swung out over the water. The wire bounced with a jerk but didn't break.

I twisted around, locked my ankles over the wire, and worked my way over to the telephone pole like a skinny tree sloth on meth. It got a little tougher when I had to climb up the last ten feet going at a forty-five degree angle. When I got to the top, I reached out and grabbed one of the protruding steel bars that serves as rungs on wooden telephone poles.

I rested a moment and looked back to Misty. She held her wounded hand and watched me. Flames were now peeking out through blackened spots in the roof.

I edged out to the wires at the top of the telephone pole. Thoughts of getting electrocuted by grabbing the wrong wire crossed my mind— and wouldn't *that* have been a goddamned dumb way to die—but I didn't worry about it, I just reached out and grabbed the nearest wire and moved out, hand over hand, feet dangling this time, until I was directly over Misty's pickup, or as best as I could tell. It was hard to try and look directly down with my arms straight up. By then, my arms were screaming and my hands were threatening to let go whether I was in position above the pickup or not.

So I let go.

And almost landed in the pickup bed.

Instead, I hit the water next to the truck. The water was four, four and a half feet deep; it still felt like I was landing on concrete, boots hitting the water in a muddy splash, then falling forward, arms flailing, anything to keep my face out of the water. It didn't work, and I hit the surface with an impact that drove the breath out of my lungs. My knees buckled as the rest of my weight came crashing down, and I slipped under the water. I jerked my head out and scrabbled up the side of the pickup and fell heavily into the plastic tray lining the bed.

After a couple of panicked seconds checking myself for worms, I stood and looked back to the restaurant. Flames licked at the roof overhang and thick black smoke rolled urgently out of the front windows. More smoke seeped out from under the shingles, and I hoped it wasn't getting too hot up there. Misty crouched at the crest, half obscured by the swirling smoke.

I ripped the gloves and duct tape off, pulled Misty's keys out of my pocket and leaned over the side, trying to fit them into the driver's door. I didn't want to get back into the water again unless I had to. I had just slipped the key into the slot when I looked up to check on Misty and saw Junior crouched in the back of his truck, watching me.

I flinched. The keys slipped out of the lock and disappeared into the water.

CHAPTER 34

Junior's shirt had been burned off. The skin on his chest looked charred and loose. Most of his pompadour was gone, leaving nothing but a burnt scalp and a few scraggly strands around his black ears. He had Bert's Rambo knife clenched between his teeth, like a pirate who had leapt from a burning ship. He watched Misty for a moment.

She hadn't seen him yet through the thick smoke.

Junior whipped his bald, smoking head around and stared at me. When he took the knife from between his teeth, I could tell he was grinning. I couldn't believe he wasn't dead. His nose had been broken twice, Fat Ernst had kicked in him solidly in the head, and the last time I'd seen him, he'd been on fire. It didn't make sense. Then I remembered those scars on his chest. And what Pearl had said. She claimed to have brought Junior back from the dead three times. Maybe that was true. Maybe he'd built up some kind of resistance, sort of immunity, to death itself. Smoke poured from the rent in the front wall, rolling down over the Cadillac, over the truck. Junior turned back to the truck's cab and ducked down. I lost him in the smoke.

"Misty!" I screamed.

wormfood

She stood at the top of the roof, waving the smoke away from her face. Flames were now breaking through all over the place, erupting out of the roof in pools of embers and flames surrounded by blackened shingles.

"Junior's alive! He's right there!" I screamed hoarsely, jabbing my finger at the Sawyers' truck. Misty instantly dropped into a crouch, watching the front of the building. For a brief moment, nothing moved but the black smoke.

Junior eased his way onto the roof of the cab. With his chainsaw.

"Motherfuck—" I stepped back, preparing to jump and swim the fifteen or twenty feet to the restaurant. The keys were gone, and I didn't know what else to do. But even as I grabbed a deep breath and held, I knew I wouldn't make it in time. Junior was going to kill Misty and there wasn't a damn thing I could do about it.

Then I saw my rifle in the rack in the back window of her pickup.

I kicked at the glass as hard as I could and heard a teeth-rattling crack, but it didn't break. I glanced up; Junior was leaping from the truck's hood to the roof, his skin still smoking or steaming in the rain. I kicked at the back window again. And again. It finally cracked on the third try, and I spent another couple of precious seconds knocking the loose glass out of the way. I ignored Misty's Anschütz and went for Grandpa's Springfield instead.

I straightened, rifle in my hands.

Junior yanked on the cord and the saw started with a hungry roar. Misty backed slowly along the crest of the roof, still cradling her left hand with her right. Junior hit the trigger a couple of times and the sound of the revving engine echoed back across the floodwater.

Junior made his move and the rifle found my shoulder.

As he scrambled up the roof, chainsaw screaming, I settled, zeroing in on the saw, and fired. Junior was seven feet from Misty when his chainsaw exploded in a quick burst of fire and sparks. The bullet had found its way into the gas tank, just as I had hoped. I hadn't wanted to take a chance on missing his head, and if I hit him in the upper body, I was scared that it might not even slow him down, not with Pearl's symbols carved all over his chest. So I figured I'd take out his weapon first, give Misty a fighting chance.

The small explosion knocked Junior sideways into the roof. The chain broke loose, flipped up and over, and wrapped around Junior's forearm, burying itself deep. He slammed into the smoking shingles, blood spraying from his arm, and slid headfirst down the roof. I thought he was just going to slip right over the edge, but he caught himself with his good arm, slid around, and started creeping back up the slope.

I found a nice sweet spot at the back of his head between the iron sights, whispered, "Fucking A plus you little cocksuckers," and gently squeezed the trigger.

A dry click; the gun was empty. I had forgotten that there was only one bullet left after shooting at the squirrels yesterday.

Junior kept going, dragging himself up the roof toward Misty with his one arm. The other arm, the one that now looked as if it had suddenly grown a deep black tattoo, flopped helplessly next to him, leaving a trail of blood. Misty dropped to her haunches and kicked out, slamming her boot into the top of his head. All that did was piss off Junior even more. His good hand lashed out and grabbed Misty's ankle.

I ducked back to the broken window and jerked the .270 Anschütz out of the gun rack. I jerked the bolt back, wanting to check how many shells were left, and stupidly flung a fresh shell out into the air. It hit the top of the cab and bounced off, landing somewhere out in the water. At least the clip held three more shells. I just prayed Junior couldn't handle three bullets.

I pivoted, pulling the rifle up to my shoulder, slamming the bolt home. Through the scope, smoke from the burning roof leapt into instant, crisp clarity. I swung the rifle to the left, just in time to watch Junior jerk Misty down next to him. He grabbed her hair and rolled, pulling her on top of him.

I slid my finger anxiously around the trigger, but I couldn't fire.

Wormfood

Junior was using Misty as a shield. He wrapped his ruined forearm around her throat, and I could see where the teeth of the chain had bitten deep, right down to the bone. Blood surged out of the gash, washing across Misty's chest. Junior's eyes found mine from behind Misty's blond hair.

I let the rifle roam down their bodies, looking for something vital, anything to shoot. I realized that being on fire was the least of Junior's problems. He'd been in the water too long. The worms had been feasting. His charbroiled skin, from the waistband of his tight, ripped jeans, through his chest, up into his neck and across his face, rippled and bulged as countless worms writhed through the flesh underneath.

Misty, laying flat on her back on top of Junior, spread her legs, flattened her boots, and whipped her head back into Junior's face, cracking the back of her skull into Junior's nose. I hoped she'd broken his nose again; that would be the third time in twenty-four hours. It didn't slow Junior down a whole lot, but it was time enough to plant the cross hairs right at the bottom zipper of his jeans. If nothing else, I figured blowing his nuts off would make me feel better.

I fired but saw only a small pop in the shingles, an inch beneath Junior's crotch, realizing too late that the rifle had been sighted in for Misty's eyes, not mine. "Oh, shit," I whispered. Two bullets left.

Junior knew that I had taken a shot. He kept his bleeding arm around Misty's neck and sat up, still hiding behind her. I saw the knife. He gripped it with his good hand, brought it over and down, sinking it into the roof between Misty's thighs. He twisted the blade and pulled it tight to Misty's crotch.

I got the message. If I shot him, then Misty would slide into the blade.

Misty bared her teeth, prepared to hit him again with the back of her head. But Junior was ready. He clamped his teeth together around Misty's right ear, biting down hard. She froze. Junior let go of her, bobbed his head down, grinning at me from behind Misty's bloody right ear. A bloody ball of snot appeared in his left nostril and slid down his upper lip as the head of a worm appeared. It tested the air, then oozed out of Junior's nose about an inch. Junior ignored it and grabbed her hip with his free hand and forced her pelvis down against the sloping roof, against the knife.

The worm slid out of his nose even farther, exploring his cheek. It pulled itself away from his face, probing at Misty's ear.

You sonofabitch, I thought. *Just brush it away, get it away from her.*

But Junior didn't move. His eyes, huge in the crosshairs of the scope, flickered down, watching the worm. His grin got wider. The worm must have smelled the blood, because it suddenly darted forward and started wriggling into her ear. I could tell Misty felt it; she flinched, but whether she thought it was a worm or Junior's tongue, I didn't know.

I slid the crosshairs up to Junior's forehead and pulled the trigger, imposing my will on the universe.

The bullet struck Junior just under his nose, neatly popping the worm in half. His head twisted against the shingle with an ugly spasm. The Anschütz left an inconspicuous hole near one nostril and a slackened face and that was all. I fired again, just to make sure. Nobody in the Sawyer family died quick enough for me. This time, his head was rolled back, face upturned to the clouds, so the bullet slammed into the soft part of his neck, just under the chin, and exited through the top of his head. Junior went limp, as if someone had suddenly cut the strings to a puppet, and he collapsed against the roof. Misty rolled off Junior, away from the knife, slapping at the severed worm twisting in her ear.

Junior slowly slid sideways down the roof. His left foot got caught in the rusted gutter and hung there for a moment, long enough for him to slip off the edge headfirst. He hit the front steps, landing hard on his head. The impact snapped his neck with a satisfying, brittle crack. The rest of his body remained curiously stiff, toppling over into the water. The pointed toes of Junior's cowboy boots hit first, and then the rest of his body slapped the surface. I hoped the splash got the worms' attention. He twitched once and I jerked the rifle back up, even though it

240

was empty, but that was all. He lay still, arms outstretched, head twisted at an unnatural angle, as if he'd tripped going up the steps.

It was done. He was dead.

Up on the roof, Misty had spent a while stomping on the worm, then caught her breath. She turned, watched me for a moment, and gave me a small wave. I set the rifle in the back of the pickup and jumped into the water, not caring about the worms. I stuck my hand down into the mud blindly, felt around for a few seconds, and managed to grab the keys. I opened the driver's door and hopped in. A worm inched up my boots and I crushed it against the speaker in the door. The truck started right up, but either the brakes didn't work underwater or I didn't jump on the pedal in time, because I hit the restaurant with a dull crunch. Misty inched down the roof, through the billowing smoke and light rain, sat at the edge for a moment, then jumped onto the hood.

I leaned over and was about to open the passenger door when Bert stumbled out of the smoke onto Fat Ernst's Cadillac.

He didn't look too good. I could barely see his eyes, hiding back in deep, sunken hollows in his gray face. Fresh blood rolled down his left arm from the knotted rags at his shoulder. He swayed unsteadily on his feet, watching Misty.

"Bert. Hurt," was all he said.

Misty climbed down onto the Cadillac and took Bert's hand. He looked down at her hand, then back up at her face.

"Bert. Hurt," he repeated.

I wasn't sure whether Misty was going to give him a hug or just push him off the car into the water, into the worms. She kept hold of Bert's hand, pulled him over to her pickup, and helped him climb in the back. He followed her lead silently, like a lost and confused old man who was trying to hide his fear. Misty helped him sit down, leaning against the back of the cab.

I slid over into the passenger seat as Misty climbed behind the wheel. She backed away from the restaurant about twenty feet and stopped. Neither one of us said anything, and I got worried she might not ever speak to me again, after everything that had happened. I figured she probably hated me and I'd be lucky if she didn't just leave me here, waiting for help in the back of the Sawyers' truck.

Instead, she reached over with her good hand and took mine. It was enough. I gently curled my bloody fingers around hers, and we sat quietly for a moment, watching the flames leap and dance. She let go for a moment, reached under her seat, and pulled out a bottle. I think it was whiskey. Whatever it was, it tasted better than the stuff I'd tasted in the truck on the way to the pit.

I twisted around to face Misty. "Listen, I—"

"Shhh," she said, squeezing my hand.

She took another drink, then dropped the gearshift into reverse, and took my hand again as we drove away from what was left of Fat Ernst's Bar and Grill. I turned and watched through the broken back window as the place folded in on itself in a haze of smoke. Most of the building was now nothing but broken, burning timbers, sinking slowly into the muddy water. The flames reached nearly fifteen feet high. A twisting column of smoke, swollen and almost completely black, billowed up into the wet, dark afternoon sky like a slow-moving tornado, where it blended into the angry storm clouds, spread out, and disappeared.

CHAPTER 35

Misty drove straight to the nearest emergency room, nearly forty miles away down in Redding, where they spent a few hours straightening out her fingers. I got some blood. The doctors couldn't quite figure out exactly what was wrong with Bert and wanted to run all kinds of tests on him, but he slipped away when the National Guard guys were busy watching Misty bounce up the hospital corridor, all smiles and giggles after her pain medication had kicked in. I told them we'd picked Bert up along the side of the highway and had no idea who the hell he was.

Everybody was too preoccupied with the flood to worry about much else anyway.

A few days later, when the rain had finally stopped and the floodwater had settled into nothing but miles of mudflats, somebody finally figured out that Fat Ernst's restaurant had burned down. I don't think many people were all that concerned, but with Ray's police cruiser, the Sawyers' truck, and especially Slim's pickup scattered out in the parking lot, somebody had to take a look. Then they started finding bones. It took a week, but several skulls got unearthed. Two of them had a couple of large bullet holes. Somebody jumped to the conclusion that

Junior and Slim had killed each other, and that goddamn idiot Ray had made things worse. Heck and Pearl got caught in the cross fire. That suited me fine.

The county made some half-assed attempt at an official investigation, but everybody assumed that either the flood or the fire had killed whoever had been there when Slim and Junior started shooting at each other. The flood had washed pretty much all of the evidence away. Nobody asked me and Misty anything, and we didn't exactly volunteer any information.

A few days later, they found another skull out by the ditch. It was Grandma. They identified her back molars. I spent a day sifting through the mud and charred timbers, wearing Grandpa's boots in case any worms were left, and eventually found her walker and the shotgun. The next day I buried Grandma's skull next to Grandpa. Her skull looked lonely in the casket, so I put her walker and Browning .10 gauge in with it.

Nobody ever found the buckle. Or the worms.

I figure that most of the worms got washed down into the wide, flat fields of the Sacramento Valley and once the rain stopped and the floodwaters receded, they buried themselves in the mud, escaping the warm, dry rays of the sun.

I'm careful. I only drink bottled water. I don't fish anymore. I wear Grandpa's heavy boots all the time.

And I'll never eat meat again.

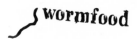

wormfood

One More Moment

Check it out! There is a new section on the Medallion Press Web site called "One More Moment." Have you ever gotten to the end of a book and just been crushed that it's over? Aching to know if the star-crossed lovers ever got married? Had kids? With this new section of our Web site, you won't have to wonder anymore! "One More Moment" provides an extension of your favorite book so you can discover what happens after the story.

medallionpress.com

THE FRENZY WAY

GREGORY LAMBERSON

In every hardened cop's worst dreams there lurks a nightmare waiting to become reality. Captain Mace has encountered his. When a string of raped and dismembered corpses appears throughout New York, the investigation draws Mace into an interactive plot that plays like a horror movie. Taking the lead role in this chilling story may be the challenge of his career, testing his skills and his stamina, but even a superhero would find the series of terrifying crime scenarios daunting.

Unlike anything Mace has experienced, every blood-spattered scene filled with body parts and partially eaten human remains looks like an animal's dining room strewn with rotting leftovers. Only Satanic legends and tales from the dark side of spiritual oblivion resemble the mayhem this beast has created in his frenzy. In the wake of each attack is the haunting premonition of another murdering onslaught.

As Mace follows this crimson trail of madness, he must accept the inevitable conclusion. Whoever—or whatever—is responsible for this terror does not intend to stop, and it's up to him to put an end to the chaotic reign of a perpetrator whom, until now, he's met only in the annals of mythology. The mere mention of the word would send New York into a panic: *werewolf.*

ISBN# 978-160542099-8

Mass Market Paperback / Horror

US $7.95 / CDN $8.95

AVAILABLE NOW

www.slimeguy.com

MEDALLION

P R E S S

Be in the know on the latest
Medallion Press news by becoming a
Medallion Press Insider!

<u>As an Insider you'll receive:</u>

· Our FREE expanded monthly newsletter,
giving you more insight into Medallion Press

· Advanced press releases and breaking news

· Greater access to all your favorite Medallion
authors

Joining is easy. Just visit our Web site at
<u>www.medallionpress.com</u> and click on the
Medallion Press Insider tab.

medallionpress.com